A BAD BOY STOLE My BRA

"... ...et, funny and with a surprising heart... Bra kleptomania aside (what the actual fudge is that all about?!), teenage-me have killed to live next door to Alec Wilde."

ELEANOR WOOD, author of *Becoming Betty*

"... ...ook is a joy to read. Smart, hilarious and full of fun!"

KATY BIRCHALL, author of *The It Girl* series

"... ..., funny and seriously cute, this book will make you ... make you cringe ... and have you cheering for Riley ... start to finish."

MAGGIE HARCOURT, author of *Unconventional*

A BAD BOY STOLE MY BRA

LAUREN PRICE

INK ROAD

First published 2018 by Ink Road
INK ROAD is an imprint and trademark
of Black & White Publishing Ltd.

Black & White Publishing Ltd
Nautical House, 104 Commercial Street
Edinburgh EH6 6NF

1 3 5 7 9 10 8 6 4 2   18 19 20 21

ISBN: 978 1 78530 178 0
Copyright © Lauren Price 2018

A CIP catalogue record for this book is available
from the British Library.

Typeset by Iolaire, Newtonmore
Printed and bound by CPI Group (UK) Ltd, Croydon, CR0 4YY

To all my Wattpad readers, thank you for believing in me.

1

Mario Wins Again

"Mario wins again!"

As the cheesy, overplayed music comes to a close and the screen goes dark, I drop my controller into my lap in defeat. Be it the stuffiness of this room or the fact that this is our sixth tournament today, I lost my first game of *Mario Kart* in months ... to my eight-year-old brother. I watch through narrowed eyes as Jack catapults around the room in victory, lifting his shirt over his head to reveal his pale torso. Seriously, what is it with boys and showing their chest when they win something? Is it some sort of animalistic display of dominance originating from our monkey ancestors? I can't help but snort in amusement as I consider this. He's such a little show-off. My hands dart out to grab him by the sides and I tug him down to tickle him.

"You wish, monkey boy," I scoff. "We both know that I kicked your butt on the other games."

Jack squirms to free himself from my hold, shooting me a glare as he brushes himself down. He hates me tickling him. "Monkey boy? I beat you with Mario, not Donkey Kong."

I'm way too lazy to explain my thought process to him so I just roll my eyes.

"Riley, can you come here please?" Mom calls from downstairs. If it wasn't for the urgency I can hear in her voice, I would probably make more of a scene asking why she can't just come upstairs to me, but she sounds excited about something. There's a spark of vitality in the words that I haven't heard in a while and it intrigues me.

Mumbling my protest instead, I swing my legs from the beanbag and give Jack a warning look with a clear subliminal message: *Steal my seat, I steal your life.* Of course, by the time I've reached the door, he's already sitting there. Oh, how I miss the days when I had some kind of authority over him.

As I enter the kitchen, I'm hit with the heart-warming aroma that signals Mom's baking: cupcakes and coffee, like the inside of a Starbucks, but much cosier. It's something that I haven't smelled for quite a while, and my sourness at having to walk *all the way* down the stairs disappears in a second at the sweetness of the nostalgia. I can't help but smile as I see her standing behind the kitchen counter in an apron. She looks up and brushes her hands off immediately. There's icing sugar in the curls of her hair.

"Come and look at this," she says, beckoning, abandoning her half-iced cupcakes. She leads me over to the kitchen window and pulls back the plaid drapes ever so slightly, just enough for me to peek through. Shooting her a look of bewilderment and wondering if this has anything to do with the new geraniums she bought yesterday, I squeeze my head into the gap and look out at the neighbours' driveway. I was expecting a potted plant, so what I see instead surprises me greatly.

We have new neighbours.

2

Parked next door, in the house that has been empty for almost six months now, is a large removal truck. The giant green anomaly overshadows the small car beside it, and my eyebrows rise further upwards as I watch the family climbing out of the vehicle. A woman steps out first, and reaches into the back to grab a small girl from the back seat. Her dark curls are scraped back into a clasp, and her features are delicate and feminine. It's nice that someone around Mom's age is moving in next door – my mom could use someone to talk to living so close by. The girl the woman carries is around the age of four or five, with the cutest baby face I've ever laid eyes on and two brunette bunches on either side of her head. Adorable.

I'm not sure who I was expecting to see get out of the car next, but it definitely wasn't the alluring, moody boy that I see now. He looks around my age, and from what I can see of his ebony hair and angled jaw . . . he's hot. No doubt the entire population of the student body will completely swarm this one. I can't help but watch as he threads his fingers through his hair, slightly entranced. I'm a bit of a scientific hermit when it comes to the species of "the hot", so the fact that I have an attractive male now living next door is enough to make my stomach flip.

I pull the drape further to the side, but to my complete horror, the boy's head snaps up at the movement. His eyes latch onto mine as he notices me ogling. *Oh.* I pull away quickly, bumping back into Mom's shoulder. I can already feel a blush burning my cheeks. He must think I'm such a creep. Surprisingly though, by the time I've recovered enough courage to peek through again, he doesn't look affected in the slightest. Bored almost, which reassures me.

3

Out of fear of being spotted again, I withdraw from the drapes – finally this time – and pull them closed. It was only a matter of time before we got new neighbours, I knew that, but it still comes as a surprise. The house next door is fairly large – a two-storey cream-coloured family house with a front porch and unruly yard. I had grown quite used to it being empty, and definitely never pictured someone of my own age moving in. Mom chortles at my puzzled expression and tucks my long hair behind my shoulders. It warms my heart that she's so excited about this.

"What do you think, eh?" she says. "New neighbours."

I smile half-heartedly, heading over to the fridge. "I haven't seen them around Lindale before. They must be new to town."

Lindale is one of those fairly small, well-kept communities where most people know of each other and the sense of town pride is strong. There's a school for each age group, lots of community fundraisers and with surroundings of dense Oregon forest in almost every direction away from the beach.

My eyes scour the shelves of the fridge, but I'm left disappointed. "No orange juice," I murmur, peering at the remnants of food. All that's left is wafer-thin ham, flavoured water and an old lettuce. Not much I can make there.

Mom shrugs in reply, batting my hand away as I reach for a cupcake instead.

"We need to go shopping, Ma," I grumble. "There's no food in this house."

"The order is coming later!"

She sticks her tongue out at me, and I'm momentarily stunned by that simple action, something that she hasn't done in a long time. It seems like today is going really well

4

for her. Mom and I are similar in more ways than one. Along with our almost matching appearance – auburn curls and fair skin – we're both sarcastic and jokey with an abnormally weird side. Mom only shows her weird side when she's in a good mood nowadays, so when she does, that makes it all the more special.

"So, you felt like doing some baking today then?" I probe, peering over her shoulder as she ices the cupcakes.

Her hand falters slightly as I ask, and she nods. "I missed it. Figured I can't mope for ever." She looks back at me with a small smile.

"Good," I say. "I love you. I'm going upstairs to do some studying." I brush past and grab a lollipop from my sweet jar, just as my phone begins to vibrate in my pocket. Amusement curves my lips as I see Violet's particularly horrific caller-ID picture show up on the screen. She and I have a bit of a tradition about how we answer the phone. It takes me only a second to think of an opening line before I pick up.

"Tampax tampons – for your need to bleed. How may I be of assistance?"

"This is no time for jokes, Riley!" Violet replies in a hushed voice. It's only then that I remember that she's on a blind date. Knowing her pickiness when it comes to guys, it's probably going badly. "I'm in the girls' toilets at the moment. Hiding. Stupid period had to come today, when I'm wearing white jeans! Plus, he has the table manners of a complete pig. He spilt water all over me."

"Okay," I snort at my eccentric best friend. "Dry yourself off a bit. If you have a jacket, tie it round your waist and just tell the guy that you have a stomach ache or something. If he's got a brain, he'll take you home."

Violet mumbles in agreement, and I can hear the rustling of her jacket down the line.

"Thanks so much." She sighs gratefully. "And hey, nice line. I better get back out there before he starts worrying. Text me later?"

"I will," I promise, before hanging up.

Violet and I have been best friends since the very beginning of Freshman year. We sat next to each other in our first Math class, where she slapped a jock for making fun of her dyed purple hair. I respected her attitude from that moment onwards. Unlike me, she's gabby and confident and shamelessly herself – she's magnetic. I, on the other hand, am known to be a bit of a dork. Just a little socially awkward, my role in our friendship is often to advise her from afar while she faces the horrors of social interaction.

I head straight back upstairs to my room and shut the door behind me. My bedroom is my haven. It's not particularly glamorous or artsy, but it's rustic and it feels like home. The entire far wall is dedicated to tacked posters of bands and TV shows. Everything in this room, from the mess of books to the mix of old vinyl records, screams introvert and I love it. My skateboard and old guitar sit propped against the wardrobe, and my double bed, complete with Star Wars sheets, sits in its usual unruly state just opposite my window. Funnily enough, my window exactly mirrors a window in the neighbouring house, separated only by a couple of metres.

Now that I have neighbours . . .

Oh crap.

I tiptoe towards the window and cautiously peer round

6

the window frame into the room opposite. If my luck is as bad as I estimate it to be, I can't risk being spotted staring at Neighbour Dude again. Sure enough, as my eyes rest on the room opposite, I have to fight to restrain my groan. *Of course* it's the guy. I guess my drapes will have to remain closed from now on. I tug the purple material further back to see that he's packing away his things. He hasn't noticed me this time, at least. It's only this close up that I realise quite how attractive this guy is. With a strong, chiselled jawline and defined cheekbones, his face is angular and, dare I say it, sexy. Inky locks curl over his forehead, and his eyes are a deep cobalt.

He turns to face the other way and I snap out of my daze, a little surprised with myself that I have stared at him so much already. I will be the first to openly admit that I haven't had the best experiences when it comes to boys, so it's really out of the question for me to have a crush. I guess there isn't any harm in looking, but I close the drapes and walk away just to be on the safe side.

Putting on my music, I settle down to do some studying. My grades dropped a lot last year, and I'm determined to get back on track in time for Senior year. Studying is a way to focus my energy so that I feel like I'm actually accomplishing something in my free time. Twenty One Pilots blast through my docking station. I nod my head in time to the music and stare down at the equations in front of me until my eyes blur. I've never been good at Math, and now I'm having to fight my hardest to keep up. Nothing seems to click. I just hope this extra work will be worth it in my final exams next year.

My phone buzzes. It's Violet again.

I escaped from that hellish date! I'll tell you all the details on Monday xx

Don't get distracted by the phone. Ugh go on then. May as well reply.

I type in a hasty message before turning my phone off. No doubt if I didn't, Mom would walk in, see me texting Violet and think I'd been doing that the entire time. We have some major trust issues in our relationship – mainly due to the bowl cut she made me get when I was twelve. Yup, it looked just as bad as it sounds, if not worse.

After a solid hour of studying, I finally finish and it's getting late. I stifle my yawn and begin to get changed ready for bed, ensuring the drapes are firmly closed before I strip. I would not want Neighbour Dude to get more than he bargained for by moving into that room. I don't think that's the kind of first impression I want to make, funnily enough.

I slide into the covers in my pyjama top, frowning as I realise that the music next door is playing pretty loudly. Surely that heavy metal couldn't belong to the mom of a toddler. No, my bet is placed on the boy in the room next door, which would explain why I seem to be taking the brunt of the volume. Judging by the raucous laughter and heavy rock music, Mr Neighbour has friends over. He hasn't even been here for a day, and already he's having a party. If this isn't foreshadowing, I don't know what is.

I sigh, frustrated, and slam the pillow over my head in an attempt to muffle the sound, curling further into the soft sheets and hoping for the best.

Twenty minutes later, I'm still unsuccessful.

Looks like this will be a long night.

I stir to a small sound near by, and groan quietly. The music from next door still hasn't stopped! Can a girl not get her beauty sleep any more? Blinking to clear my vision, I prop myself up on one elbow and turn on the lamp beside my bed. Light floods the room, and I survey the lit scene quickly, my jaw slackening in surprise at what I see.

I stare wide-eyed at the boy, who seems just as paralysed as I am.

His eyes lock onto mine in shock and we stare at each other for what feels like hours. He's positioned halfway through the window, reaching out towards the opposite sill, with my Minnie Mouse bra swinging in his closed fist.

What. The. Actual. Fudge.

2

Come and Get It

My first instinct is to scream. Unfortunately, the boy is one step ahead of me. By the time I snap back to reality, he's already darting out of the window. He doesn't look back as he climbs nimbly over the frame, and my paralysis turns to pure confusion and rage.

"What the absolute *hell* do you think you are doing?"

I yank the covers back and swing my legs out of bed to chase him to the window. He gives me a single unreadable glance back before making the final leap towards the opposite ledge, landing so gracefully that a cat would be jealous. My bare legs tingle with goosebumps in the chilly night air, and I fold my arms across my chest as I turn to face the window. Inside the opposite room is a group of boys, all laughing uneasily as they stare at me. They're barely recognisable in the dim lamplight, but I know who they are.

One of the boys approaches the window, the breeze in the frosty air ruffling his golden locks. *Dylan Merrick*. He's in my grade at school, although I've never really spoken to him. He's one of those effortlessly sociable types whom everybody adores. Dylan offers me a sheepish, reassuring grin which would usually melt any girl in a second, including myself, but this time my anger seems to have immunised me from that angel-carved expression.

"You must be really confused," he says, taking in my mixed expressions.

"No shit, Sherlock," I hiss. "Care to tell me what the hell you think you guys are doing?" I feel so uncomfortable knowing they have my tattered old bra in that room.

Dylan cringes slightly. "It was a stupid dare. We didn't think you'd wake up."

"He stole my freaking bra!" I cry, fisting my hands. "You thought you could break into my house in the middle of the night and steal my bra for some stupid dare? I don't even know you!" I watch him wince at my crazed tone, and I'm suddenly aware of how loud my voice has grown. I have a right to be crazy, surely?

"Very nice bra by the way." Joe Travis pops his head up beside Dylan, all scruffy hair and mischievous blue eyes. He's one of the class clowns at Lindale High. He's mostly popular for the amount of times he's played pranks on the ex-principal – itching powder in the underarms of her cardigan, superglue on her chair and stuff like that. He hasn't performed any tricks on the current principal, but I think he's waiting for the right moment to attack. This guy is legendary in our school. He raises his eyebrows in faux sincerity. "I do appreciate a girl who loves Disney."

"Dude." Dylan gives him an almost pained look. "Shut *up*."

11

My cheeks flame red. Of all the things, of all the bras in the world, this guy had to steal my freaking Disney bra. Not a pretty one. Not even a plain one. I mean, even *I* didn't like my Minnie Mouse bra, but it was old and comfy and felt too familiar to let it go in the trash. Surprisingly, most of my anger has diminished by this point, leaving me embarrassed and a little bit overwhelmed.

A stupid dare.

"Were you at least planning on giving it back?"

Dylan looks uneasy and glances back at Neighbour Dude, who has remained strangely silent for this entire encounter.

"Are you serious?" I groan. I consider climbing over the gap, but another gust of chilly wind alerts my senses to my bare legs and Batman pyjama top. No retrieving it, then. My eyes narrow on my neighbour and I scowl.

"You. You're the grasshole who took it. Give it back, now."

"Grasshole?"

Chase Thatcher stands up from the corner with a grin on his face at my insult, and my attention shifts. He is possibly the most notorious ladies' man of our school. I don't know much about him, other than his string of dates and unquestionable charm, although I did hear one rumour that he doesn't have the best home life. Three out of the four boys in that room are some of the most popular in my year – how has my neighbour managed to climb his way to the top of Lindale's social ladder in less than a day?

"Y'know, I'd say Chase is more of a grasshole than Alec," Dylan jokes.

Alec. His name is Alec.

12

"Be careful there, Merrick, or you might just hurt my feelings."

"Nah, your ego is way too big for that."

The boys clear away from the window, shoving each other playfully, and my eyes immediately settle onto the boy who stole my bra: Alec. My curious gaze turns icy. This boy doesn't even know me and he's already broken into my room to steal my underwear. Shouldn't he be apologising and handing it back by now? I caught him in the act after all.

"Who has it?" My tone is demanding. At this point I just want to go back to bed, with my bra stuffed into the back of my drawer and my window firmly locked.

Chase glances at Alec, biting his knuckle to restrain his smile. Joe, spinning round on a desk chair, is looking sheepishly at his knees. I am left with a clear suspect, and unsurprisingly it's the boy who committed the crime. I look to Alec for my answer, and sure enough I receive it . . . in the form of a smirk.

Of course. Was it ever likely to be anyone else?

"You have my bra, don't you?" I ask him tiredly, running a hand through my bed hair.

"Yes." His voice is smooth and confident. It irritates me already.

"Are you going to give it back or am I wasting my time?"

I'm unable to prevent the irritation from seeping into my voice. This situation is going on for so much longer than it should be, and I'm tired. If it wasn't for sleep deprivation, there is no way I would be able to stand up and talk to these guys as easily as I have.

"I'm afraid I can't do that. The dare was to keep it."

13

"What's your name, Sleeping Beauty?" Chase interrupts.

"Riley Greene," I reply suspiciously, fighting back my blush. My cheeks have a tendency to flush crimson at even the slightest compliment – it's like my body just rejects the notion.

"You're in our year, aren't you?" Chase asks. "I don't think I see you around much."

I bite my lip slightly. Generally, I fly under the radar. I have a limited amount of friends and don't draw much attention to myself aside from my occasional – and often unintentional – witty comments in class. I also took a lot of time off school last year, which meant that I unconsciously withdrew from the more social elements of my life. It should not surprise me that I'm not particularly memorable.

"Chase, stop flirting," Alec scoffs. A casual grin settles on his lips, and his eyes flicker to me momentarily. My body stiffens in annoyance.

Joe laughs. "That's like telling him to stop breathing."

Chase scowls and pushes the desk chair round so that Joe is facing in the opposite direction. "Much better."

"Look." I turn to Alec, growing even more impatient. "I don't know who you are, but I just want to go to bed. Can I have my damn bra back please so I can forget this ever happened?"

"My name is Alec Wilde," he says smoothly, his lips twitching upwards at the corners into an annoyingly cute half smirk. "It's nice to meet you, neighbour."

"Shame about the circumstances," I quip.

Alec's eyebrows rise slightly, but he doesn't look angry. He looks almost impressed. It's difficult not to notice the silence of the other boys, absorbed in our conversation.

14

"Bullshit isn't your colour," he replies smoothly.

I huff with impatience. "Just give it to me."

"Wow, you're forward." Alec laughs.

The boys shift uneasily as they watch the two of us.

Damn, I fell right into that one.

"You know that's not what I meant. I don't care about your stupid dare. Just give it back."

Alec's mouth drops open to reply, but no words come out.

I feel a slight tug on my pyjama sleeve.

Spinning round, I'm surprised to see my little brother standing behind me. He rubs his eyes as a yawn escapes his mouth.

"Riley, I'm trying to sleep," he grumbles in a low voice. He stiffens a little bit as he notices the presence of the boys next door and his eyes widen. "You're talking to boys?" He sounds flabbergasted, and I wince, wanting nothing more than to die of embarrassment in this very second. "Why are you talking to boys in the middle of the night, Riley? Does Mom know –"

I slap a hand over his mouth, pulling my hair over my face in an attempt to conceal my reddening cheeks. "Right, time for bed then, Jack!" I chime, feigning happiness. I usher him out of the room as quickly as possible, muttering profanities under my breath. It takes everything I have not to headbutt the door as I close it behind him.

With one glance at Alec's smug expression, I slam the window shut and pull the drapes closed. I think I've had enough embarrassment for one night. I dive into the bedcovers, smothering my face in the pillow to release a muffled scream. It takes a while but eventually I begin to fade

15

back into the land of dreams, one thing running through my mind as I drift off.

I'll get that bra back.

"Come on." My mom tugs on my arm, dragging me towards the porch. "It's only polite to welcome the neighbours."

She tries hard to conceal it, but there's a small smile on her face; she's excited about this, and that is possibly the only reason that I'm going along with it. I eye the house in front of us sceptically. Mom doesn't know that I've actually met Alec already, nor the somewhat bizarre circumstances in which that meeting took place. I'm absolutely exhausted from last night, but I stretch on an elasticated friendly smile. Mom rings the doorbell, holding twelve of the cupcakes she made yesterday packaged neatly in a box. I clasp my brother's hand for dear life. This is going to be horrific, but at least I can ask for my bra back.

"Riley, why are you holding my hand? I'm not five," Jack grumbles beside me, trying desperately to retrieve his hand from my tight grip. Suddenly, the russet door of number nineteen swings open, revealing the woman we saw getting out of the red car yesterday. Her mouth bursts into a smile as she sees us. She's even prettier up close.

"Welcome, welcome! I'm Marie Wilde; it's a pleasure to meet you!"

She ushers us inside and a cinnamon smell hits me as we enter the hallway. Her dark curls hang wild around her porcelain face, the exact inky shade that Alec's hair is. It's quite obvious that he gets his appearance from his mom's side, although his skin isn't that pale.

The hallway is wide and airy, with a couple of boxes

stacked neatly against the wall. My mom's vitality fills the space as she gushes her introductions.

"It's a pleasure to meet you too! I'm Ruby, and these are my children, Riley and Jack."

I smile at the sight of her happiness. It would be so good for her if she had a friend living next door, someone she could talk to. When my cousin Kaitlin died . . . well, we lost contact with all of Mom's side of the family, especially my uncle Thomas. Mom never speaks about it, but I know exactly how lonely she is. She lost her niece and her brother in the short space of a year, and it's taken a massive toll on all of us. Just the thought of the family I used to be so close with brings a lump to my throat, and my stomach twists.

"Hi there." Marie smiles warmly. "You live next door right?" When we nod in reply, Marie continues, "I have two children as well. Millie is at a friend's today so that we could keep unpacking, but Alec is home. He's around your age, Riley. I'll call him down in a second. Come on in and I'll make some drinks."

I trail behind my mother into the living room, settling daintily at the edge of a plump couch as I take in my surroundings. The house is cosy and warm, despite its lack of furnishings. Candles and dried flowers are set up on the mantelpiece, giving the fireplace a rosy glow. As for the layout, well it's exactly like our house, but the opposite way around. A mirror image.

"Coffee? Do you take two sugars or one? Milk?" Marie says hurriedly, running a hand through her untamed curls, her bright eyes flickering between me and my mom.

"I'll come and help if you'd like?" my mom offers, and the relief on Marie's face is immediate, but is quickly masked with denial.

17

"Are you sure? You're a guest, I –"

Mom interrupts her with a firm nod, and together they walk over to the kitchen, leaving me with my annoying little brother. I glance over at Jack to see that he's playing on his iPad.

"Jack," I hiss. "That's rude! Put it away, now."

"But she's not even here!" Jack protests, his eyes still focused securely on the brightly lit screen. Jack lives on his gadgets – I guess his way of dealing with reality is by escaping into the virtual kingdoms. I can't say it isn't appealing. I gently press the iPad's lock button.

"Jack. It's rude."

"Fine, I'll put it away, *Mom.*"

As much as Jack and I do fight, he can be a cutie some-times. Unfortunately for me, he inherited all the good genes. His scruffy brown hair and wide green eyes somewhat resemble my dad, whereas his faint scatter of freckles and snub nose are inherited from Mom. Even I admit that he's adorable, but in my defence, he's the devil incarnate behind that angelic face.

"Here you are, guys." Marie places a plate of cookies on the coffee table and a large jug of lemonade. I thank her quickly, and she shrugs it off with a smile before calling Alec down from the foot of the stairs. Then she settles on the couch opposite us, next to Mom. "It's just us three at the moment," she explains. "My partner's away with the army."

"What is it, Mom?" I hear Alec groan loudly, before the patter of footsteps down the stairs catches my attention. My breath hitches as Alec enters the room, wearing some faded jeans and a black T-shirt which hugs his torso. His gaze

18

locks onto mine, his eyes widening in recognition before becoming confused. "What are you doing here?"

"You two know each other?" my mom questions, looking between us.

"No!" I rush out, just as Alec claims the opposite.

"We met last night," Alec explains, glancing at me. "Our windows are opposite each other."

I look quickly to my mom to assess her reaction, but she doesn't seem particularly fazed. Sat comfortably on an elegant mink-coloured couch next to Marie, she seems a little vacant from this discussion. I think she's more focused on making a good impression.

"That's nice!" Marie says chirpily. "Alec's joining the high school on Monday, so it'll be good for him to have another familiar face. Maybe you can even walk to school together."

"I'll be going on the bike, Ma," Alec says quickly. "Unless Riley likes motorbikes."

I feel eyes fall on me and I slowly shake my head, wincing slightly. I watch Jack reach for a cookie, a knowing smile on his face.

"I'm happy walking."

Alec smirks. "I thought so."

"Still," Mom says. "It's so nice for you both that you have someone your own age living so close. Especially if you're taking any of the same classes – it could be handy."

Alec takes a seat next to me and throws an arm around my shoulder.

"We can be as close as Mickey and Minnie," he jokes.

He doesn't look at me but I *know* that's a dig about my bra. The bra is red and polka dotted, with a small version of both of those very characters on the left cup. My cheeks flame and I slowly adjust my elbow to press uncomfortably into the side of his ribs. I can't believe he took it. Unluckily for him, he's just reminded me about what I'm really here for. Marie and my mom begin to make small talk about careers, and he gradually removes his arm from my shoulder, pushing my elbow away. I see him smile, still not facing me.

"Where's your bathroom?" I ask, nudging him in the rib again. I know where it is, based on my house. I just want to get him alone so he can give me back my bra.

"Would you like me to show you?" He turns. His face is close and his eyes glint with something closely resembling humour. He's clearly picked up my motive.

Considering it for a second, I nod. Alec stands up, quickly grabs my hand and pulls me up from the couch. "I'm just going to show Riley where the restroom is."

"Be good, kids," Marie jokes, and Mom chuckles beside her.

I fight back the blush forming, but it's no use. Alec pokes my cheek annoyingly as we head up the stairs together, dodging stray moving boxes. This guy knows no boundaries at all.

"Someone's a little embarrassed."

"Why would I be embarrassed?" I cough, turning my burning cheeks away.

"Oh of course, it's not like I have your bra or anything."

"Ever heard that sarcasm is the lowest form of wit?"

"Actually, sarcasm is the ability to insult idiots without them realising it," Alec retorts.

"Are you calling me an idiot?"

"Of course not." Alec grins adorably. Obviously, when I say adorably I mean annoyingly.

I purse my lips as we step into Alec's bedroom. The walls are block navy and white, with a few posters scattered around. I recognise Metallica and some other heavy metal bands. Other than that, his room is eerily bare, still filled with cardboard boxes from yesterday's move. Must have been quite a party in here last night. I notice the box of empty cider bottles.

"Right, where is it?" I cut straight to the chase, scanning around. I can't see it anywhere. It must be hidden in his bureau or something. I march over and pull open a drawer. I'd feel uncomfortable doing this if it wasn't for the fact that he invaded my privacy last night. If he tries to call me out on it, he's a hypocrite. The top drawer is filled with boxers and quickly I grab a pair, flinging them at him. "Don't tell me I have to take boxers in exchange for my bra."

"Who says I have it?" he replies cautiously. He's watching me with a completely vacant expression, too icy-cool for my liking. I know he has it. He admitted yesterday that his dare was to steal it, not borrow.

"Oh come on," I groan, throwing my hands up a little. "I'm tired of this game now."

"Maybe you should play." He shrugs. "It's pretty fun."

"I'll get my bra back."

"You seem quite confident. It's not in here, I'll tell you that much." He collapses down onto his bed, still watching me calmly. I bristle. I don't know if he's telling the truth.

"I'm not letting you just keep it; you're a jerk for not giving it back straight away!"

"Jerk." Alec repeats the word, tasting it in his mouth. He leans back against the wall. "Yeah that seems about right. Unfortunately, a dare is a dare. I have to follow the rules." He closes his eyes, completely at ease.

"Whose dare was it?"

His eyes open. "Private information."

"Screw you."

"Is that an offer?" He smirks.

"I'll get it back, and I'll get you back, just wait and see."

Alec's dimples flash and his eyes close once more. "That's more like it."

3

Sweet Metallica Lullabies

"What's up with your fine ass this morning?"

I turn to face Violet with an acknowledging grunt, slamming my head into my locker with more force than intended. I whimper as I feel the ache emerge in my temple, and my fingers automatically rise up to massage the pain. Have you ever loathed something so much that the mere thought of it wipes the smile off your face and instantly makes you a hundred times more irritable?

Ah, then you understand my mutual relationship with Mondays – specifically Monday mornings.

"You look like crap, you know," Violet says bluntly, leaning against the lockers beside mine and casually crossing her arms. Her hair is newly dyed and her dark skin is flawless, unlike my scruffy bun and the dark bags under my eyes. I scowl in response.

"It's not my fault that Alec freaking Wilde doesn't know what time is acceptable to play music," I grumble under my breath. My hands dart into my locker to retrieve my books, and I shut it with a satisfying slam. Amid the ambient noise of chatter, the buzz of cell phones and the screams of stressed students, my display of frustration goes completely amiss. I'm actually looking forward to the peace and structure of lessons today.

"Seriously though, did you get dressed in the dark or something?"

I peer down at my pale blue skinny jeans and Yellow Submarine T-shirt. My usual home attire. I don't have anything against this outfit – it's comfy, casual and cal. Violet, however, has a signature style and a differing opinion on my classic clothing choices.

"Not now, Violet. I'm not in the mood," I murmur, rubbing the skin under my eyes in an attempt to wake myself up. Sure enough, I know I look like crap. I didn't even bother dragging a brush through my hair this morning, and my Converse are beginning to get tatty from overuse. I blame my dishevelled appearance on Alec. He was the one playing Metallica until God knows what time last night. I blame everything on Alec really.

Suddenly the atmospheric chatter of students seems to hush. I twist round with a knowing groan. *Speak of the devil.* Alec saunters along the corridor with Joe and Dylan, a folder clutched loosely in his right hand and a leather jacket slung over his toned arm. I can practically hear the drool collecting in girls' mouths already, and my teeth clench. He looks so smug, so confident – and it's his *first day*. I don't know how someone can seem so carefree.

"I heard he was expelled from his last school."

"Lisa told me that he's got a history of violence. Just look at him – he's so intimidating."

"Intimidatingly hot!"

I roll my eyes at the gossip I can overhear, somewhat

relieved when Alec turns the corner and disappears from sight. It was almost too easy to predict what kind of reaction he would receive at school. A hot new boy, confident and witty and best friends with three of the most popular students? He'll be swamped with attention, despite his rumour record. He's got his fast pass to the top.

"So, did you happen to know that there's an incredibly attractive new guy at school?" I hear Violet say over my shoulder. I turn round to face her. "Rumours are saying that he's your next-door neighbour," she continues. "Of course, I told them where to stick it, because I know that if that were the case, my best friend would have at least *mentioned* that a complete hottie has moved in right next door. Am I right in making that assumption?"

I can hear the teasing in her voice.

I cringe as we begin the slow walk towards Math, popping some gum into my mouth to cover the fact that I forgot to brush my teeth this morning in my dazed, sleepy state. I probably should have told my best friend, but honestly the idea never occurred to me. The events of this weekend were short and intense. Violet, taking my silence as an answer, chatters on beside me.

"Of course I'm wrong, but you know, I don't even care. I can't believe you live next to Alec Wilde and you didn't tell me. Dammit, you're lucky. You probably don't even realise how lucky you are, you know that? You might even –"

"Stop right there!" I pull her to a halt. "I don't care that this new guy is living next door to me, I really don't."

She raises an eyebrow. "You should care. This guy is new to town, apparently very confident and definitely very attractive. This is a good thing, surely?"

25

"No, it's not a good thing."

My best friend looks at me for a long moment and laughs. "Just because you're allergic to boys."

"I'm not allergic to boys!"

"You know, Riley, I honestly think it would be healthy for you to start dating again," Violet's tone becomes serious. "I know you've been repulsed by the idea of crushes and relationships since the Toby Incident, and I get that, but you shouldn't have to punish yourself for what happened with Kaitlin –"

Immediately my heart rate increases, and I find myself shaking my head viciously to try to eject the words from my brain. I don't want to talk about this. I hate it when she brings it up, and I don't know why she still pushes me.

"It's not that easy," I cut in sharply. "Besides, that isn't why Alec moving next door is a bad thing . . . I'm not repulsed by him in that sense."

Just every other sense instead.

"Then what is it?"

"Well basically, I was woken up on Saturday night be-cause –"

"Riley!"

My eyes jolt towards the source of the voice. Dylan Merrick stands further up the corridor of blue lockers, flanked by Joe, both of their gazes fixed on my disgruntled form. At the sound of his husky voice, people immediately zone onto me and before I know it, I've gone from my safe spot below the radar to hot topic for gossip in a matter of seconds. I cringe as the two head towards me, shrinking back into the lockers and hoping that there is some other Riley standing conveniently behind me.

26

"Hey there." Dylan greets me with a small smile as he nears us, leaning on the locker beside me. "How are you?"

Is he completely oblivious to the curious stares we're getting? Maybe he's just grown used to it by now, what with him being popular and all. Suddenly self-conscious under multiple gazes, I flush and tuck my hair behind my ear.

"I've been better." My voice comes out surprisingly strangled and croaky as Joe steps into my only escape route. Help required, sharpish. I hate being the focus of attention.

"So has Wilde given it back yet?" Joe asks me, shooting a sideways glance to an incredulous Violet. Her face is puckered in confusion, and it would take a blind man not to see the barrage of questions ready to tumble out of her. Yay.

"Nope," I grumble. "Yesterday, when I was at his house, I tried to find it for a solid fifteen minutes while he watched me, before admitting defeat. Infuriating grasshole."

"You know I could help you get him back . . ." A spark of excitement flares in Joe's eyes as he says the dreaded words.

"Er . . . no thanks." I chuckle uneasily. "Helping isn't really your forte. Your forte would be fire, danger and exclusion." I glance uneasily to my side. Thankfully, not many people are looking over any more.

"I'm just a dial tone away if you change your mind." Joe gives me a wink.

Beside me, Violet straightens up from slumping against the lockers. "I feel like my best friend hasn't told me something. Something pretty big," she says. "Can someone please explain to me what the hell is going on, because you two didn't even know Riley existed until now and all of a sudden you're flirting? What happened on Saturday night?"

She looks between us, demanding. I look to Joe and Dylan

27

for help but remain unsuccessful. Dylan shifts uncomfortably under my pleading gaze, and Joe just grins, amused by the situation.

Just me, then. I take a deep breath. *I'm going to need it.*

"Basically Chase, Dylan and Joe were all at Alec's house last night. I was asleep in bed, but I got woken up in the middle of the night because Alec was in my room . . . He had my bra, Vi! And he was like a cat and he ran away, but I chased him to the window and then, um . . . I met these guys. He stole my Mickey Mouse bra. Now if you'll excuse me." I scarper from the scene and, without another word, escape into my math classroom.

"What?" Violet shrieks in a hushed tone. "Alec Wilde stole your bra? Why? And more importantly, how come I didn't know about this until now?"

"I will answer any questions you have in Math, just please don't decapitate me." I wince, raising my hands in surrender.

"Okay, we're discussing this in class. I want every detail." Violet's eyes narrow.

"Every detail get you shall."

"And that's my sad, sad tale," I finish off in a hushed voice, peering warily over at the teacher to ensure she hasn't heard us. Although Violet and I sit in the furthest corner of the classroom from the teacher, Miss Thompson, she has eyes like a hawk, and I hate the idea of her listening to us from behind that large lacquered desk of hers. She hasn't looked up from her marking, luckily, and I sigh in relief as I turn back to Violet, but the sigh quickly diminishes in my throat as I take note of her expression.

I wasn't exactly sure what I was expecting Violet's reaction

28

to be after I told her about my weekend, but this wasn't on the agenda. A fangirl squeal? Interrogation? Sure. But instead I'm faced with something a lot scarier: Violet is thinking. You might think it strange for me to be worried about that, but nobody quite understands how opinionated Violet is. She's loud, confident and she knows her mind clearly. Very rarely do I ever see her actually thinking before she says something, hence my nervousness. Whatever Violet is about to say is going to be profound. I knit my fingers together.

"You want to get your bra back, right?" Violet asks hesitantly.

"Of course I do!"

"Well then I think you need to play his game." Excitement becomes more prominent in her dark, glittering eyes. "He's not going to give it back – accept that and move on. You need to pull out the big guns if you want that bra back, and I understand why you do. I mean, that Disney thing shouldn't be allowed to exist, not to mention in the hands of a sex god." She pauses to cringe, before continuing with a scary amount of enthusiasm. "Trick him, steal his boxers, embarrass that pretty little face of his and knock him down a peg or two."

I nod, fighting to restrain the evil laugh bubbling up my throat. Violet's right – did I honestly think he was going to give it back without a fight? No, I need to get my revenge.

"Should I be taking notes?" I say. "I feel like I'm at a boot camp or something. This is going to be so much fun."

I don't realise that my voice has risen too much until it's too late and I've gained the attention of the teacher. The clearing of someone's throat has never sounded more intimi-dating. "Miss Greene, have you got something you'd like to share with the class?"

"I, um . . . no, Miss."

"And do you think it's acceptable to be talking throughout my lesson?" Mrs Thompson sneers at me from behind her thick-framed glasses. I shake my head meekly. People are turning around to watch the encounter. She's never really liked me, but I think that's her general consensus on teenagers rather than a personal matter. Most teachers like me. Her brown hair is long and pulled back into a low ponytail, and her teeth are dashed with crimson lipstick. *Probably because she's always so busy snapping at students that she forgot she was applying it.*

"Excuse me?" Her eyes widen in sheer shock before brimming over with liquid fire.

Shit. I didn't just say that aloud.

Her face flushes pink with anger, and I know that somehow, idiotically, I must have. Eyes are wide around the classroom and a hushed chatter flares up. Stupid, Riley, stupid. I never get into trouble; I'm a good student and I work hard. I'm not usually this *idiotic*. I close my eyes as I pray silently that the floor will swallow me whole.

"Detention!" she barks, her musty breath fanning my face so much that I have to fight to keep a straight face. "I will not have students disrespect me this way!"

Bitch.

Thank goodness I didn't say *that* out loud.

My hand knocks timidly on the door of the detention room, and a deep feeling of disappointment stirs in my gut. Cautiously, I take a few steps in to face Mr Harris, a fairly nice teacher from my Philosophy class a few years ago. Quite a strange man actually. I mean, you just have to take a look at his socks and sandals to know that.

30

He is funny though, in a wacky Russell Brand kind of way.

"Take a seat, Miss Greene, and complete the detention slip."

I turn to face the quiet room of people, English posters screaming punctuation and rows of pale blue desks. Tiana Cooper is sitting at the front. She taps her fingernails in a menacing manner, and her cold eyes are fixed precisely on me in one hell of a glare. Tiana and I aren't exactly best friends, and I try to avoid her as much as humanly possible. Feeling uncomfortable, I look away. Behind her is a boy commonly known as 'Greasy Damon' due to his lack of contact with a shower. Finally, there's the couple in the back who I can't make out because they're huddled over a notepad. A fun bunch, all in all.

I make my way to a seat by the window, a fair distance away from Damon's body odour and Tiana's glare. Leaning my head against the cool glass, I attempt to clear my mind a little. After six murderously long hours at school, I just want to be at home, but I can see why Miss Thompson sent me out. I must have embarrassed her a little bit. As much as that woman seems to hate me, I do owe her an apology.

I can't believe I'm in detention. I *never* get detention.

I wince as I hear the door opening, a fatigued sigh escaping my lips. I just want to go to sleep. Preferably not by succumbing to Metallica lullabies.

"Sit down, kid, and complete the detention slip." I hear Mr Harris's gruff voice speaking, but frankly I cannot be bothered to move an inch and see who my new detention buddy is. My head is killing me.

"Well, look at what the cat dragged in," a familiar voice says with a chuckle beside me.

31

My head darts up, despite the pain, and I groan loudly as I see who it is. Alec raises an eyebrow, clumsily pulling out a chair and plonking himself into the seat to my right.

"Just for that outstanding enthusiasm, I'm going to come and sit next to you."

"Abracadabra," I mutter under my breath, before pausing to assess the damage. "Nope. You're still here."

"Don't even pretend like you don't love it," Alec retorts playfully. I don't feel like going along with the joke. How is it possible for a boy to be this annoying?

"What got you in here on your first day then?" I ask bluntly. It's not typical for a new student to get a detention on his first freaking day. Maybe the rumours are true.

"I had a little argument with Mr West on the nature of his teaching," Alec replies casually.

"The nature of his teaching?"

"The idiot insisted a kilometre was longer than a mile. I disagreed."

"Right."

"He didn't appreciate the manner in which I disagreed." Alec grins.

"Of course he didn't." I roll my eyes but a small smile lifts the corners of my lips before I can help it. Silently, I fish my phone from my pocket as a distraction. I have a horrible habit of scanning through my messages to avoid socialising.

"Well that's antisocial," he says, poking me. "Why are you in such a bad mood, Greene?"

"Not antisocial, just anti-idiot," I grumble. "And I'm not in a bad mood." I'm in such a bad mood, I don't know why I even bother denying it. It has something to do with

32

this detention, my lack of sleep and a lot to do with the girl glaring at me from the front of the room.

"Are you Google?" Alec asks me bluntly.

"What?" I turn to him, squinting at his random remark. Where did that come from?

"Because you have everything I'm searching for."

I blink. "Are you ins –"

"I was reading a book of numbers yesterday, and I realise I don't have yours."

"What are you –"

"Do you believe in love at first sight? Or do you want me to walk by again?"

"Alec, seriously –"

"Are you a parking ticket? Because you've got 'fine' written all over you."

"Stop!"

"Stop what?" Alec asks me innocently, despite the malicious grin curving the corners of his lips upwards. "Giving you compliments? Cheering you up? Is a guy not allowed to hit on his crush these days?"

Did I just hear that? I begin to choke on my own saliva. "Crush! What?"

Alec snickers. "Sorry, I didn't think you'd fall for that. You are pretty, Greene . . ." He leans closer to my face. "Pretty stupid."

My face hardens into a humiliated scowl. What a jerk. I turn to look at my phone again, unlocking it quickly and flicking through my photos as my method of ignoring him. People like him feed off attention and for that reason I won't give him any. I can't wait for this detention to be over. Alec frowns beside me. Of course, he can't possibly deal with the silent treatment.

"Riley," he whines, poking me. My head throbs again.

"You are immensely irritating, do you know that?"

He smiles almost proudly. "I know. What are you doing?"

I roll my eyes. "Just looking through photos."

"Can I see?"

Sighing, I angle the phone towards him, flicking through photos of myself and Violet, food in idyllic cafés, screenshots of my favourite Instagram posts. I hesitate on a particularly fond photo from a couple of years ago, of Violet grinning at me over a latte, and I smile at my best friend. She's a kook, but I adore her. Alec shifts beside me to get a better look at the phone screen.

"Best friend?"

I nod. "Her name is Violet."

"She looks nice."

I give him a sideways glance and he chuckles. "Not like that – calm down."

Smiling slightly myself, I click onto the next photo on my camera roll and instantly freeze.

"Whoa," Alec breathes. "She looks so much like you."

I release a strangled breath, a lump of pure panic forming in my throat. I thought I'd deleted this. *I thought I had deleted this.* The photo is of me, about the age of twelve, while I was on holiday with my family. My hair is shorter, my smile is wider and there's a spark in my eyes that seems to have disappeared for ever by now. Beside me is my cousin. I can't even bear to look at her half of the photograph, so I lock the phone and hide it from sight. My eyes sting slightly. Alec shouldn't have seen that. "That's my cousin," I state as firmly as I can manage, composing my facial expression.

34

"Kaitlin couldn't hold onto her man either, could she, Riley?"

The smartass little comment comes from none other than Tiana Cooper, her icy voice cutting in from a table over. She faces me challengingly, and I instantly wilt under the weight of the words. Guilt festers in my stomach like a fungus, and I feel my vision start to tint red at the nerve of what she just said to me. She doesn't know what happened.

She has *no* right to even mention Kaitlin's name.

My hands shake with the anxiety of confrontation. I clench them away from sight and face Tiana, fully aware that she's intending to wind me up and it is working. Anger, I was taught in therapy last year, is one of the ways of expressing the amount of emotion and guilt I've built up. The only thing preventing me from jumping out of this seat and punching Tiana is the steady gaze of Alec resting on my face. I don't want the questions. I can't answer them.

"Say something like that about her again, I dare you." I breathe out slowly. *She just wants the confrontation.* My jaw is locked. I'm not sure whether my threat scared her, or whether she just felt I didn't have the nerve to do anything in front of these people, but Tiana just gives me a smug look and turns back to the front of the class. She thinks she's won, and maybe she has. Her words burn in my mind like fire, a rotting sick feeling in my chest.

She doesn't know anything. How can she?

I want nothing more than for Alec to go back to his normal jokes, and to think nothing of that picture and what he just saw. I need the distraction, the happiness, to get over what was just said to me. Luckily, he seems to realise this and doesn't comment on the showdown between Tiana and I.

His eyes turn playful again, replacing the cold shock of my bad reaction.

"Can we keep looking at your photos?" he asks. "I was actually enjoying that."

"What are you, five?" I sniff, sliding my cell back in my pocket safely.

"Yup. I could be your toy boy, baby." He wriggles his eyebrows suggestively. "The effect I have on you is adorable."

"What, you mean wanting to rip your head off your shoulders?" I reply, voice still shaking. My heartbeat is slowing as I relax into my chair again. *It's okay, Riley, he didn't think anything of it.* My headache has somehow got worse.

"You look like an angry kitten. Don't get me started on that blush."

"Shut up," I say. I can't deny it though – what he's saying is working. Distraction.

"Hey, Riley?"

"What, Alec?" I sigh.

"Is your face from McDonalds? Because" – he pauses to wink at me – "I am lovin' it."

Alec, infuriating as he is, is just what I need at this moment.

4

The Plan

"I can't believe she said that," Violet fumes beside me.

I remain silent. We're walking along the main corridor in school towards our lockers. It's Tuesday morning and the raucous chatter of teenagers and busy surroundings are doing nothing to lift my mood. I knew when I told Violet about Tiana that she'd be as angry as I was. After all, Kaitlin was Violet's best friend too. Even thinking about yesterday's encounter is twisting that guilty feeling in my stomach. I have the feeling it might remain there for a while.

"I also can't believe you didn't give her a good slap," Violet grumbles on, her face twisted into a scowl. "She walks around you like she owns you, Riley, and you have every right to hate her. If I were you, I'm pretty sure I'd have busted her pretty pink lips by now, at least once."

That brings a slight smile to my face. "Oh it's tempting."

"You're so nice to people." Violet shakes her head. A cluster of folders is rested neatly on her hip, and as she strides confidently through the corridor I watch her gather the usual amount of attention. Violet is so logical, so confident. She walks, proud of who she is, and people love her for it. She continues on, oblivious of course. "It's admirable, but she is the one person in the world you can afford to hate. And yet you don't."

"I just don't see the point," I sigh. "I don't want to spend my time hating her."

As we reach our lockers, we stop. We're near the hub of Lindale High School now, and the corridor is busy with students. I open my locker and quickly slide a couple of today's folders in.

"Saying that, a black eye would go nicely with those boots of hers," I add.

"That's the spirit!"

The sound of wolf whistles to the left catches my attention, and Violet and I peer over to see Alec merely ten lockers down, kissing a girl and drawing a fair amount of attention. He's only been here a day, but just as predicted, he's gone straight to the top of the food chain. He breaks away from her, and some but not all people move on and the attention diverts.

"Control your *whore*mones," I mutter under my breath.

I look on as the girl presses one last lingering kiss to Alec's lips.

"Chelsea!" I hear a horrified voice exclaim. "What do you think you're doing!"

Tiana marches down the corridor, and Chelsea seems to shrink suddenly against the lockers with an expression of horror. A hushed silence falls over everyone as Her Royal Bitchiness stops in front of the quivering girl. High-heeled black boots, an icy glare and smudged mascara make for a very intimidating Tiana Cooper.

"That's it," Tiana hisses. "We are no longer friends. I told you to stay away from him."

"But T-"

Chelsea's pleas are interrupted by Tiana shaking her head. "Save it."

Almost as soon as the drama has begun, it diminishes. Tiana turns away and a natural conclusion settles over the crowd. Throwing me a glare, she then stalks back down the corridor with Chelsea running and yipping behind her like a little lost puppy. Everyone seems to remember to breathe once they're out of sight. Tiana is universally feared, by everybody except maybe Violet. She's a power figure, with lots of money and a fierce attitude. She's crushed on by a fair amount of boys. Strangely enough, they tend to like that kind of badass Megan Fox vibe she has.

"Hey there, Greene."

I feel a tug on my sleeve and turn my head to see Alec standing next to me, also watching Tiana storm away. "Hey," I reply a little awkwardly. "Alec, meet Violet." I push my locker shut and lean back to watch the interaction. I'm quite curious as to how this is going to play out. Alec's eyes fall onto Violet and he nods, tousling his dark hair.

Violet stares blankly at him for longer than it's comfortable. Finally she says, "I've heard lots about you."

"All good things I hope."

"Some good, some bad, some bizarre."

"I have no idea what you're referring to," Alec scoffs, adjusting the strap of his rucksack. I'm pretty surprised he's over here talking to us actually. I didn't know he'd actually make an effort to talk to me. "That Chelsea girl," he continues, "she says someone's throwing a huge party

39

tomorrow night. Are you guys going? I don't think it's Tiana's." He glances at me.

I open my mouth to say no anyway, but I'm hastily interrupted by Violet.

"Yeah we're already going," she says nonchalantly, even though I'm pretty sure this is the first she's heard of it.

"Violet." I turn to her dubiously. This definitely does not sound like a good idea. Plus, I don't know any of Chelsea's friends well at all, and I'm not exactly the partying type. I'll be left on my own in a room full of strangers, knowing me.

Violet simply raises an eyebrow slightly. I know what she's trying to say. She thinks this is a good opportunity to get one up on Alec. She also knows I haven't been to a party since . . . well, since that night. She's trying to tell me I need to get back out there and push myself, and I know I should, but my anxiety is holding me back more than a little bit. The doubt is still clear in my expression.

"Chicken," Alec teases from beside me.

"I'm not a chicken!" I defend.

Alec begins to make clucking noises. If I wasn't so irritated, I'd be laughing.

"I'm *not* a chicken," I spit out through clenched teeth.

"Who lit your fuse?" he teases. "It'll be fun. Me and the boys will be there too. You might actually enjoy yourself." He gasps in fake shock to emphasise his point. I feel a slightly nervous twist in my stomach. I hardly know these guys, so that was not particularly comforting.

"You only have to give it a shot," Violet reminds in a slightly softer tone, bumping lightly into my arm. "Come on, you know I'll look after you."

Alec begins to cluck again.

40

"Okay, enough from you," says Violet immediately, stepping towards Alec, who immediately pipes down.

"Okay, okay," I surrender. "I'll come. On the condition I get my bra back."

I think that's pretty fair.

"Nice try." Alec grins, with a furtive glance at Violet, who is still standing to attention. He hastily adjusts his rucksack again and begins walking down the corridor to his first lesson. "Have a nice day!"

As soon as he is safely out of range, I turn to Violet with a look.

Now it's time to fight fire with fire.

Stage one of the plan for revenge: get my bra back.

I peer behind my curtains curiously. Alec went to bed twenty minutes ago, and I'm pretty sure he must be fast asleep by now. I'm clad in a typical burglar outfit – leggings and a black and white stripy top. I may look like a third grader at a costume party, but I figured the people in the movies did it for a reason.

The plan is simple. Break into Alec's room. Find the bra. For stage two, get some revenge for the prank he pulled, and come home safe and sound in stage three. What could possibly go wrong? Well, I guess jumping out of the window could potentially cause some issues, but we'll cross that bridge when we come to it. Or don't come to it, as the case may be.

I pull back the drapes, looking out through the open window at the gap with a gulp. Sure it's only a tiny gap, but if I fall then I will probably die. Taking a deep breath to ease my nerves, I climb nimbly over the window frame and stretch across onto the opposite sill. *Don't look down, do not look down.* I'm not exactly the biggest fan of heights. As I prepare to launch myself over the gap, I begin to sense the familiar build up in the back of my throat. Oh no, oh no, shoot no –

"Achoo!" I sneeze loudly into the silence, freezing in my position. Did he hear that? Crap. Crap, crap, crap. I stay still for a few more seconds, but nothing stirs in the room, so I decide to take my chances. I project myself from my window ledge to his, not even giving myself time to get nervous again. Luckily, I land pretty niftily on his sill and grab his window frame to steady myself. Maybe I should pursue burglary as a career. I've got the uniform after all. I swing myself into his room quickly, landing softly on my feet.

His room is dark, crowded with shadows from mahogany furniture. His bed is plain white, and his desk is cluttered with photos and homework assignments. The boy himself is sprawled attractively on top of his covers, fast asleep. It's time to find my bra, and I've got to be as quiet as humanly possible. Adrenaline shoots down my veins; my heart speeds up at the thought of him waking. I could never live it down if he did.

I check all the obvious places first. Under the bed, in his bureau and in his closet. Unfortunately, I can't see anything except dustballs and deodorant. His whole room reeks of the stuff. It's then that I turn to the more unlikely places like under his desk or on his bookshelves, but yet again I come up empty. And as time stretches on, I feel myself getting more and more jealous of the boy asleep in bed. I'm exhausted, thanks to him.

I search around the room for what feels like hours. Maybe

he's hidden it somewhere else. Is it in a different room? Or maybe it's under the floorboards or something . . . I sigh in frustration. I think this is a mission failed on the bra front, but at least I can get revenge on him for not giving it back. My eyes have already pinpointed a permanent pen on his desk, and I know just what I want to do with it.

I grab the pen from the desk beside me and tiptoe back over to Alec's bed. He looks oddly peaceful when he sleeps, and it's disconcerting to see him without a smirk on his face. Cautiously, I press the felt to the skin of his upper lip and draw a long, swirly moustache. Although this idea is really overused, it's the only one I have energy to think of. Next, I fill in the space between his eyebrows, before printing "RG" firmly in the middle of his forehead: my initials. I have to leave my mark somewhere, right?

I admire my work for a second as I place the pen back. I think that's quite a reasonable revenge actually, considering all he's done to me. I take a photo on my phone. If this turns into some kind of a prank war, I have ammunition.

Suddenly, Alec grunts below me and rolls over in bed. His giant arm swipes through the air, knocking the pen out of my hand. I lunge for it clumsily in the darkness and the next thing I know, my petite figure is sprawled on top of the bed, scarily close to Alec's sleeping face. *Do not move. Do not breathe.* Chanting the words to myself internally, I watch through squinted eyes as Alec shifts again. He wraps his strong arm protectively round my waist, and he lets out a small snore, completely and utterly lost in his slumber. Wow, he's a deep sleeper.

Once I'm sure it's safe to move again, I grab for the bedside table and shift my leg back over the bed.

43

Alec's eyes open.

He blinks at me. Once. Twice. Thrice. And then it hits him. He jumps a mile back in bed, cursing loudly. "Holy shit! What are you doing?"

If he hadn't got marker all over his face at this current moment, it would be a hell of a lot easier to take him seriously.

"Riley?" he yelps, flicking a switch and filling the room with light. "What the hell are you doing in my room? Please don't tell me we slept together, because I don't remember a thing –"

"Are you insane?" I say, choking on the words. "Slept together? Of course we didn't!"

Realisation dawns on his face as he wakes up more. It's a school night. He wasn't drunk, and I definitely didn't sleep with him. His eyes meet mine, hardened this time. "Why are you in my room then?"

Dammit. I should have told him we slept together.

"Um, well –"

"Tell me."

"I thought I saw a hornet in my room?" I try weakly.

"It's the middle of the night, Riley."

"Actually it's kind of morning, because it's almost 2 a.m. so, you know, that's not really night any more, is it?" Taking one look at Alec's face, I stop blabbering and sigh. "I was trying to get my bra back."

"Dressed like a cat burglar?" Accusation seems to fade from his expression, replaced by obvious amusement.

"Shut up, grasshole, it was part of the plan," I sigh.

"The plan?" Alec laughs. "What did you do, plan out stages?"

No comment.

44

"Freaking hell, you did!" He's howling with laughter now, oblivious to the noise he's making. I can feel my cheeks burning in embarrassment. If he doesn't shut up, Marie's going to come in wondering what the hell is wrong, and if I'm there that's a whole lot of awkward that my poor crimson cheeks can't stand.

"Alec, shut up – your mom's going to wake up!" I hiss at him, batting him on the arm.

"This is going straight onto all of my social media." He ignores my warning.

"Don't you dare!" I snarl, but Alec is already reaching for his phone with a boyish smile. "No!" I lunge forward to grab it, missing by a whisker. If he posts that, my life will be over for good, but if I stay in here much longer then Marie might come in and see me. I need to go.

I dart towards the window and swing my legs over, not thinking of the danger before I jump swiftly onto the opposite sill, leaving Alec typing hurriedly in his room. He doesn't even seem to notice I've disappeared. Despite the embarrassment of having yet another status written about me, something makes me think that being caught in Alec's bedroom in the middle of the night by Marie would be somewhat worse. Panting a little, I slide into my own room and draw the curtains, collapsing against the heater. Now that was an adrenaline rush!

In Alec's room I can hear Marie's muffled voice as she tells him to shut up through his door. I escaped in the nick of time.

As if on cue, my phone buzzes.

Alec Wilde has mentioned you in a status.

Looks like I've just been cat-burgled! @RileyJGreene can't
keep her paws off me . . .

Alec freaking Wilde, I am going to kill you.

5

Hiding in Plain Sight

The next day at school, I avoid Alec like the plague.

No doubt, he will have become aware of my permanent pen drawings on his face by now, and I don't feel like being there to see his reaction. I've tried to stay under the radar as much as possible and go about my usual business, but there's only so much I can hide when the whole school is wondering what that status meant. I've been attracting attention all day, from people I know, as well as people I don't. They want to know why their new attractive boy has the initials 'RG' written clearly on his forehead. This was perhaps not my brightest idea, in hindsight.

I roll my eyes at the curious attention, walking down the corridor towards my lesson and trying to hide how much anxiety is building in my chest. Since it is common knowledge that I drew all over Alec's face, Tiana and her progesterclones are leading a movement against me. The majority of the attention has simply been curious, but on the bright side, I've had a couple of boys high-five me for my prank. Alec did totally deserve it, so I have nothing to hide. Witnesses have told me that the pen is still very much on Alec's face, and he came to school looking rather pissed off this morning. Looks like I'm not the only one who's been trying to stay under the radar.

"Riley!" Dylan catches up with me, grasping my forearm lightly. "How's it going?"

"Hi, Dylan. Not too bad, how are you?"

He looks gorgeous today – angel blonde hair lightly pushed back, as if he's run his hand through it too many times, and wearing a clean grey jumper which is no doubt expensive. I can't deny, I do see why Dylan gets the attention he does. He's cute, smart and, most importantly, really nice to people.

"I'm all right." He smiles lopsidedly. "Any luck with the bra?"

I grimace. "Not as of yet. I broke into his room last night and couldn't find anything. I don't know where it is but he's not stupid enough to keep it in his room. I got a bit of revenge though, so at least there's that."

We turn into the corridor leading towards my English room, the students dwindling now to reveal the polished wooden floor and cheesy inspirational quotes of a high-school hallway. I need to be careful or I'll be late for my lesson.

"I saw your prank – nice job by the way. Alec told us about you breaking in. You dressed like a cat burglar?" Tones of disbelief and amusement colour his voice.

I scoff. "Of course not. He's making that up."

"Well, I thought I'd give you a hint." He pulls my elbow lightly to stop me in my tracks.

"A hint?"

"I do feel a bit bad for the whole bra thing," he admits,

shoving his hands into his pockets and rolling back on his heels. "If it wasn't in his room, then I think you should check his bag. Alec's got exactly the kind of guts to carry the thing around with him. He's in football now, so if you went to the boys' changing rooms you'd be able to find his stuff."

"Oh," I say stupidly. *The boys' changing rooms.*

"I'm only helping you once," he warns. "And I don't know that it'll be there, but it sounds like an Alec thing to do. Just make sure you get in and out before their training session is done otherwise you're screwed."

"Thanks," I say in surprise. "I didn't expect you to try to help me."

"Well." He shrugs abashedly and looks away. "No word of this to Alec. It's just a suggestion anyway."

"Do you mind if I ask . . . how do you guys actually know Alec so well?"

"He lived here when we were kids. We all basically grew up together."

"Huh." The thought that he had lived in Lindale previously hadn't occurred to me.

"Anyway," Dylan drawls. "I should get to Chemistry. Good luck with the bra hunting if you decide to go." He touches my arm lightly and walks back down the corridor away from me. It was actually really nice of him to try to help. I glance towards my English classroom and bite my lip. The corridor is entirely empty now. I'm already late.

"God, I hope it's there," I grumble to myself, spinning on my heel and marching in the opposite direction.

I stare horrified at the door in front of me. I can already smell the stench of axe spray and male sweat from here. My

49

nostrils are burning, my jaw is clenched and my eyes are wide. It won't be too bad. I can just . . . not breathe for a while. I'll get used to the smell, and hopefully I won't have a lung spasm and die. *Crap, I can't believe I'm doing this.* I'm a bit worried that this is maybe taking the searching too far. Then I remind myself that he started this. I'm just going to be the one to finish it.

If this is the only way, it's time to step up and take it back.

Reluctantly, I pinch my nose and kick the door open to enter the changing rooms, letting the strong-smelling air flood over me. I'm going to die of asphyxiation in here. Wary of possible male stragglers, I peer round the corner of the wall and I'm relieved to see the room empty, albeit a complete mess. I step cautiously, dodging stray socks and sneakers that have just been thrown around. Sweat-stained towels and deodorant cans lie everywhere. The room is tiled blue, instead of purple like the girls', and is lined with benches. To the right are doorways to the showers. I begin to scan for Alec's things. I know he has a navy rucksack, but which one of them is his?

Staring at all of the bags in doubt, I feel so uncomfortable. I just want to find his bag and get it over with. I shouldn't be in here.

I make a snap decision and pick one that is as similar as I can recall, opening it to peer inside. Water bottle, folder, notepad. Nothing special. Cussing under my breath, I position it as I found it and move onto the next navy rucksack. I hiss out my breath through my teeth. I'm not sure if I can continue to do this. It feels wrong. Frustration begins to escalate in my chest. For all I know, Alec might not even be at football training today. Dylan could have made a mistake, or sent me here as a trick. I'm in the boys' changing rooms, potentially searching through some random guys' bags!

If Alec would just give the damn thing back, I wouldn't be doing this! I can't believe that boy had the nerve to take it in the first place, never mind keep it from me. He's undoubtedly the hottest but also most irritating guy I have ever met. I hate that a part of me is growing fond of his warmer, playful side. I can't allow myself to be hurt again, and this guy is evidently an utter grasshole.

I freeze. My blood runs cold.

That's the sound of footsteps. Guys cheering and hooting, doors closing.

The football team are coming back.

Scrambling to push the navy rucksack I was looking at back into place, I search frantically for somewhere to hide. The showers have no cubicles. I can't hide under the benches. Beginning to hyperventilate, my gaze rests on a set of metal storage cupboards. These are my only hope. I frantically dash over, open a door and clamber into the bottom amongst the dirty footballs and team sweaters. It stinks of stale sweat in here, but at least the axe-spray smell is less strong. I pull the door shut in front of me, curl up into a ball and sit in the darkness, listening. My heart is racing.

The next sound I hear is the bustle of the team coming into the changing rooms – the smack of soles across the tiles, the jostling of sweaty bodies. Boys are so loud.

"That was one kick-ass game," someone yells, echoed by howls of agreement. Shin pads and shoulder guards clatter against the floor. I realise I'm holding my breath, too scared to make a noise, despite the clamour that they're making. This was so *stupid*.

"Guys, round up any borrowed shin pads. I need to put them back in the cupboard."

Please be talking about a different cupboard.

I can hear footsteps getting closer, and somehow it's louder than all of the other noise. Cringing back into the shadows, I find myself covering my face, as if that will make any difference. As if it isn't enough to be known as the girl who broke into her neighbour's bedroom, now I'm going to be the girl creeping in the boys' locker rooms too! The footsteps stop outside of the cupboard and I can see the shin-pad box being placed down through the gaps in the lining.

Crap, crap, crap.

And just like that, all my panicking is replaced by downright fear. The door swings open, revealing a load of half-naked, muddy and sweaty guys in a changing room. Light floods the cupboard, meaning even the darkest crevices are exposed. They haven't spotted me yet, but it won't be long. I peer up, wincing as I see the aghast face of a bulky football player staring down at me. His curly hair is slicked back with sweat, his jaw is slack and his eyes are bulging impossibly wide. Way to make an impression, Riley.

"Girl!" he roars, and it's as though everybody within a fifteen-metre radius jumps a mile in the air. Havoc ensues as boys turn to stare at me openly, shrieks of a pitch that I didn't even think was possible for boys are released and guys are jumping around, pointing at me and covering up their junk. Cheeks burning, I stare at the chaos in front of me.

I cuss under my breath, standing up from my position in the cramped cupboard and holding my poor back. Just that simple motion seems to send the havoc into overdrive. Everywhere I look, boys are shouting and cussing at me or screaming with laughter, and quite frankly I'm so over-whelmed that tears begin to prick my eyes. Do not cry. That will just make this situation ten times more embarrassing.

"I'm leaving, shut up. It was a dare!" I repeatedly shout out my lie, making a beeline for the door.

I freeze in my tracks.

Alec Wilde is standing at the entrance of the boys' locker rooms, staring at me in shock. He's sweaty and his skin is reddened, but the pen is still evident. Every guy in the room is staring at me, and my cheeks have never been so scarlet in my life. He has caught me, quite literally, in my most embar-rassing moment. Meekly, I step past Alec to get out of the changing rooms. At this point, I am ready for death.

"I've got you," he whispers, coming up behind me with his hands on my shoulders and gently pushing me into the fresh air of the corridor. As soon as we're out, he spins me round, pressing my back against some sports lockers.

I take a few gulps of fresh, clean oxygen, feeling totally shell-shocked.

"Why were you in there?" I hear the incredulity in his voice.

"I was looking for my bra," I answer almost robotically. I can't believe that just happened. I can't *believe* I didn't leave when I should have.

"Did I even need to ask?" He chuckles dryly to himself. "Anyway, are you okay?"

His question surprises me, and I don't fail to show it. My head snaps up painfully to stare at him. He actually cares, despite what I did last night. Why? "I'm fine," I say breath-lessly, blushing and glancing back down to the floor again. I'm snapped out of my daze when he shifts beside me, and slowly but surely I'm pressed into the lockers. What is he doing? I glance up curiously and freeze. Alec isn't saying anything, he's just looking. Just looking at me.

"What are you doing?" I stammer.

He begins to lean in. His face is sweaty, his eyes are beautiful.

My heart stirs into overdrive, pummelling against my ribs at a speed I never knew was possible. My breath dissipates in my throat. My lungs are on fire, my pulse is going crazy and my blood feels like it's boiling in my veins. What –

He leans right past my lips to my ears.

I release my breath in relief, but not for long. Alec's breath tickles my earlobe, reminding me that I am still smack bang in the centre of an incredibly compromising, awkward situation. I await his words nervously. Surely he's going to say something, right? He's not just going to stand there and breathe awkwardly into my ear?

"I will get you back for this, Greene," Alec murmurs.

It's only when he leans back that I take notice of the marker pen on his face. It's faded a little, but it's still quite prominent, even on his olive skin. I sense a laugh tugging on the corners of my mouth but hurriedly try to restrain it. Now is not the correct time for laughing, but the more I try to restrain it, the more it escapes. Giggles turn into full-blown cackles, and Alec has a horrified glare on his face. "Riley, stop laughing!"

"I'm sorry," I wheeze, unable to look at him for fear of laughing even more. I think I'm losing my sanity.

"What the – ?" Dylan's voice butts in from beside us, and I look up to see him staring at both me and Alec with a slightly baffled expression. Alec shrugs in reply. Even I don't know why I'm laughing like a donkey in the middle of the corridor, but this is the perfect time to escape. So, as I burst into another round of giggles, I make a break for it. I run so fast I'm afraid my legs won't carry me and I'll fall over. I can just about hear Alec's cry of surprise behind me, but it's too late now because the air is whipping past my ears and I'm focused and concentrated on my running – on my running and nothing else.

Dodging gym teachers and tennis balls, I sprint through the gym as fast as my legs will go, fully aware of Alec catching up to me. In one last burst of adrenaline, I slam straight through the girls' restroom doors and into the beige interior of the school bathrooms, knowing Alec wouldn't dare follow me in here. A few girls look up at me in surprise, but all I can concentrate on is catching my breath. I did it! I'm saved!

"I'll see you at the party tonight, Riley," Alec calls from outside. "I know where you live."

And they'll say I'm the creepy one.

6

The Party

Violet pulls up outside the party and my heartbeat thunders inside my chest.

I stare through the window, making no effort to exit the vehicle just yet. We're parked, like many other cars, on a long gravel driveway at the foot of a stone mansion. There are people everywhere I look – passed out on the grass, dancing or making out. The music is so loud it seems to shake the ground. This party is huge. Why did I ever think this was a good idea? My palms are slick with sweat as I wipe them down my unusually-for-me bare legs, and I take a deep breath to calm myself.

"Riley, you can do this," my best friend reminds me, leaning over to squeeze my hand.

"You sure about that?" I ask breathlessly. A large part of me is dying to go home, but I won't allow myself to cower out of this. To defeat my anxieties, I have to confront them. But son of a biscuit, I'm scared right now.

"I'm positive." She squeezes again. Violet's eyes are lined with kohl, and her hair is in an intricate French braid. She looks gorgeous. I turn to look out of the window again at the scene. We're in the more expensive part of Lindale, towards the cliffs. The houses here are all worth a lot of money, and this one is no exception. It almost seems a crime to litter it with teenagers. You can tell this place looks magnificent in the daytime.

"Okay, I'm ready."

I force myself out of the car and we walk up the long driveway towards the party. I watch Violet teeter slightly in her heels, thanking heaven that I've stuck with my trusty ankle boots and dungaree dress. The music seems to grow louder with every step I take, alongside the thrumming of my heart in my ears. We receive only a few disinterested glances as we make our way up to the door – people are too absorbed with their own business to notice that anyone else has arrived.

"Greene," a familiar voice calls from behind me. Standing at the top of the steps leading to the entrance, I spin on my heel to see Alec making his way towards us, freshly scrubbed from the permanent-pen disaster. He wears black skinny jeans and a low side-cut tank top. His hair is messy, and he's got a can of beer in one hand. His other hand is behind him, hidden from my view. I feel an instant wash of relief once I see him. "Hey," he says, looking me over. "You look great."

What? He just complimented me. He just told me I look "great".

"Oh . . . thanks," I stammer. "You – you do not look bad either."

My eyes wince shut the minute the words leave my mouth. That is quite possibly the most awkward response I could have given. Why does the filter between my brain and my mouth seem to crumble into ash sometimes? I practically burned myself there.

Alec snorts with laughter, and I crumble further.

"Such sweet words you speak."

"She means you look hot," Violet intercedes. She flicks back a braid teasingly. "I would just like to remind you adorable kids that I'm here too!"

"Go on, Riley, give her a compliment." Alec grins.

"No, no, it's all right," says Violet dramatically. "No need to compliment me. I'm the Victoria sponge and she's Victoria's Secret, I understand."

"Oh shush, you." I laugh, batting her arm lightly. "Where are the others?"

"They're inside," Alec says, although he makes no move for us to join them. "Do you want a drink?" He brings the can forward, pushing it into my hands, and I wrinkle my nose. I've never been the biggest fan of alcohol full stop – but beer is just *foul*. I don't understand why anyone would want to drink it. Seeing my expression, Alec sticks his tongue out immaturely. "Loosen up a little. It will help you have fun, I promise."

"This is peer pressure," I mutter, but nevertheless I bring the can to my lips. I take a long, dry gulp of the disgusting liquid, squinting my eyes shut at the taste. As expected, it's vile, but I swig down some more of the can anyway and push it back into a surprised Alec's hands. I can't believe I'm doing this, but if there's any way I can calm my nerves about tonight, it'll be through a little bit of alcohol. "That was vile."

"It's gross," Alec says, grinning. "But we drink it anyway." He glances at Violet and offers her the can, but she shakes her head.

"Designated driver tonight."

Alec looks at me. "So you're the designated drunk? This should be interesting."

"If you find me chugging back vodka like no tomorrow at any point during this party, please stop me."

"No way! Drunk Riley could be fun. More fun than sober Riley at least." Alec offers me the beer again and I throw some more back without question. The only alcohol I really like the taste of is strawberry cider. Beer, wine, vodka or anything else just puts a bad taste in my mouth. The beer I'm chugging down is helping me to relax a bit, though. Or maybe that's just Alec's presence. The blue eyes that seem to dissolve a little bit more of me every time I see them.

"Drunk Riley would cry all over you, or faint." Violet laughs. "Not fun."

"Body shots?" Alec winks at me. "I'll let you use my abs if you want."

Tempting.

"I don't think potatoes get abs," I mutter under my breath, albeit loudly enough for Alec to hear me.

Violet snickers.

"Who said I was a potato?" Alec grabs my hand before I can move it away, flexing his bicep under the warm skin and forcing me to feel the arm tighten significantly. I try not to broadcast the fact that I want to melt right here right now, and tear my hand away instead.

"Mr Potato Head," I blurt. "Your arms aren't quite as impressive as you think."

"Liar," Alec says as he leans in, challenging me. My breath seems to leave my body quite rapidly, and I almost forget to breathe again. *Being so close to him makes me uncomfortable. It*

59

makes my heart race and my palms clammy. I don't like feeling like that.

"Shall I just be going, you two?" Violet interjects bluntly. "I'm a bit of a third wheel."

Alec moves back instantly and I scoff. "You can't third wheel unicycles, Vi."

She rolls her eyes. "I'm going to go inside and see who's here. Meet me in the kitchen in five minutes okay?" she says to me, before fixing Alec with a cold stare. "And don't call me 'Vi'."

"Deal," I affirm, but truthfully I'm a little uncomfortable. I don't want her to leave me with him, and I especially don't want to be alone at this party. I watch her walk away for a good few seconds before I turn to Alec. "You can go back to your friends now."

"I would but I have to speak to someone about something first." Alec pouts slightly. "You should go after Violet." He places the can of beer on the wall at the side of the steps and brings his other hand forward into my view. I stiffen as I register what he's holding. Is that a cigarette?

When he lights it, I realise what it is. A joint, which he brings to his lips, puffing out a sweet and seductive smoke that burns my nostrils.

"Is that a spliff, Alec?"

He stares blankly back at me. "So what if it is?" There's no playful ring in his voice any more. But judging by the defensive edge to his eyes, I'm treading on dangerous ground. I get nervous around people taking drugs, but I barely know him so I hardly have the right to tell him to stop. I analyse him for a few seconds before shaking my head.

"Nothing."

A flicker of surprise flies across his face. I think he was expecting me to blow through the roof in righteous anger, but in all honesty I know that I haven't got a say. It's his decision. He stares at me for a few seconds, and I look back unblinkingly. I can't help but wonder what he's thinking about. After a while, he cracks an empty smile.

"Good."

That's the only thing he says to me, and I've barely had a chance to register it before he walks away, into the party.

He drops the hardly smoked joint on the floor before he leaves.

Something about that small action makes me smile stupidly.

"Chug, chug, chug, chug!" the crowd cheers around me. I watch aghast as the person standing on the table gulps heavily from the bottle, spurred on by everyone's rowdy support. As he turns to face the crowd, I see his face, and laugh when I recognise it as Joe's. He's going to have a killer hangover tomorrow morning. Next to him, a boy called Adam is sheepishly mopping up a cider he spilled on the expensive carpet. Judging by the amount of people in this room, I have no doubt this gorgeous house will be trashed in the morning.

"Hey." Someone taps me on the back. I whirl round to see Dylan there, a coy smile on his slightly blurry face. "How are you finding the party?"

"It's all right, thanks, how about you?" I say, grinning back at him.

I've spoken to Joe and Chase tonight, alongside various other people, but I haven't spoken to Alec again since we first arrived. He's currently in the corner of the large room with some of his friends – that Chelsea girl included. Being the new boy at his first party, he is the focus of rather a large amount of attention. The current rumour spreading about Alec is that he went joyriding in his ex-principal's car. Whether or not that's true I have no idea, but everyone seems to have decided he's some kind of bad boy, so I guess it doesn't even matter. Because people love a bad boy.

I've drunk a fair amount at this point. The buzz seems to dissolve my stress the more I consume. I'm glad I came, but I think that feeling's only because of the alcohol.

"I've been good. Can I get you a drink?" Dylan offers politely. Violet is off getting me more vodka now, but I nod anyway. He passes me a can of cider, unopened.

"Thanks." I beam. I can't deny I'm a little bit tipsy.

"I never really pictured you drinking," Dylan notes, watching me take a gulp.

I nod in agreement. "I don't drink very often, fear not. Wanted to let loose a bit tonight, though." My gaze drifts back to Alec in the corner, and I feel a surge of irritation rise up in me. Why is he so attractive when deep down he is a monster?

"To try to fit in?" he questions. "I guess we're all guilty of that."

"Yep," I confirm, drinking from the can of cider again. "But there's the perk of having no social life. I don't have to try to fit in very often!"

"You have got a social life," Dylan says, rolling his eyes. "You know me, Alec, Joe and Chase. You've got Violet, and I'm betting you have friends in your classes. Plus, correct me if I'm wrong, you're at a party right now." He gestures around to the mass of people dancing. The room is large and smells of money, alcohol and an undertow of sweat.

"I guess." I wrinkle my nose. "But I've only just met you and the guys."

"Yeah but we like you. You're funny."

"Funny?"

"Yeah. And you're nice to be around."

My heart stammers a little with that phrase. *I'm nice to be around.* I guess I've forgotten what it feels like to have many friends outside of Violet. I've never been close to what anyone could call popular, but the events of last year pretty much put an end to any friendships that I did have. I didn't really think of trying to make new friends again. I'm lucky to have stumbled upon some.

"Alec isn't talking to me."

Uh oh. Alcohol talking, alcohol talking.

"And that upsets you?" Dylan raises an eyebrow skyward.

Yes. No. I don't know.

"I don't like him," I say hurriedly, taking another gulp. "He's a jerk. He seems to play around with girls a bit too. You're actually nice."

I need to start filtering what I'm saying out loud.

"He's not that bad," Dylan drawls, but I can see him smiling at the compliment. His hand goes out to hold my arm as I wobble slightly, but I don't focus on the contact. Everything feels blurry, a little cloudy round the edges. Is Alec angry at me? Why do I care so much what he thinks? "To be fair, it's not him that usually initiates anything. He has them under a spell at the minute."

"People are all so superficial," I sigh. "Alec and his reputation, and girls feeding off his reputation. Who cares?"

63

The fame and attention Alec has received tonight – all week, actually – as the "new guy" verges upon sickening.

"Not the sane people." Dylan shakes his head. "They don't care."

I finish the last of the cider and he takes the empty can.

"Hey, Riley." Violet comes up beside me, but her gaze is focused on Alec in the corner. I think I mentioned to her at some point that he hadn't spoken to me. I can't remember. He's kissing a girl now, but I don't think she's Chelsea. Violet holds a newly filled cup out of my reach as I try and grasp at it. "How are you feeling?"

"I feel good," I sing, snatching it from her. "A bit buzzed."

"Just let me know when you want to go home." She rests a hand on my shoulder and looks at Dylan. "Hey, I'm Violet, Riley's best friend. It's Dylan, right?"

"Nice to meet you." He smiles. "Think your best friend would want to dance?"

Violet glances at me, smiling. "I think she'd be silly to refuse."

When I nod, he grabs my wrist and leads me further into the crammed dance floor, away from Violet. I teeter, hissing out a breath as the crowds jostle me back and forth. Maybe this wasn't such a good idea. I gulp down the strong lemonade in my cup eagerly. I'm going to be fine. The alcohol will take it away. I won't be awkward and dorky any more.

Dylan and I dance and talk for a while, but I can't seem to stop my eyes from straying to Alec in the corner. It seems the more I look, the more I drink. The fuzzier my head gets, the less I feel when looking at him. When Dylan asks me if I want to come with him to get another drink, I nod. He grabs my hand, and I eagerly stumble after him through the

64

crowd. Alcohol is great. It makes everything so funny. I feel like Tony Stark in *Iron Man*, when he's drunk and he blasts the watermelon and stumbles all over the stage. I love *Iron Man*.

My leg hooks round some other girl's and I trip, landing awkwardly on my side. Everything shifts ninety degrees. I begin to giggle.

"Riley!" I hear Violet call.

People around me move. Dylan has released my hand. Strong arms hook up round the small of my back and I'm lifted onto a chair that has magically appeared behind me. My head spins as I struggle to make sense of my surroundings. Why is it so busy in this room? Some guy waves at me from the crowd, and I wave back. I wonder if anyone has any watermelon.

"Dude, did you not notice how much she was drinking?" I hear Alec groan at Dylan.

"I did notice, but she was good at disguising it!"

Violet kneels down before me, looking at me with her kohl-rimmed eyes. "Right, I'm going to get you some water and some food okay? Then I'm taking you home." She looks over my head at something behind me. "Please look after her – don't let her move."

"I can't go h-home," I hiccup. "Mom will be *soo* angry."

"Right. Well, we'll figure something out, okay? I'll be right back."

"Please get me some watermelon," I beg her.

She rubs my knee consolingly before she leaves. I don't want her to leave me alone. I continue to hiccup. A warm hand follows the length of my arm and Alec sits before me, staring up at my face dubiously.

65

"How did you get so drunk?"

"I drank a lot. A bit too fast."

"I got that. Why?"

"Because I wanted to," I hiccup, looking around. "I don't like parties."

"Look . . ." He runs a hand through his hair, still assessing me. "You're going to stay at mine tonight, okay? Violet can drop me and you back at my place, and I'll make sure you're safe. She has a test tomorrow and something tells me you're going to be late to school. We can speak to your mom in the morning to smooth things out."

"You can't take advantage of me," I warn.

Alec laughs. "Don't worry, I'm not a *complete* prick."

My head rolls back and I begin to giggle again at the sight of the ceiling. Violet and Dylan stand behind Alec with a cup of water and I eagerly reach for it. My throat is so dry, which is weird because I *swear* I've had loads to drink tonight. Gulping down the whole cup in essentially one go, I hiccup again. I kind of just want to go to bed now. I want brownies too.

"Right, time to move," Violet announces. She moves before me, blurring a little around the edges. "Riley, we're going home now okay?" I feel Alec slide an arm round my back, and I'm lifted from the chair into a standing position.

I nod.

"Dear lord, you're drunk," Alec mutters beside me as he helps me walk to the door.

"So *not* drunk."

"You're staggering."

"Thank you." I smile. "You're not too bad yourself."

66

Dylan begins to laugh, and I join in, although I'm not quite sure why.

As we make our way out into the hallway, the cold night air hits. Someone has left the front door open. There's a boy throwing up in the plant pot and a couple kissing in the corner. Alec's arm is warm round my back and he pulls me towards the door after Violet and Dylan, but that's when something, or rather someone, catches my eye.

"Toby," I murmur, staring at the figure.

"My name is Alec," Alec sighs beside me.

"No, that's Toby," I repeat. Standing by the door with an easy smile on his face, as though this isn't the one thing, as though he isn't the *one person* that could blow my mind into oblivion and shock me to the core. He looks the same as he always has. Cold blonde hair and hazel eyes that are locked on mine. "That's *Toby.*"

I resist against the front door as we pass him, craning my neck back to look at the boy. I glance forward but Violet is already outside. She hasn't heard me. She didn't see him.

"Come on, Riley." Alec tugs me by the waist. "It's time to go."

Locked in the grips of an alcohol-infused daze and the warm arms of an attractive boy, I don't resist.

7

Unexpected

Everybody that knows me knows that I am far from a morning person.

Awakening from a serene slumber into a blurred sense of reality is definitely not my ideal, much less what I look forward to. I always kind of envy those people who can wake up and think of nothing but the beautiful possibilities of the day ahead, of what they're going to do and who they're going to see. The word I'm looking for is positivity. These people have positivity in the mornings, and it's a shame to say that I . . . well, I am the polar opposite. On a normal morning I am a sight for sore eyes, but on this morning in particular? Well this one is something spectacular.

Let's just say that I don't usually wake up feeling like I've been hit by a truck. Twice.

I release a loud groan as I open my eyes. I don't think I've ever experienced a headache of such ferocity before. What the hell have I done to myself to cause this kind of pain? I sit myself up in my covers, squinting as my eyes adjust to the morning light, only to regret it completely. When I scan

68

my surroundings, my breath hitches in my throat. This isn't my room. The scent of cologne hangs in the air. The navy walls, the bed, the lamp – all of it is familiar to me. A warm presence is sleeping soundly beside me.

I'm in Alec's bed.

I cuss loudly, pushing the covers off me as soon as I realise. I claw the interior of my mind for anything, any information as to why I'm here. There was a party last night, but that's all I can remember. I've woken up with the world's worst hangover, albeit clothed, *in Alec Wilde's bed*. I'm praying to God that this doesn't mean what I think it does. I cautiously push the covers back from his sleeping form. He's shirtless. I cuss again.

Panic bubbles tauntingly in my gut. How long have I been asleep? My mom is going to freak. I look down at the clothes I'm wearing. Baggy leggings and a male's shirt.

Fudge.

"What's with all the swearing?" Alec mumbles drowsily. He turns to face me, squinting in the light. His hair is messy and his exposed chest is tanned, and as angry and scared as I feel right now, part of me wants to curl up in his arms and fall back to sleep.

"You grasshole," I hiss at him, enraged. "How could you take advantage of me like that? I don't know what the *hell* happened last night, but for you to—"

"Jeez, turn the volume down a few decibels," Alec grumbles, pushing himself up to sit next to me, leaning against the headboard. I daren't look at him, focusing instead on the white covers in front of me. How on earth did I let myself get into this? I don't remember drinking much at all. How did I even get here?

I force myself to speak calmly.

"What happened?"

"Of course you don't remember." Alec rolls his eyes. He sighs for a few seconds. "Let's just say you got completely hammered last night. You didn't want to go home because your mom would be angry, so Violet dropped you back here with me. And I promised her I'd look after you."

"Why am I in your *bed*?"

"Well, actually, you specifically requested to sleep on the sofa so that's where I left you," Alec says with a yawn. "You slept down there for less than an hour, and then came into my room at about 3 a.m. and climbed into bed with me. When I tried to go downstairs, you started crying. You pinned me down and fell asleep and, well, here we are now." He gestures at the two of us, lying in bed together. I can hardly believe what I'm hearing right now. What got into me?

"I'm sorry," I croak. My throat is dry, and frankly, I have no idea what else to say. First of all, he had the decency to take me home after I apparently obliterated myself on alcohol. Then, he leant me clothes and put me to sleep, only for me to climb into his bed in the middle of the night and try to spoon him? I thought even my drunk self had a little more dignity than that.

Alec finally turns to look at me properly. "How are you feeling?"

"Not fantastic," I mutter. "Hangover symptoms. I told you drunk Riley wasn't fun."

"I don't know, I thought it was pretty amusing to be honest," he teases. Pushing the sheets back entirely now, he shuffles down to the end of the bed and climbs over my

70

feet. His bare feet, bed head and sweatpants make him look frustratingly adorable as he stands and looks at me. I must have drunk a *lot*.

"I'll give you a minute to sort yourself out while I grab some breakfast. I woke up earlier and called your mom to let her know you were okay. She's called you in late for school, so we've got a bit of time. She wants to speak to you as soon as you're ready." Yawning and tousling his hair, he steps out of the room and I'm left alone, my impending doom settling in on me.

I climb out of the bed and stare at myself in the mirror. My hair is sloppy, my make-up smudged around my eyes, but what is really striking is the soft expression on my face. As much of a son of a biscuit Alec can be at times, there's no denying that he's got a sweet side. Not many people would do so much for a girl who completely embarrassed herself. I tame my hair into submission with my fingers, doing the best I can to remove my make-up with a dry tissue from the box on Alec's nightstand. The rest can wait until I get home.

Alec comes in after about five minutes, carrying a tray complete with toast, pills, orange juice and two cups of coffee. I perch daintily on the edge of the bed, unsure of what to say when I have so many questions running through my mind. Alec sets the tray between us and instantly reaches for a piece of toast.

"You should eat, Greene," he says, through a mouthful.

I pick up the coffee and hold the warm mug in my hands. "So where's your mom? Where's Millie? Do they know I'm here?"

"Mom left early to go to work; she dropped Millie at

71

kindergarten. I guess we're lucky that she didn't walk in this morning – she might have had quite a shock."

"You're going to keep this from her?"

"She would kill me if I told her."

"Fair enough," I say. I sense that he may want to change the subject. "I must have really gone overboard if I can't remember anything."

"You were pretty bad. You said it was because you didn't like parties."

"That seems about right," I murmur. I think about last night and begin to remember slightly – at some point I decided it was a great idea to drink myself through the ordeal. I was also upset that Alec wasn't talking to me, even though I had no real reason to be. *Mental note: you need to stop that.* I guess it just spiralled.

"My mom will never let me go to a party again," I think aloud.

To be honest, this has deterred me from another party anytime soon anyway. I'll stay at home next time. Nothing good ever happens to me at parties. I reach for the pills and gulp them down quickly, not quite sure how something so small can prevent the throbbing in my head but willing to give it a shot. I pause. "They're not laxatives or something, are they?"

Alec snorts on his orange juice. "Jesus, Riley, talk about kicking you while you're down. No, it's just aspirin! That would have been good, though . . ."

We chew on our toast in silence, both of us lost in thought about the events of last night. I feel so uncomfortable. I hate that he saw me like that.

"I need to speak to her," I say finally, standing up. I can't begin to describe how touched and surprised I am by Alec's actions. Never in a million years did I think he would do any of those things for me. The breakfast, taking me home. None of it.

"Okay, come back when you're ready and I'll drive you to school."

I hesitate for a second as he stands up.

"Hey, Alec?" I say. As he looks at me, his eyebrows furrow in confusion. "Thank you," I continue, before shyly leaning forward to give him a hug. "You know . . . for taking me home and stuff. Dealing with me."

He stands frozen for a second as he evaluates the situation, but slowly his arms wrap round my back and he squeezes tightly.

"You're welcome, Greene."

"Mom?" I call as I open our front door, taking hesitant steps into the hallway. "Are you still here? I'm home."

"Riley?"

Her voice rings out from the kitchen and it doesn't sound too happy. I brace myself for the inevitable and shut the door behind me with a click. All I have on me is my clutch and last night's clothes, and I'm wearing a pair of Marie's leggings and an oversized T-shirt belonging to Alec. Heaven knows what she's going to say to me. I can only hope that Alec's explanation this morning has helped to ease some of the anger.

A moment later, the monster herself emerges with nostrils flared and a phone clutched in her hand. "What happened to you last night?" she fumes. "I told you to go easy on the drink, and stupidly I assumed you would listen to me and *stay safe.* You know that drinking isn't good for your anxiety, and you're also underage! Then I get a call from Alec this morning telling me you're passed out and hungover, and you're going to be late for school! What were you thinking? I was so worried!"

"Mom," I say, clutching my head and wincing, "I'm really sorry, but please don't shout."

Mom blatantly disregards my plea, and glares at me. "What happened to you?"

"I don't remember."

"You don't remember?" She curses aloud. "Did you really drink that much?"

"I don't remember drinking much *at all*," I say in my own defence. "I just remember feeling uncomfortable and sad, and wanting it to go away."

"You could have called! I would have come to get you!" Mom's voice cracks and the expression on her face is one of complete disappointment. I realise quite how much I must have hurt her by doing this, on a night so similar to Kaitlin's death. By attempting to feel numb, I disregarded her feelings about my safety. I disrespected her simple requests for me to stay safe.

"I'm sorry, Mom, I really am."

"Don't do that to me again," she says finally, turning away. "Listen to me and be careful, or call me. Drinking that much when you're so vulnerable, and it's against the law! After what happened with Kaitlin . . . she went to a party and didn't come back. I need you to stay safe when you're out. Booze makes people do stupid things – including you. You have no idea of the things going through my –"

"Mom," I say. Guilt eats away at me. I didn't even think.

74

I'm so stupid, I'm so freaking stupid. "I'm so sorry, Mom, I didn't even think. I didn't mean to worry you."

"You understand there'll be consequences to this," Mom warns. "I allowed you alcohol, I told you that you could drink. I expected you to be responsible with what that decision means to me." Her arms are folded across her chest. She's dressed for work in a fitted suit with her hair twisted above her head. I stopped her from going to work on time.

"I understand."

"You're going to help out more around the house, okay? You want to be treated like an adult, you have to start acting like one."

"Okay."

"I mean it – dishwasher, cleaning. Everything."

"Okay." I nod. "I'm really sorry, Mom."

"Yeah me too," she says with resignation. There are bags under her eyes. She must have not slept very well. "Make sure you say thank you to Alec."

Then it dawns on her, and her warm expression turns cold once more.

"Riley, is that a boy's T-shirt?"

"It's Alec's T-shirt, so yes, I guess that would mean it belongs to a boy." I twist my hands together and fiddle with the chain on my clutch.

"Don't sass me." Her eyes narrow. "Why are you wearing his T-shirt?"

"Not for the reason you're thinking." I make a face, but my cheeks are flushed pink. "He just lent it to me, so I wouldn't have to wear last night's clothes. It's a sweet gesture, that's all."

"I don't want to know about the sweet gestures you two made, Riley."

75

"Mother!"

"I know what young kids are like these days, and nobody can deny that you and Alec have chemistry," she finishes. "I just want a warning if you ever decide to do that stuff, okay?" Mom raises an eyebrow, and I curl further and further into myself at her accusing stare. "Make sure you give him his shirt back. Have you taken any aspirin?"

"Yeah, I've had some aspirin," I say, grateful for the change in topic. "And I will, don't worry. I need to get changed for school now – I'm late enough already."

I tug myself away from her, kiss her on the cheek and head to the stairs. If I get to school in the next fifteen minutes, I'll only have two lessons to catch up on. Something tells me this hangover is going to last for a while and I don't want to be up late studying tonight.

"Stay hydrated, Riley," Mom calls up after me. "I'm going to work now. Take it easy today." I hear the rustle as she collects her bag. The cupboard door slams.

"I will, thanks, Mom," I call down from the top step, still cringing at the previous conversation. "I love you! Have a good day at work!"

"Have I ever mentioned to you that I don't have a death wish?" I say, biting my lip as I stare at the death trap on which Alec is currently sitting.

"You want a ride to school, don't you?" he retorts, patting the seat behind him on the motorcycle. "Hurry your sweet ass up and get on the bike, Riley." I continue to stand there staring doubtfully at him, and he releases a groan before repeating his actions. I've never thought about motorcycles personally – with my lack of balance I'll be lucky if I manage to even stay on the bike. My mind screams in protest, but the only alternative is to walk to school on my own, and I'm too lazy and too late for that right now. Begrudgingly, I walk towards my doom and slide on behind Alec. He passes me a helmet, and I can practically feel the smugness radiating off of him.

"You ready?" he asks, as I clip the helmet on.

I wind my arms round his waist and squeeze my eyes shut. "Ready as I'll ever be."

The vehicle roars beneath me, coming alive, and the next thing I know we're reversing back onto the road. I clutch Alec for dear life as we turn, and his muscles tense at the contact. With one final roar, the acceleration kicks into gear and we're off. My hair streams behind me like a banner, the wind silencing my cries of surprise. It's scary, but at the same time exhilarating – I didn't think I'd be able to experience both of those things simultaneously for a very long time. It makes me feel excited, and my embarrassment about last night drifts away. I'm proud that I managed to do this. My heart is in my throat.

"This is awesome," I shout to the boy in front of me.

He nods furiously in reply. Resting my head against his back, I watch fascinated as the Lindale scenery rushes by. Trees and large stone houses, neat sidewalks and dog walkers rush by, until I recognise the familiar roads leading up to the school. My abdomen seems to contract with nerves at the prospect. What will people say if they see me and Alec walking in together this morning? Especially if we left together last night. Acting spontaneously, I tap Alec's shoulder and call for him to stop the bike.

He glances back at me in concern but obediently pulls

over to the side of the road. Ice runs down my spine. Once we've stopped, he turns round in his seat, frowning. I swing my legs back over from the seat and hitch my schoolbag up on my shoulder, handing him back the helmet.

"What are you doing? Don't you want to get to school?" Alec asks me.

I shake my head, looking down at my feet. "I think it's better if I walk from here."

"Why?" Alec asks.

"Alec, what will people say if we walk in together this morning?"

To my surprise, Alec's eyebrows shoot up and he stares at me in hurt. I hurriedly try to patch up my mistake. "I mean, you have a reputation –"

"I get it," he interrupts me icily, every trace of emotion now extinct from his expression. "Can't have me tainting your perfect little track record, can we?" He laughs, but the sound is bitter. "Whatever, Riley. I'll see you at school."

I watch in shock as he puts his helmet on, kick-starts the bike and rides away.

"Wait, Alec . . ."

But he's gone before I can even finish my sentence.

The day passes slowly without Alec, as much as I hate to admit it.

Seeing him around school, he either doesn't notice me or pretends not to. I should've known that the nice treatment I was shown this morning was a one-time thing. It's frustrating that when he acts like he doesn't care about me, it's okay, but the minute it *appears* like I don't care about him – he shuts off completely.

I relay my fears to Violet as we sit in the canteen at lunch, but she merely scoffs at my worries. "He's manstruating and being stupid, Riley. He doesn't deserve you to care so much. He'll realise that he overreacted and come running back to you, I promise, and then you can make babies and everything will be swell."

"Aside from the 'making babies' part, I hope so." I stab a piece of pasta with my fork, eyeing it up without actually planning to eat it. "I hate that I care so much about what he thinks of me. I've only just met the guy, I don't need this extra anxiety in my life."

"Then try not to let it affect you – you haven't done anything wrong, Riley. You've been doing so well recently."

"That's true," I admit.

Violet stirs her milkshake with the straw. We're sat at the very edge of the canteen, at our usual table. It's slightly quieter here. "I actually have a proposition for you. It's something good – a distraction, and I honestly think you're ready for it."

Uh oh. That doesn't sound good.

"You see," she explains, "a friend of a friend is looking for a date this Friday night."

Here we go.

"Violet, you know I'm not the dating type," I cut in with a whine. "Let me be single and happy."

The truth is, dating terrifies me. As a socially awkward teenage girl, with a personal vendetta against dresses, I can just imagine that dating will be my individual version of hell. My last relationship ended miserably, and I can't relive that all over again.

"Are you happy, though, really?"

79

"That's beside the point," I admit. "I don't think I can manage it."

"I know you don't want to date again after last time," Violet probes softly, her expression one of sympathy. "I know you miss your cousin, and you hate Toby for what he did. This could be your fresh start, Riley. You have to start somehow, and Kaitlin wouldn't want you to stop living just because of how your last relationship ended."

I scrutinise Violet for a few seconds.

She's right about one thing. Kaitlin would be so pissed off at me if she knew that I hadn't moved on since Toby. She'd say that I should start dating again soon anyway, and it's not like I'm doing too much too fast. It's just one night. If I hate it, I don't ever have to do it again.

I hear myself giving in. "Okay. I'll do it, but if it's bad then you owe me chocolate."

"Riley, I wouldn't be suggesting it if I didn't think you were ready. And if you do decide to cancel, then I'll understand." Violet nods supportively. "I think this is the right thing for you, though. My friend says the guy is really charming and cute. It can't be that bad, can it?"

"I guess not," I grumble. "I hate it when you're right."

"I'm always right," Violet teases. "Friday night it is."

I miss Alec Wilde's presence.

I've only known this guy a little while, and already I've adapted to having him peppered throughout my day. Somehow, the fact that he's a player and that he pranks me constantly has been removed from my consciousness. Am I just another brainwashed fangirl to him now? I can feel myself slowly growing irritated at him. Irritated that he is

80

allowed to treat me badly, but he gets angry when he misunderstands a simple sentence coming from me? It's conceited of him and hardly fair, yet still I can't seem to shake the feeling that I miss him. I don't know why, or how, I just do.

Sitting here in Psychology, I can't help but let my mind stray back over to the incident this morning, as it has been doing all day. I feel bad, but I wish I didn't. I wish I didn't care about what he thinks of me. I shouldn't let him affect me so much. I bite my lip, playing with the end of a chewed pencil.

I shouldn't have even cared enough about his reputation to tell him to stop that bike.

I shake my head to clear my thoughts – I really can't be dealing with this right now. I've got a Philosophy test coming up next period, and I can't afford to be distracted. I'm not a straight-A student naturally; I have to work hard for my decent grades. For Chrissakes, I've been studying for a week and I am not risking this grade over a stupid little falling-out. I stare intensely at the whiteboard, trying hard to absorb what the teacher is saying, but I can't help but be distracted by a certain pair behind me.

"Mr Wilde! Miss Wilson!" Miss King shrieks from the front of the classroom. "Pay attention!" He's sitting at the back of the room with Minnie Wilson. They're leaning in close, *very* close, talking. My grip tightens on my pencil.

"So, what's going on between you and Alec?" I look up, just as Dylan slides into the seat next to me with a concerned expression. "Obviously something's gone wrong." He checks that the teacher isn't watching us, but luckily she is now typing on her computer. No doubt she's emailing the principal but at least the angry colour is fading from her

81

face. The class is free to talk, so long as we do the work set.

"Where do I even begin?"

"Uh oh." Dylan grimaces. "So he is avoiding you then."

"Like the plague," I grunt.

"I'm sure you guys will make up eventually, but in the meantime you still have me to talk to."

"He needs to let me explain." I exhale sharply, before going on to describe the events of this morning. Dylan's eyebrows raise further into his hairline the more I talk, but by the end he looks much more assured and confident. That makes one of us, I guess.

"Don't worry," he reassures me. "I'll speak to him and explain what you meant. In future, though, I think you need to learn that Alec doesn't give a crap what people think of him. If he wants to give you a ride to school, he will." Dylan reveals his teeth in a winning smile – the kind that makes mere mortals like me swoon. If there's ever a boy who embodies sweet, attractive, clever and funny, it's Dylan Merrick.

"Thanks, Dylan," I say, grateful for his wisdom.

"Okay, so that's what's up with Alec. What about killer queen over there in the corner?" He subtly motions to Tiana, who's been sitting in the back glaring at me for the entire lesson. I've kind of grown used to her cool glower every time I turn my head, but I shift uncomfortably when Dylan questions it. "What's her problem with you?"

"She's hated me ever since I wore the same dress as her to one of our formals," I bluff, not meeting Dylan's eyes. There's no way I'm getting into the Toby incident with Dylan. *No way.* "She glares but she never does anything about it. I don't even realise she's doing it any more." The last bit is true, at least. But as if I'd ever wear the same style of dress as Tiana. To me, my lie is clear as water, but Dylan doesn't notice a thing.

"Wow, okay." Dylan frowns. "She's very superficial. How could she not like you for that?"

"Yup," I mumble in agreement, then hurriedly change the subject. "Anyway, enough about me. How are you? Any exciting plans for this weekend?"

"Not really." He clicks his tongue. "What about you?"

"I'm going on a blind date actually." I force out a laugh, and observe Dylan's hoarse cough at the statement. I guess it is shocking that I actually have a social life, considering I'm a socially awkward monster.

"So you're on the hunt for a man, Riley Greene?"

"Maybe, yeah I'm not sure." I bite the end of my pencil.

"Who are you going on a blind date with?" Dylan asks, and I give him a blank look. "Dumb question." He curses his mistake. "Forget I asked."

I chuckle a little bit at Dylan's dumb moment, but the truth is that not even he can cheer me up while I know that Alec is still angry.

And I have to do something to fix this.

8

Sweet and Sour

The two simple doorbell tones ricochet through the chilly air, and I shiver in my woolly sweater, rubbing my hands together for warmth. *Please don't answer the door. Please don't answer the door.* It's pointless hoping, I know. The door swings open, light cascading onto my frozen figure.

"Riley! Come in, come in! You must be freezing." Marie ushers me inside with a beaming smile that I find myself returning unconsciously. How can a mother and son be so different? I wonder.

As soon as I got home after school today, my mom decided to spring it upon me that I'd be babysitting tonight for Marie, as a way to make up for my escapade last night. I'll be meeting and then looking after Alec's four-year-old sister Millie. I can't help but be more than the tiniest bit nervous. Kids that young are unpredictable, fragile and brutally honest if they don't like you. What if she's a handful? The only experience I've had with kids is my brother.

I was hoping that I'd be able to kill two birds with one stone while I was here and talk to Alec, but apparently he's out. I suppose that makes sense. I'm in this babysitting business alone, and knowing my luck, it's not going to go well.

"Thank you so much for coming on such short notice!" Marie smiles at me. "You're a lifesaver. It's such a shame Alec can't be here helping you – I get the feeling that you two are getting close. It's lovely to see him have friends again."

Again? Marie skips over her confusing remark, and hurries me into the living room to meet the baby I will be sitting.

The adorable little girl, who I haven't seen since the day they moved in, is sitting in the centre of the rug having a tea party with her dolls. The room is much more established now than when I last saw it – there are cushions on the sofas, flowers on the coffee table and the whole room smells like cinnamon and glows with fairy lights.

"Millie, this is Riley," Marie says as we step into the living room. Millie looks up immediately, her porcelain face turning rosy and coy as she evaluates me. She tugs at the bottom of her pink dress, hiding her face behind a wall of thick dark ringlets. But I can see that her eyes are the exact colour of her brother's.

"Hiya," I greet her softly, walking forward to kneel down beside her tea party. "I like your dress. Did you choose it yourself?"

"Yes," she replies shyly, her wide eyes peering at me as though measuring me up. "Are you going to look after me? Where's Alec?"

"If that's okay with you! And I think Alec's gone out to buy some new perfume. He's a bit smelly, isn't he?" I whisper teasingly.

She giggles, delighted at my joke, her timidity disintegrating almost instantly. She shuffles closer to my side in front of the tea party and offers me an adorable toothy grin, which I gladly return. In my peripheral view, I sense Marie leaving the room quietly. It's nice to be accepted.

"Do you want to join the tea party?" Millie asks me.

"I'd love to; thank you for inviting me."

"Would you like some tea?" she asks me in a singsong voice, picking up the teapot and leaning over to pour 'tea' in my cup. "This is my best tea set so we need to be careful not to break it." She leans over to whisper in my ear. "But the tea is only pretend. Mommy says I can't have real tea or I might get burned."

I nod understandingly, restraining myself from beaming at her cuteness.

Marie returns to the doorway, chuckling. "Okay, I'm leaving now to go to the dinner party. Riley, Millie's bedtime is at eight o'clock, but you can push it to eight thirty at the very latest if she's being a good girl. You can watch TV, films, play. There's food and drink in the fridge so help yourself." She checks her watch absent-mindedly. "I should be home by about midnight."

Millie gets up to charge across the room and hug her mom's legs. Marie looks down adoringly at her daughter. "Are you going to be okay with Riley, baby? You've got to be a good girl for her, remember? When she says you go to bed, you go to bed."

"Yes." Millie nods. "We're going to play princesses next."

"Of course you are," Marie says, laughing. "Well, have fun, Riley. Thanks so much for this. My number is on a sticky note on the fridge – call me if you need anything."

"Got it." I walk over to Millie's side, hooking my fingers round her smaller ones. "Have a good time, Marie. I'll see you later." Marie gives one last wave, before stepping out of the door and out of sight. I turn to Millie with an excited smile.

"So, what's your prettiest princess dress like?"

Bang bang bang.

I awake with a start at the sequence of loud noises, shooting up from my curled-up position on the couch. After putting Millie to bed about half an hour ago, I settled down to watch some of the latest *Teen Wolf* episodes, only I must have drifted off. Marie isn't due back for a few hours yet, and it sounded to me like Alec was planning on staying the night at his friend's house. I shake off my blurry stupor, then jump in shock as the loud banging sounds again. By this point I'm beginning to get scared. If it's a burglar, then I need to protect Millie. I scan the room for a weapon. Something cal I mean, not a toothbrush or something stupid like the victims grab in films. You know, before they get their insides stewed.

The house is deathly silent apart from the noises coming from the window, behind the drapes. I hold a can of body spray in my hand, left by Marie in her rush to leave the house, and step cautiously towards the noise. My heart is in my mouth, my stomach constricting in apprehension. If the burglar does anything, I can spray him in the eyes. I try to comfort myself with my future bravery. Then I knock him out with a frying pan and call the cops. I take a deep breath as the window rattles again; my hands are shaking with nerves. A loud groan sounds from outside, before the snap as the window opens. I brace myself as the drapes shift, as if concealing a body. *This is actually happening. There is someone in the house.* I raise the frankly useless can of body spray in front of me.

The drapes are pulled aside. "Hello?"

I scream at the sound, spraying the can and closing my eyes. I'm so ridden with panic that my feet are frozen to the floor. A voice curses, and I let out another yelp of fear as they stumble back. I need to call 911 right now. I need to get to Millie.

"Shit, my eyes!" a familiar voice shouts.

My heart stops as I realise who it is.

I open my eyes and, sure enough, Alec is coughing and fanning the air around him blindly, his eyes squinted shut in pain. He hasn't seen me yet. With a strangled whimper, I catapult up the stairs and into the first room I see, which happens to be Alec's. What do I do? If he sees me then he'll know it was me for sure! I curse silently, diving under his bed. His floor is hard and the impact is painful, but I'd rather bruise myself than get killed by Alec. I hold my breath to keep from coughing and think about what to do next. I feel like I'm in a horror movie.

Footsteps up the stairs.

"Whoever you are, you better show your face right now, or I'm calling the cops," Alec's voice threatens as he steps onto the landing. "I'll get your ass landed in jail quicker than you can say 'guilty'." I gasp at this, cringing into the hardwood of the floor. He's going to spot me, it's inevitable, and this is going to be one awkward conversation.

Any hopes of making up with him are out of the window now.

Slowly, I crawl out from under the bed. This could not get any worse. Why do I get myself into these situations? And more importantly, why did I think hiding under the bed was a good way to resolve this one? I accidentally hit my head on the bureau on my completely ungraceful exit. The action makes a loud bang and I wince, partly from the immense pain and partly from knowing there's no hope left for me now. I'm basically already dead. No more than a second later, Alec sprints into the room, amazingly with a frying pan held at the ready.

I stumble backwards, but luckily his eyes land on me before any serious damage is done. "Riley?" Alec's eyes become wide and confused, before hardening over in anger again. "What the hell are you doing in my house?"

"Skipping the pleasantries, I see," I joke half-heartedly. Alec glares at me in reply, the frying pan still a threat in his hand. "I was babysitting, and there were these noises, and then you burst through the window and I thought you were a burglar no I ..."

"Almost blinded me?" Alec finishes angrily. "Jesus, Riley! At least double check it *is* a burglar before you spring into attack mode! I'm lucky I closed my eyes before too much of those chemicals got in them!" He turns away from me in fury. The muscles are tense in his back, like wires pulled taut underneath his skin. Oh, I've really done it this time.

"Well, I figured you'd have a house key on you," I protest. "Plus, I wasn't expecting you back this early . . . I thought you were staying with your friends or whatever." I use Alec's bed to stand up, wincing at the pain in my knees from throwing myself onto the floor so rapidly. "You misunderstood me earlier, by the way."

Hearing this, Alec freezes. "What?"

"I didn't want to walk in with you because I thought it would damage your reputation," I admit sheepishly. "I didn't mean it in the way that you think – you didn't let me finish. I didn't get a chance to say that it's probably embarrassing to go into school with me the morning after a party, especially with all the rumours. I don't care about walking in with you, but then you aren't an outcast so –"

"Why would you think that?"

"Because I'm lame," I semi-joke.

"That's the furthest you can possibly get from the truth." Alec spins round to face me. All anger seems to have faded from his expression, and instead he just looks vacant. Stoic. The room is dark without the lights on, lit only by the hallway glow. There are shadows in the contours of his face. The intensity of this subject matter crushes me, and I instantly look away and release a breathy laugh.

"Riley, listen to me."

"What happens if I don't?" I laugh again, still not facing him.

His hands grip the sides of my jaw and he turns my head to face him. He isn't taking any of my goofiness right now, it seems.

"Riley, you aren't an outcast, and I wouldn't care if you were."

I remember Marie's words from earlier.

"Alec, what was your last school like?" I ask quietly. I'm genuinely curious, but also somewhat relieved to think of something to detract the attention from myself.

His answer is curt. "It wasn't like here," he replies.

"In what way?"

"Riley." Alec releases a pained breath. He turns his face away, and I recognise it as something I do when I'm uncomfortable facing a certain topic. "I got in a fight with someone at school and it happened to be the wrong someone. I didn't have many friends."

90

"Who did you get in a fight with?" My voice is soft.

There are rumours that Alec's been in a fair amount of fights. However, there are also rumours that he's stolen cars, that he's a drug dealer and that he's stabbed someone, so I never really gave anything I heard much merit.

Alec looks at me. "I was an angry kid. My dad had just left, I'd been taken away from my home and my friends to join a different high school a month or so in. I punched a kid in my first week. He was a popular jock-type and his dad wasn't happy about it – I did some detention service for the school and set off on totally the wrong foot. I never made any friends. I was an *actual* outcast."

"I'm sorry, I didn't mean to offend you when I said that."

Alec chuckles, running a tired hand over his face. "You think I care what people think of me, Riley? Four years at that school, it toughened me up. I kept in contact with Dyl, Joe and Chase, but every day I felt alone. I was looked at as the angry kid, the kid your parents wouldn't want you around. If I kept caring what people thought, it would have broken me entirely."

"It's strange," I admit. I sit down on the bed, and stare at my hands, clasping the covers. "Knowing you were like that. It doesn't add up to the boy I see you as now."

"People like me here." Alec shakes his head, sighing. "It's different. I had established friends already. That doesn't mean that I give a crap about what people say about me. Walking into the school the morning after a party with a quiet girl – you think I'd care? They can talk all they want. That's what people do."

"You and Violet," I say quietly, "you both have a very similar outlook."

91

"You should have the same one." He still has the same detached expression on his face.

"A girl can dream."

"Just" – he closes his eyes for a second – "don't say something like that again. You don't need to protect me. If I'm doing something, I'm doing it because I want to."

"Okay. I'm sorry you had to go through that." I watch my fingers knit together, gather my courage. "What exactly happened with your dad, if you don't mind me asking?"

"I don't want to talk about it."

Alec clambers onto the bed beside me, and slowly a hand pulls my chin up to face him.

"Sorry about the body spray too." I cringe as soon as our eyes meet.

He smiles slightly. "Oh don't worry, I'll get you back."

"No you will not."

His dimples flash. "Do you feel like a Chinese takeaway? I'm starving."

"Always."

It's a shocking fact, but I'm blushing. Am I flirting with him? I duck my face beneath my hair. When I look back up, Alec is inches away from my face. For a mere millisecond, I think I forget to breathe.

"I knew you couldn't resist me, Greene," he says. An arrogant smirk plays out across his lips, and I push him away with a laugh.

"I can't resist chow mein," I say. "Get downstairs and order my food."

He smiles crookedly at me, before skipping out of the room and slapping his palms against his bedroom door as he exits. I take a deep breath as soon as he's out of the room.

Alec actually kind of opened up to me there. It sounds like he's dealt with a lot over the last few years. Suddenly his whole attitude – the bike, the PDAs with random girls, the pranks. It all fits together a bit more. My heart, it feels warm, and I frown as I recognise the emotion. No, Riley. You can't allow yourself to feel like this. Not about him, not about anyone. I force myself to think about the girls he flirts with. *That's* who he is interested in.

I don't want to be heartbroken again. I don't even know if I'm ready for a crush again. My life is a bit of a shambles at the moment.

Taking a deep breath, I stand up from Alec's bed and pull my sweater sleeves down over my hands. As I step into the glow of the landing, I hear Alec talking downstairs. He must be ordering the takeaway. And yet, as I approach the top steps, I freeze.

"Tiana, I'm really not feeling well," I hear Alec say.

I peer through the banister rails and watch him lean against the wall with his phone pressed to his ear.

"I really don't think you should come over. No. No. I'm just going to stay in and get an early night. Maybe another time. Yeah, okay. I'm sorry. Night." He hangs up.

My heart squeezes in my chest and I sigh.

I'm doomed.

"I want to watch *Mean Girls*."

"No way, I refuse to watch that disgrace of a movie. *The Avengers* is so much cooler."

"But Regina George is so hot," Alec whines. "Girls in short skirts, bitching about each other and fighting? That is what they call quality entertainment." He attempts to use the puppy-dog eyes on me, but I'm too strong for that. I'm basically the Hulk.

"Really?" I drawl sarcastically. "I know a Regina George you could talk to."

He clocks my meaning straight away. "What is the thing between you two anyway?"

My smile fades. I let myself in for that, dammit.

"Something happened, a long time ago," I say vaguely. "We just don't really get on."

"What happened?" Alec probes.

"Oh, we argued about who took the best topless selfies one time in the bathroom."

Alec's head snaps to the side. "What?"

"Yeah, her symmetry is *all* wrong." I roll my eyes. "I'm kidding, grasshole."

"Thanks for the mental image anyway."

I crinkle my nose, hoping he's successfully distracted from the initial question.

"Anyway, we obviously can't decide between these two so let's watch something else instead," I say. "What do you suggest?"

"Let's see how you handle a horror, eh?"

The mere mention of a horror movie brings an amused smile to my lips. Oh, Alec, if only you knew.

"*Paranormal Activity*? *The Conjuring*? *Carrie*?" Alec wriggles his eyebrows at me, and I bite my nails to add to the authenticity of the "nervousness" he expects me to have. Judging by Alec's victorious smirk, it's worked. "Or perhaps you'd like some *Final Destination*?" Ah, the gore. Of course that will terrify me.

Eventually he settles on *Scream*, thinking that of course

the man in the mask brandished so often in Halloween costumes will terrify me. Does he really expect that from me? Throughout the scary movie adverts, Alec keeps sending me sideway glimpses to observe my reactions, and I obligingly pretend to be nervous about them all.

Then the first scene kicks in.

I begin to mouth the lines as the actors say them.

It takes a few seconds for Alec to notice but when he does, his mouth drops open in surprise. I still don't look at him of course; I'm watching him in my peripheral vision as my lips curve round the familiar lines. But after a few more lines, the temptation is too much to resist.

"Who are you trying to reach?" I quote.

I can't take it any longer. My composed exterior crumples into giggles at the shock on Alec's face. *Scream* is not one of my favourite horror films (I find it a little repetitive and tedious), but I still know it back to front.

"How did you do that?" Alec demands.

"Believe it or not, I'm actually a fan of horror movies. Heaven forbid."

"Have you watched *Paranormal Activity*?"

I yawn in reply, and his face moulds into a mask of determination. Now he's going to try to find a horror movie that I haven't watched, and good luck to him is all I can say.

"*Insidious*?"

"I can quote it backwards."

"*Sinister*?"

"One of my personal favourites."

"*Saw*? *The Blair Witch Project*?" Detecting my glee, he moans. "You know what? Don't even answer that. I give up trying. You win."

I jump up and shake my hips in a boastful victory dance. He can test me on any movies or TV programmes – from horror, to science fiction, to anime. I'm a very cultured dork on that front. A lot of my free time is spent watching things, and gaming online too.

The doorbell rings, interrupting my moment of glory.

"Food's here," I say.

Alec rolls his eyes moodily, still upset about my victory, and gets up.

"Don't answer the door, Alec!" I scream in a high-pitched tone, chuckling at the sight of his raised middle finger. A minute later, he comes back in holding a paper bag of Chinese takeout.

"This is for me, this is for me and this is for ..." He turns to survey me. "Me as well. So none for you then. What a shame."

He collapses into the couch next to me with a proud sneer, and I boil over with annoyance as I watch him begin to deliberately eat some of my chow mein. His eyes glint with malevolence. This means war.

First, I attempt to grab the food by reaching across Alec, but obviously fail. So, my next method is somewhat more forceful. Launching myself onto him, I snatch the bag of takeout and successfully pin his hands down. He writhes and struggles beneath me. I've trapped him to the couch. Now, sitting on his lap in an awkward slouch, I grab a cushion from beside me and shove it into Alec's face, muffling his curses and profanities, before leaning back into it. It's actually quite comfortable.

"You know what I feel like watching? Disney princesses," I declare deliberately loudly. Instantly, Alec's hands are unleashed from underneath me, darting towards my sides and tickling me frantically. A cry escapes my lips and I squirm like I've just been electrocuted, before hysterics follow. My eyes water with unshed tears of joy. I hate being tickled. Helpless to his merciless fingers, my hold weakens and I go crashing to the floor with Alec following behind.

The bag of takeout is soon forgotten as this morphs into a tickling war. He straddles my legs and attempts to pin my hands, his eyes glinting deviously as he leans forward. "Did you honestly think you'd get away with that, Greene?"

I writhe under his legs, the knowing churn in my stomach telling me that there's much worse to come and my jaw is already hurting from all the laughing. I don't understand why we laugh when we're tickled. It's not like we enjoy it. Keeping my chin up and maintaining the shred of dignity that I have left, I grumble, "Bite me."

Alec laughs. "Just tell me where, sunshine."

Unfortunately, my plan to surprise him and jump back up fails the moment that I hear a new voice coming from the living-room doorway.

"Well, well, well. What have we got here?"

Alec and I spring apart, and I land on the floor with a hard thud. Rubbing my backside, I groan and attempt to shield my face from the chuckling boys in the doorway. Joe and Chase are standing there, laughing their asses off at the two of us.

"Idiots," Alec groans, leaning back on his elbows. "I thought you guys were my mom."

"Yeah well, we all know how much you love your mommy, Alec," Chase teases. "Sorry to disappoint. We brought beer. Can we join?" Both boys look between us in anticipation. I

97

sense Alec's gaze on my face seeking approval, and I shrug. I am slightly uncomfortable with the idea of being part of a lads' night, with a group of boys I'm not exactly best friends with, but maybe this will be a good chance to get to know them better. Hopefully my night has just got a bit more interesting.

"Why not?" I say.

9

Intellectual Badass

I sit in silence in my car, aware of the minutes ticking by, as I stare at the Elephant Bar in front of me.

Somehow, miraculously, I've made it this far. It's Friday night. After school today, Violet crammed me into a dress, curled my hair, and now I'm sitting outside of the place where I'm supposed to be meeting "the man of my dreams". I can't bring myself to move a muscle. All I can think of is the time I helped get Kaitlin ready for her first date with Toby. Her hair was tied up, she was wearing a yellow sundress and she had a smile from ear to ear. She was so excited. I feel a pang of guilt, deep and sharp enough to make me feel sick to my stomach. I'd do anything to have my cousin here now, preparing me for this. Maybe if she were, I'd have the confidence and inclination to get out of the car.

It's this thought that brings me to suck in my nerves, exit the car and walk to the entrance of the restaurant. Violet told me earlier that he's meeting me just inside the entrance. I exhale slowly, straightening out my blazer and striding with my head held high into the restaurant. The music engulfs me, followed by the chatter of customers. This restaurant is small, lively and gorgeously rustic. Kaitlin would have loved it.

I glance around, but by the looks of things he hasn't arrived yet. I'm not sure if I'm glad about that fact or not. I don't think I'm early; he just might be a little late. Or maybe he won't show at all. *No, no, no, I'm not going to get stood up. That's a stupid thought. He's just a little late, that's all.*

Or maybe not so late.

I watch, fighting the urge to drool, as a guy walks through the entrance. His tousled chocolate locks and big brown eyes definitely make him cute. Maybe this is him? If so, he's way out of my league, but I'm definitely not complaining. My heart falls to my feet with nerves as he approaches.

He's not as good-looking as Alec.

I ignore my senseless thought and focus instead on my potential date. The boy looks over at me, offering me a small smile, but carries on walking. I exhale quickly in relief. A girl with red hair waits for him at the bar, her hand resting on the swell of her stomach. Oh, she's pregnant! Well, they are going to have the most attractive babies ever.

Just like you and Alec would.

I have no idea where these particular thoughts are coming from, but the truth is that I'd much rather be watching a movie of any sort with Alec right now than standing on my own. I feel more comfortable and happy when I'm with him, and that's a big deal for me considering everything I've dealt with over the past year. It's too good to give up. I frown and glance at the entrance again. I'm beginning to consider whether I may have been stood up. In all honesty, I'm kind of hoping I have been. I just want to go home and watch *Sherlock*.

100

"A beautiful girl like you should never frown. You never know if someone's falling for your smile," a voice sounds from behind me.

I spin round quickly. I wish I could say that the guy in front of me is a tall, dark and handsome stranger. I wish I could say that I've never met him before, and that he was a sweet dark mystery for me to unravel. After all, that's what the concept of a blind date is, right? Meeting a stranger and getting to know each other, no expectations and no strings attached. The thing is, I don't think I can call this a blind date any more. The person standing in front of me is most certainly not a stranger.

"Toby."

I stare at the boy in front of me in horror. Toby is here; he's back. My ex-boyfriend moved to Chicago six months ago after breaking my heart, and I've not heard a word from him since. His mom got some hotshot job there, and that was his escape ticket. Something must have gone wrong. *He's back.* I clutch my head, trying to cram the memories and thoughts back into my brain but it's no use. They're bursting out, a flood of all of the things that I wanted to forget. Things that are best left forgotten.

He hasn't changed that much since I last saw him half a year ago. Same steely hazel eyes, tousled blonde hair and strong jawline. But the circumstances have changed more than my much-younger self could have ever imagined.

"Fancy seeing you here," he says with a smile.

I skip one beat and bolt for the door.

"Riley, wait!" Toby calls after me, but I've taken off sprinting. I need to escape. I shove the entrance open and rush out into the chilly night, dodging diners making their

101

way into the restaurant. I can feel my eyes stinging, but I refuse to cry. Not now, not in front of him. His feet patter behind me, and I know he's closing in. Stupid damned quarterback. I need to get away, to outrun the thoughts worming their way inside my mind. Does he not understand that I don't want to see him? It hurts. He's opening a wound again, a wound that hasn't healed properly even now.

"Riley, stop!" A hand clamps onto my shoulder, bringing me to a skidding halt, before I'm forcefully turned round. Toby stands way too close for my liking, staring into my eyes in disbelief, as though he can't understand that I'd want to run away from him. I flinch away, and hurt flickers in his eyes. Does he not see that he's hurting me just by standing here?

"Why are you here?" I ask brokenly.

"Mom didn't like the city. It took us a while to get it all sorted." He huffs out a breath, his eyes wide and pleading. "Riley, you must hate me. I know that. I'm better now though – and I want a chance to make it up to you. To make things a bit better between us."

His voice cracks on the last word, and that's how I know that he feels it too. Her presence. But she's not really here. I wish she was.

"It's too late, Toby." I feel fragile, trembling. Like a piece of glass waiting to shatter. It hurts so much. Too much.

"It's never too late."

"No, this. This is what too late looks like," I hiss. "After Kaitlin last summer, you cracked. You were weak. You cheated on me, then you left for Chicago as if you could just write off everything that you did. You broke her heart, and you broke mine."

102

I turn to walk away, but he grips onto my forearm to prevent me from leaving. How dare he! I spin round and shoot him an icy glare, until he finally, reluctantly releases his grip.

"Don't even try to stop me from leaving," I hiss. "You turned your back on me; it's only fair that I should get to do the same to you."

The guy has the nerve to look ashamed, after all of this time. "Riley, you don't understand, I had to! I was falling to pieces. I couldn't deal with it."

"That's right," I whisper, placing my finger in the centre of his chest. "You would have broken, just like the rest of us did. Just like I did. Your friend died, but she was *my cousin*. She was like a sister to me, and it was *our* fault. I had to stay and face the consequences, I had to live with the aftermath of my mistake, and where were you? You disappeared. I don't forgive you for that and I never will. Leave, Toby. Now." I release him and take a step back, staring at him in disgust and pain.

I can hear the sob gathering in the back of my throat, but I refuse to give him the satisfaction of seeing me cry. *Be stone, Riley. Cold, hard, untouchable stone.* I turn and walk away, leaving Toby standing behind me with the wounds of my words. I walk as quickly as I can, despite the fact that I know he's not following this time.

"You think I didn't have to deal with the aftermath?" he yells.

"There's a difference between reading the flyer and watching from the front row!"

"I'll make it up to you, Riley Greene," he shouts after me. "We're meant to be, Riley. We were when I was with

103

Kaitlin, we were when I was with you, and we still are right now. I'm willing to do whatever it takes to get you back."

I don't look back, but my teeth are gnawing so hard into my lip that they're drawing blood.

"See you at school!" he has the nerve to shout.

I shoot the middle finger at his back as he walks away.

It doesn't take long for the tears to come.

I return home quietly, slipping inside and hoping no one will notice. It's only about 7.30 p.m. I got myself back together pretty quickly after my meltdown in the street, but it's clear that any evidence of make-up has been erased from my face. I tiptoe up the stairs to my room and shut the door with a sigh, slumping against it. The curtains are closed, so I quickly change into a pair of leggings and a baggy sweater. I'm not in the mood for anything at all. Even a little visit from Ben and Jerry doesn't seem appealing right now.

Toby. My cousin. Tiana. Alec. Everything is crashing down on me, and I can't breathe. I can't breathe.

I choke back the rise in my throat as the thoughts enter my head again. I need some air. I need to breathe. I can't have another panic attack right now; I won't allow myself. I've improved so much, and I'm not falling down this hole again. I head over to the window. My throat feels red raw. I open the window and breathe in deeply, attempting to calm my senses, distract my thoughts. I wish I'd never gone on that godforsaken date.

Remember what your therapist taught you.

A few tears dampen my cheeks. I can't seem to hold them in. Toby. Kaitlin. Tiana. Toby. Kaitlin. Tiana. Toby. Toby is *back*.

"Riley?" A soft voice comes from in front of me, and I jump wildly, almost hitting my head off the window. Alec is standing behind his window, watching me with a concerned and wary expression. I offer him a weak half-smile, as though he didn't just scare the life out of me, then wipe the tears from my cheeks in an attempt at nonchalance. I completely forgot that by going to the window, I'd be giving him a front-row seat to my breakdown.

"Hi, Alec. What's up?"

"Seriously?" Alec chuckles bitterly. "Don't even start with that crap. What's wrong? Who hurt you?" He searches my face for any clues in my expression, while I try to keep it as void as I can. The last thing I need right now is to go all hormonal teenage girl on Alec.

"I just found out the next season of *Stranger Things* isn't out for another year," I joke half-heartedly.

"Answer me seriously, Riley. Stop rebuffing."

"Nothing, Alec," I sigh, leaning back. "I've just had a hard night, okay?"

He analyses me for a second longer. "I don't believe you."

"You don't have to."

"Put on some warm clothes and meet me outside in five minutes. I want to show you something."

With that parting sentence, he disappears from his window, and I'm left with no choice but to gawk after him. What can he possibly have to show me right now, when I'm dealing with this? I don't want to meet him!

It takes me a few minutes to calm down, until the curiosity finally gets the better of me. I get changed and put my shoes on as fast as I possibly can, and dash down the stairs two at a time. It'll be easy to sneak out because nobody knows that I'm back yet. Plus, it's not like I'm going to be gone for long. I hesitate for a second as I consider how much trouble I could get in if Mom did find out, but it's not enough to prevent me from slipping out into the night.

I ensure my tears are all wiped from existence before I face him again.

Alec leans against the tree at the bottom of my yard. "C'mon," he gestures and strides over to the motorbike.

This time, I don't even hesitate in following his lead. I sit down and wrap my arms round his waist. I'm actually excited to see where Alec is going to take me, and surprised that he cares so much as to take me anywhere. I continue to underestimate him, and I really need to stop that.

I watch the scenery on the journey. I'm not sure if it's the distraction or what, but Alec has managed to calm me down. My chest no longer feels constricted, and although my head is pounding, it's a small price to pay for being able to breathe again. As the town fades into rural forestry, it strikes me just how strange it is that we're driving down these quiet country roads. They go on for miles, with no real ending. Why would Alec take me into the forest?

I don't hesitate to ask him as soon as we stop; we're seemingly in the middle of nowhere, by the side of the road. The streetlights are oddly far apart, setting the scene in gloom, and there's no one else in sight.

"Alec, why are we stopping here? If you're planning to murder me, just know that I always carry pepper spray – and it stings a lot more than Abercrombie body spritz."

Alec raises an eyebrow and begins to walk into the forest. I rush after him, scared of being left alone. We all know how that horror movie ends.

"If I was going to murder you, it's probably not a good idea to tell me that you have pepper spray," Alec says, unfazed by the creepy surroundings.

I glance desperately back at the motorcycle. Seeing me, Alec chortles. "Scared, Greene?"

I ignore him, adopting a surly expression as I glare at the tree roots I'm trying so hard not to trip over. It's dark under the canopy of trees, not to mention eerie. What could be so interesting, out here in the middle of a forest, that Alec found the need to bring me here?

"It's not far now, don't worry," Alec interrupts the silence, reassuring me.

After what seems like forever, the trees begin to thin out and a small clearing comes into view. It's set quite far back from the cliffs – I can just about see the coastline in the far distance, but that's not the focus of my attention. In front of us lies an abandoned railway – a gorgeous stone bridge smothered in ivy to the left, with a rusted track running down the middle. It's beautiful, and old, and the kind of thing you see on the front of stunning photography magazines. It appears untouched and completely idyllic.

My mouth pops open in reaction to the view, and Alec turns to look at me with a smile which is almost as breath-taking as our surroundings.

"You like it?" He grabs my hand and pulls me down the hill towards the tracks, and we stop just a few metres in front of it. He's still holding my hand.

"I love it," I whisper as we sit down, staring at the gorgeous stone bridge. "Who introduced you to this place?"

Sadly, he lets go of my hand at this point, but the skin still feels warm and tingly from his touch.

"This was our hangout spot – me, Dylan, Joe and Chase. I've started coming again quite a bit since we moved back."

"It's nice."

Alec glances sideways at me. "You're the first girl to make it up here."

"I feel honoured," I tease, elbowing him a little in the ribs.

"So, are you going to tell me what was wrong now? I brought you here, to my thinking space." Alec gestures at the scenery and ignores my joke. "So it's time to tell me why you were crying. It's obligatory."

I bite my lip. I should tell him, but it's difficult. It's not like I broadcast this often.

Seeing my conflicted expression, Alec brushes his shoulder against mine and smiles. "I'm waiting." His voice is teasing, but at the same time there's an undertone of curiosity. He really does want to know.

"There's quite a bit of background first," I warn him. "But I'll try to sum it up as best as I can." I rub my damp palms dry on my legs.

"Okay." He leans back to rest on his elbows, waiting.

"When I was thirteen, a boy moved to town," I begin. My voice is shaky with nerves, but I trust him. I tell myself I have no reason to be nervous. "His name was Toby, and he was my first real crush." I glance down at the grass. "He was in most of my classes, and he was really sweet to me. It was only natural that we became friends. Our moms became close too, and one thing led to another and finally one day, Toby asked me to be his girlfriend. And I said yes."

The last word comes out as a sigh. I feel a painful twist in my gut at my own voice. I struggle to curve my lips round

108

the next words. "Then, around a year ago, something big happened."

"What was the big thing?" Alec asks.

No. No, no, no.

"I don't want to get into specifics tonight. It was hard for me, harder than I could ever describe, but it was hard for Toby too. A few months passed and we were both in bad places. Toby cracked . . . he cheated on me, and then moved away to Chicago six months ago."

"Wow," Alec exhales. I guess he's struggling to find words to respond with.

He thinks I'm so brave by telling him this, but he doesn't realise that this isn't even the worst part. He doesn't know anything.

I take a deep breath and continue. "I went on a blind date tonight . . . and it happened to be Toby. He's moved back to town, and he's coming back to school. Just seeing him has awakened all the memories of what happened. He wants another chance," I trail off, picking at a piece of grass. "I'm kind of scared because I don't want him to worm his way back into my life again. I'm not ready for that to happen."

Alec looks at me for a little while, and the silence envelops us. It's like he's trying to absorb the information, get a better grip on what I've just told him.

"I won't let him," Alec says at last. "He's a dick, and he doesn't deserve another shot, Riley. Don't give him the satisfaction." Alec's face grows hard with determination, and suddenly he's speaking a little more quickly and assertively. "We'll help you avoid him. If you stay out of his way, and if he sees you've moved on, maybe he'll drop it. I'm not an expert on these things, but I won't let him intimidate you. None of the guys will. We'll keep an eye on him."

"Thanks." I smile without meeting Alec's eyes, turning away from him to stare at the scenery. I don't want him to see the guilt and hurt in my eyes. He thinks I've told him everything.

"You're welcome," Alec replies. He sighs, his eyes trailing over the landscape too.

"So." I clear my throat, bumping his shoulder with mine in an attempt to lighten the mood. The sooner we move on from this topic, the sooner I can allow myself to feel happier again. "What about you? Any toxic relationships you'd like to share?"

Alec glances at me flatly. "You think I've had relationships?"

"Not even one?"

He turns back to the view in front of us, staring intensely at nothing. "I didn't get near a girl at my old school. I wasn't interested and neither were they. Aside from the few 'girl-friends' I had when I was, like, twelve, nobody."

I think how it's perfectly normal not to have had a relationship before at our age, but not to ever have had feelings for someone . . . that's a little more unique. Crushes do suck, so maybe Alec is taking the more intelligent route, but still I can't help but feel disheartened.

"Do you think you'll ever be interested in one?"

"Why?" Alec looks at me and suddenly grins. "You interested?"

I splutter. "What? No! Of course not –"

"Yeah I know, you hate me." Alec rolls his eyes. "It was a joke, Greene."

"I don't *hate* you. I'm just not necessarily excited by your existence," I say, offering him an innocent smile to prove that

110

I'm only joking. I hope he knows I don't really dislike him. Sure, he's annoying a lot of the time, but would he honestly think I don't like him after he brought me here and was so understanding about Toby? After he looked after me at the party? He's warming on me faster than I care to admit. Fast enough that my whole body is screaming to press the brake pedal. Sure, we would never have even spoke if he hadn't rather cruelly stolen my bra in the dead of night – which, this reminds me, I *still* don't have – but since then he's actually been kind of great. To be this comfortable around him so quickly is shocking me, because it's been a long time since I trusted anyone but Violet.

"The feeling is mutual." Alec pulls a face. "So today we've clarified that I have no relationship experience, and you've had no sexual experience," Alec points out, way too casually for my liking.

"Who says I've had no sexual experience?"

Alec gives me a blank look.

"Okay, I'll shut up."

"And on that note . . ." Alec stands up, brushing the dust from his jeans, and offering me a hand. "We should probably get you back. Can't have your mother sniffing us out, can we?" I nod in approval and I take the hand, only for it to be pulled away quickly, leaving me to fall back on the dusty floor. I probably should have expected that. Alec keels over, laughing at me, to which I scowl.

"Grasshole."

10

Concrete Heart

"Riley."

I grit my teeth and ignore the voice; instead I carry on collecting my books from my locker.

"Riley, c'mon. Answer me."

Why can't some people just get the message? Maybe if I slam the locker and run now, he won't chase after me. Or is that just wishful thinking? I tell you what I wish – I wish he'd freaking leave me alone. I release a short sigh, grabbing my Math book and slamming the locker door closed. I don't want to face him, but maybe if I yell at him some more he'll get the message and leave me be. It's a fat chance, but I'll try anything.

"What do you want, Toby?"

"Nothing much." He shrugs nonchalantly, but I can see the delight in his face that I actually turned round and answered him. I know him that well, unfortunately. "I just wanted to know how you've been recently."

I grit my teeth even more fiercely and shove the last of my books in my backpack, turning to walk down the corridor towards my first lesson. Annoyingly, Toby follows.

"I've been just great," I mutter. "No thanks to you."

You'd think he'd have given up by now, but no. Toby has been insistently friendly since the moment I stepped into school this morning. All day pestering. Toby hesitates before speaking, and I can almost see a guilty sheen in his eyes. "Yeah, I deserve that one," he admits, "but I'll make it up to you, Riley. I promise."

"Go and preach it to someone who gives a shit, Toby," I glower. "Leave me alone."

Toby's act drops, and he gives me a stony scowl. "You aren't going to make this easy for me, are you, Riley? All I want is to be friends."

You should have thought about that before you cheated and moved cities without telling me.

"You should have thought about that before you cheated and moved cities without telling me," I hiss in a low voice, trying to prevent anyone nearby from hearing us. "Now leave me alone." I shoot him a final icy glare, as I step into my Physics room. No sooner have I stepped in, however, than I'm yanked out again with a sharp and painful tug. I curse under my breath and spin round to start yelling at him, but the person standing in front of me is the furthest from "him" that you can get. Toby stands by my other side, but it's not his hand that's currently clawing my arm. Not unless he's suddenly got silver acrylic nails and a diamond bracelet, that is. Toby stares shell-shocked at the girl, but her eyes are fixed on me.

Tiana Cooper. What the hell does she want?

With a small sigh, I stretch on an elasticated smile. Here we go again.

"Tiana," I greet, my cheeks aching. "What a pleasant

surprise." I grab her hand and slowly detach it from my forearm, only making her smirk widen. My fingers trace over the marks on my skin, bruises in the curve of perfectly manicured fingernails.

"Riley, sweetie, you look gorgeous today," Tiana purrs, her icy grey eyes running over my body, scrutinising every flaw. The compliment is completely flat, that is abundantly clear. What does she want with me? It's not like we make a habit of associating with each other – we hate each other's guts and that's no secret.

"Thanks," I say, "I'd say the same for you but . . ."

My heartbeat jumps with nerves.

Behind her smile, Tiana's eyes turn stormy. Good. "Please could I talk to you? It'll only take a second, promise." Her gaze drifts from me over to Toby, and her eyes widen as if she's only just noticed his presence. "Toby. Nice to see you again."

"I'm going to leave," Toby mutters, flushing bright red. He doesn't even have the courage to look me in the eye. Cowardly man-whore.

Tiana turns to me and I nod, glancing reluctantly into the Physics classroom before following her away from the door, further into the corridor again. The walk is eerily silent apart from the thud of Tiana's sneakers against the polished flooring, and my eyes narrow in concentration. I've stayed as far away from her as possible and still I've managed to rub her up the wrong way. It's pretty obvious that she doesn't want to compare lip-gloss brands and talk this week's crushes.

After she's checked that we're far enough from all of the classrooms she turns to face me and I stop walking.

"So, what is it you wanted to talk to me about?" I ask,

mocking her with no shame. Her steely eyes show no hint of fake friendliness now, and her full lips are curled into an unattractive sneer as she flips her dark ponytail over her shoulder. Alas, the true Tiana Cooper comes out for me.

"Drop the act, Riley," she snaps. "I think you know what I want to talk to you about." She steps a little closer, but I refuse to give in to the temptation to step backwards. That would only make her think that she intimidates me, and although that may be slightly true, there's no way I'd ever let her see it. I stand tall, staring directly into her eyes. *Don't give her the satisfaction, Riley.*

"No, actually, Tiana, I really don't know why you've dragged me here with those garden shears that you call fingernails."

"Don't you dare play dumb with me, Greene," she hisses, stepping right into my face this time and shoving me back into the lockers. "I want you to stay away from Alec Wilde, or so help me God, I will make sure you regret it. We almost had a good thing going until you got in the way."

My eyes narrow back at her.

What? Does she think I'm stepping in her way or something?

"You can have Alec," I snarl. "Get the hell out of my face, Tiana."

"Really? I can have him? Then back off. He doesn't want you." She leans down further, her icy glare searing holes into my skin. I've never seen a look filled with so much hatred before. Someone has a case of the green-eyed monster. I don't know what she has to hate me about; if anything I should hate her more. She's the one that Toby cheated on me with; she's the one that has single-handedly made me feel worse and worse about myself ever since by rubbing it in my face.

I frown after Tiana as she slithers away. Does she think she's winning? I am not prepared to obey orders from her. She's taken so much from me, and my new friendship with Alec is not going to be another item added to her list.

With that thought in mind, I jog back to my last lesson for the day, determination hardening my concrete heart.

"Psst, Riley," Alec whispers, poking me in the arm softly.

I raise my eyebrows, ignoring him like the badass I am and staring instead at the teacher's demonstration at the front. Ignoring Alec is surprisingly fun.

"Riley," he whines, poking me again, harder this time. "Riley, what's the answer?"

This time I scoff, unable to restrain myself. No chance am I giving him all the answers. Physics isn't an easy subject; it took a chunk out of my weekend to do these! He can work them out on his own. Alec seems to sense my defiance and he groans quietly, poking me hard enough to leave a bruise, desperation showing through. He knows that if he hasn't completed the homework, he'll get a detention. My lips curve up in amusement. Oh, I can play this game all day.

Alec's hand makes a dart for my folder, but I pull it neatly away from him, my smile morphing into a full-blown grin. He's no match for my ninja skills. Alec growls low under his breath. He's figured out that I'm playing with him, and I chuckle quietly. He knows that I'm trying to get him annoyed. Jeez, he must be desperate for those answers.

"Riley," he whispers, that desperation evident in his voice. Aw bless. "Please can I have the answers?"

116

"Alec," Mr Johnson's voice says sharply from the front, "I ask you to pay attention when I'm doing a demonstration. Stop flirting with Riley and listen to what I'm trying to teach you."

A rumble of laughter spreads around the class and I blush. There's already rumours about me and Alec seeing each other, and dating in secret. I definitely don't need the teasing from teachers now too.

"I'm sorry, sir," Alec replies smoothly. "I don't understand one of the questions we had for homework. I was trying to get Riley to help me with it, but she refuses."

My jaw drops open at this. Way to make me seem like the bad guy. At least I've actually done the homework.

"Well, next time, please ask when I'm not in the middle of a demonstration," the teacher says, brow furrowing. "Riley, please could you help Alec with his homework? He doesn't understand, and I trust you to be able to help him."

I nod stiffly in reply to his request, feeling the smugness pour off of Alec like a tidal wave. I don't dare look over at him; if he's smirking, like I know he is, the urge to punch him in the face will be unbearable, so I stare at Mr Johnson instead. The teacher nods gratefully, before turning back to the demonstration to teach the rest of the class. This is beyond unfair.

"So," Alec begins cheerfully, "are you going to help me, Riley?"

"Dude, give her a break." Joe laughs from the other side of the bench. "She looks like she wants to kill you at the moment. I don't blame her to be honest." He grins slyly at me, fumbling with a piece of paper in his hands. Is he making a paper aeroplane?

"Copy my answer and I will castrate you," I tell Alec

bluntly. "But you can look at the method." I begrudgingly hand Alec my sheet, and in the meantime entertain myself by watching Joe aim paper aeroplanes at the teacher without him noticing. They sail through the air, one by one, hitting various targets but never the teacher himself. By the fifth aeroplane, the whole class is turning round to watch Joe. These guys are fun to be around, I have to admit that.

"Thanks, Riley." Alec passes me my sheet back.

"Ignore him," Joe whispers. "He's just in a particularly annoying mood because he got laid last night."

Is that what Alec told him? Alec was with me all of last night. We watched *The Avengers*, and *Mean Girls*.

"You know, I may not be incredible at Physics but I'm pretty good at Math and Biology," Alec comments cheerfully, a smug smirk growing on his lips. "Especially Math and Biology in bed. You know, I'll add the bed, you subtract the clothes. You divide the legs and I'll multiply." Alec wriggles his eyebrows playfully. "Fancy a personal tutor, Riley? Extra credit homework?"

"Ew." I cringe. "That's so disgusting! How do you manage to bring innuendos into Math? That's practically an art."

Joe grins at my comment, chucking a piece of eraser at me. Alec just smirks some more.

"You know, I'm good with art too, Riley. I'm very handy with a –"

"I don't want to know," I interrupt, slapping my hand over Alec's mouth.

He stares at me for a second, before sticking out his tongue and pressing a long lick to my palm. "Ew! I don't want your mouth herpes!" I yelp, running my wet palm against his face to dry it.

118

"Mouth herpes? Are you implying that I have a lot of o–"

"Shut up!"

"Miss Greene, please quiet down! This is the last warning for the back row!"

I'll get you back one day, Alec. I swear it.

A single piece of eraser flies through the air, hitting me on the cheek. Joe's up to his pranks again. I try my hardest not to flinch as I stare calmly into Mr Johnson's narrowed eyes, ignoring the boys' chortles to my left.

"I'm sorry, sir. Alec was making inappropriate comments to me."

I have to choke back my laugh at Mr Johnson's bulging eyes and flushed face, but apparently the rest of the class can't because a rumble of chuckles resounds around the room. Alec blushes besides me, and Mr Johnson shoots him a look. Well, there's part one of my revenge, I guess.

"Right, as we seem to be finished with this topic –" Mr Johnson shoots us all a blank stare – "we'll move on. Our next topic will be momentum. Linear momentum is defined by the mass of an object multiplied by its velocity. Can anyone tell me what the principle of the conservation of momentum states?"

I freeze in my seat.

"If objects collide, the total momentum before the collision is the same as the total momentum after the collision, so long as there are no external factors at play," a voice parrots from the front.

Collision.

"That's correct. We will be looking at force, and the conservation of momentum over the next few lessons. So, to get you all into the mindset again, explain this to me. A car of mass two thousand kilos is moving along a straight horizontal road at a speed of five metres per second to the minus one. This car collides with a standstill object of mass fifty kilos, which is at rest on the same track."

The blood runs cold, and I can hear my heart pounding in my ears.

"During the collision, the car and the object lock together and move together," Mr Johnson continues, oblivious to the horror on my face. *I'm not ready for this. I'm not ready.* I can feel the panic rising within me, and my breaths get faster and faster as I look for a relief that I can't seem to find.

"What is the speed of the objects immediately after the collision?"

I can't breathe. I need to get out of here.

"Riley." Alec stares at me as he realises that something very wrong is happening. "Come on, Riley, let's get out of here."

Without another word, he grabs my hand and pulls me from my seat. His skin is warm and rough, and I try to focus on that, to root me to a calm place. We ignore the calls of a teacher who doesn't understand why we're leaving; we ignore the eyes of students. Alec gets me to the door as fast as he possibly can, and I could never feel more grateful than I feel right now.

"Riley." Alec grips my hand tighter and leads me out further into the cool corridor. The claustrophobia has disappeared, but I stare at Alec with my eyes wide in panic as I clutch him and hyperventilate. He must be so scared right now; I know I am. I don't want him to see me like this, but I need him to help me. I need him to calm me down.

"Breathe, Riley. In, out. In, out. It's all okay, Riley. I'm here. You're okay."

My eyes fill with tears that I can't seem to choke back down. My panic attacks are fairly rare, but when they do occur, they're so overwhelming that I can't help but sob with the shock and power of my emotions. I break down in front of Alec Wilde, the last person on Earth I'd want to cry in front of, but his arms wrap round me and he supports me as I weep. He doesn't say anything. He knows that nothing he could ever say will help.

Calm down, Riley. Calm down. You're safe. You're okay.

"Riley," Alec whispers after a while, cradling me to his chest. My gasps for breath are the only sounds that fill the stagnant, quiet air, as I struggle to force my mind back to rationality. "Listen to my heartbeat. Feel how steady that is?"

His words surprise me, but grateful for the distraction, I force my head against his chest and listen to the steady thump of his life. I listen to the source of him, the thing that's holding everything together. Slowly, surely, everything else begins to fade into the background. I place all of my concentration on him. On his heart.

I'm not sure how much time passes while I'm slumped in Alec's arms, but eventually my breathing begins to slow and my eyes stop leaking.

Thud. Thud. Thud. Thud.

He smells like cologne and vanilla. His hoodie is soft, and his arms are strong. I feel safe. When I'm placed in situations like the one I was just in, it usually takes me a lot longer to calm down. It takes me a few seconds to work up the courage to pull away from his heartbeat and face the aftermath, but once I do I wipe away my tears and avoid looking at Alec. There's a hollowness in my chest, and my head is starting to hurt.

"Thank you," I say in a weak voice, still not looking at him. What must he think of me now? "Thank you for getting me out of there." I don't think he'll ever understand how grateful I am, but also how embarrassing it is to be seen like that. To be seen as so vulnerable, so messy.

"It's okay." Alec's voice is soft, and his words are adorably awkward. "You know that you can, um . . . talk to me about stuff, don't you? I won't laugh or anything. If you need me, I'm here."

I have to fight the urge to hug him tightly and never let go.

"So." Alec puts his hands in his pockets and finally I look up at him. He looks worried, which surprises me. "What was that about?"

"Panic attack . . ." I mumble. "I get them from time to time."

It's getting close to the anniversary.

Alec's eyes betray his concern. "Okay, do you want me to walk you to the nurse's office? I could speak to her for you, if you want?"

"No." I shake my head. "Thank you, but no. I think I should get home. I have some stuff I need to think about . . . I kind of need to be alone right now." I bite my lip at the look of dejection on his face, which he hurriedly disguises. I force a smile onto my lips and continue, trying to reassure him. "Maybe we can organise something after school? Thank you, again. Honestly, you have no idea how grateful I am."

"Oh, it's okay." Alec nods and scuffs his feet against the floor. "Be safe. Text me so I know when you're home."

I need you.

My heart warms and my smile becomes a little more

genuine as he backs away, towards the classroom again. "Thanks, Alec. I will."

We sit in silence at the table. Something cold and unspoken lingers in the air, weighing down upon each of our shoulders. Someone needs to talk, but nobody wants to. It sits heavy in the air above our heads, like a cloud, ready for someone to let loose the rain. Jack stares dumbly into the patterns of the wood. Violet's hand is in my lap, squeezing my numb fingers. My mom's nails tap relentlessly against the surface as we wait for someone to speak first, someone to breach the inevitable.

"Okay," Mom finally says. "We have to prepare some kind of a plan."

The rain falls.

"A plan?" I echo scathingly. Violet's grip tightens round my hand.

"Yes, a plan," Mom snaps back, looking me in the eye. Despite the circumstances, it's refreshing to see a spark about her again. To see a glimpse of the fire that burned inside her until just under a year ago. "We need to find the best way possible to deal with the upcoming anniversary, so that events like today don't have to happen again. If you know of another way we can help make things easier for everyone, please speak up."

I remain silent.

"That's what I thought." Mom sighs. The fight within her dies again. "I think everyone here knows why I called this family meeting. Riley had another panic attack today, and it's about time that we approach the subject of the anniversary of Kaitlin's death. I think it will be a lot easier to face if we all know how we're going to face it."

I glance at Violet sitting beside me. She has a small smile on her face, most likely from being addressed as one of the family. Her home life isn't fantastic, and she's been one of us for years now. Best friends with me and Kaitlin, she went through all of the events of last year with us. She knows she is my family, but it must still be nice for her to hear.

"Nothing is going to prevent me from having panic attacks, Mom," I say weakly.

Because the guilt is never going to stop.

"I know that, sweetheart, but what we can try to do is ease your anxiety by having a certain plan for things – so that you know how to deal with the feelings when they come to you. Do you think it would be worth seeing your therapist again?"

"No," I reply quickly. Jack looks up at this with an expression of confusion, but I shake my head adamantly. "We never really spoke about Kaitlin herself. She always encouraged me to keep writing about Kaitlin in my journal if I didn't feel comfortable talking aloud about her, so I'd prefer just to do that again."

Violet looks at me for a few seconds, before turning to my mom. "I think that's probably the best thing for Riley, actually. She's got us to talk to about Kaitlin, and she has her journal for her more intimate thoughts. She's progressed so much without the need of a therapist. If she feels uncomfortable with the idea, I don't see why she should need to see Julia again."

I squeeze Violet's hand as a silent thanks.

"Okay," Mom says. "No therapist. However, my compromise is that I want you to write in your journal as often as you can, Riley. I also want you to ring me if you ever think you're going to have a panic attack, or if you've already had one, and I'll take you out of school immediately. I don't think it's good for you to be there when you feel like that."

"Okay," I agree. "What about Jack?"

We all turn to the eight-year-old boy, clutching his iPad like some kind of a lifeline. He stares blankly back at us.

"I'll be okay."

"Are you sure, sweetheart?" Mom wraps a comforting arm round his shoulders. "It's a lot to deal with, so if you'd like someone to talk to about it, then we're all here. I can also ring Julia for you and book you some appointments if you want to talk to someone privately."

"No, I don't want that."

"Okay, well, Riley and Violet have offered to walk you home from school so you don't have to get a ride with Jamie any more. Is that better?"

"That's better," Jack affirms. He's always hated getting rides with his friend Jamie.

"What about you, Mom?" I ask finally, turning to look at her wearied face. "How are you going to deal with the anniversary?" It's so like my mom to make a plan for everyone else to deal with the event, but for her to tough it out herself. Her first thoughts always go to us, but she struggles just as much as we do – if not more. My stomach churns with guilt, and my eyes drop to her hands.

Mom's fingers tie themselves into a knot. "I think I'm going to book some extra sessions with Julia. Maybe throw myself into my work as a distraction. I'll be fine, Riley. It's you kids I'm worried about . . . Violet, please help keep an eye on them for me. You have my number – if you're worried about Riley at any point, just give me a call."

"I will," Violet vows.

"We should have more family movie nights," Jack suggests.

"I think that's a good idea." Mom smiles, grabbing his hand over the table. "Let's try to see this a bit positively too."

Jack pulls his hand away from hers in mock disgust, but a betraying smile slides onto his face.

"We're going to be okay," Mom assures us.

I'm not sure if she herself believes it, but the sentiment is as comforting as her arms round me.

11

Swamp Monster

"Twenty-eight . . . twenty-nine . . . thirty! Ready or not, here I come!" Alec's voice ricochets faintly around the house, causing Millie to squirm in anticipation on my lap. After the meeting I left straight for next door to see Alec. We went to pick Millie up from preschool and have just come back, and now we're playing hide and seek (Millie's favourite game). Alec is upstairs right now, and Millie and I are crammed in the storage cupboard under the stairs. The amount of shoes and sharp things I'm sitting on now should be enough to take me into hospital. Uncomfortable is an understatement for this freaking cupboard.

Above us, Alec's footsteps are enough to make Millie fidget nervously again as he treks down the stairs. What is he, an elephant?

"He's doing that on purpose," I mutter under my breath.

Millie giggles quietly, curling further up into my lap. It's pitch black in this darned cupboard, but even so I can tell that Millie's eyes are sparkling with excitement. She adores her big brother, and recently I think she's been truly warming up to me as well.

Alec's footsteps pass by the cupboard towards the lounge, and I hold my breath in anticipation. Part of me is wishing that Alec would hurry up and find us so that I can finally get out of this horrible torture chamber (I think I'm sitting on a Lego brick – the worst kind of pain), but then the other part is giggling in excitement, similar to what Millie's doing now. "Shh." I smile, putting my finger to her lips. She giggles again, more quietly this time, but it's possible that Alec heard it.

Sure enough, we don't have to wait long until the footsteps head back towards us, and Millie tenses in my arms, releasing a high-pitched quiet squeal and shielding her eyes. "I wonder where they could be . . ." Alec ponders loudly outside, obviously for Millie's sake.

I snort in amusement but Millie gasps, squirming to get as far away from the cupboard door as possible. "Is that a giggle?" Alec's footsteps get closer and closer, until I can hear him standing right outside of the door. Even I'm squirming at this point. "Is it coming from in there?" he muses. "No, can't be. They're much too big to fit in that tiny cupboard."

"Well excuse me," I say sarcastically as I hear him walking away, and Millie screams as his footsteps stop, knowing that he'll find us. He obviously heard me. To be honest, I think the whole street did – I said it purposefully loud. A smirk curves my lips as Alec swings open the door dramatically, his eyes searching for Millie.

"Gotcha," he whispers and grabs Millie by the waist. She screams loudly as he brings her up effortlessly to his chest, before blowing a raspberry on her bare stomach where her top has risen. She's giggling and squirming as he tickles her, laughing. I watch on, feeling like a creep for watching such an intimate sibling moment, but it's just too cute not to. You don't see this part of Alec every day – I need to make the most of it.

I think I need to move now. That Lego brick is imprinting itself into my ass.

I shift and stand up in the cupboard, brushing off my jeans and pulling down my beanie. Alec glances at me and something flutters in my stomach. It's getting so much more difficult to speak to him for some reason – it's so difficult to explain.

"So, squirt," I call Millie as Alec places her down. "What do you want to do now?"

Millie's eyes light up with excitement. "Can we go to the park?"

Immediately, Alec and I exchange a look as if to ask for the other's approval. We're actually kind of similar. It's only about 4.30 p.m. so it's not too late.

"Sure we can." Alec nods. "Go and put your jacket on and we'll walk. I'll even get you a lollipop if you're sharpish."

Millie beams in awe before darting off upstairs to grab a jacket and leaving Alec and I on our own in the hallway. My cheeks begin to heat the moment that Alec looks at me. I curse internally.

"Beanies suit you," Alec says softly before jogging into the kitchen.

I stand paralysed as my mind runs over those three words millions of times. Did Alec just compliment me? After a second, he returns, sliding some loose change into his pocket. He's holding a packet of wild berry Skittles in his

129

hand, and when he catches me staring at them he wriggles his eyebrows. He didn't think anything of the compliment, which reassures and disappoints me at the same time.

"Want to taste the rainbow, Riley?"

I laugh. "I'd rather not, thanks."

"Lying to yourself again, huh?"

I stare blankly at him. "You know, I'd like to see things from your perspective but I genuinely cannot fit my head that far up my ass. I mean, can you give me some tips? Is there, like, a Wikihow page I don't know about?"

Alec grins. "No, it's much more complex than that. It's all about the angle, Greene. You have to have a natural talent, like me."

"Oh, bite me."

"Just tell me where." He winks. "You ready to go?"

I nod in confirmation, just as Millie clomps down the stairs wearing her adorable little denim jacket. A wide-eyed and rather creepy baby doll is cradled in her arms.

"Is Alicia coming too?" Alec asks Millie unhappily.

Millie nods. "Of course, Alec. What kind of a mommy would I be if I left her here?"

She says it so seriously that I burst into laughter. Alec groans, ushering us both out of the front door as I continue to giggle, and I barely have time to put my jacket on before we're standing outside. Alec locks the front door behind us, and I take the liberty while his back is turned to steal the packet of Skittles from his jacket pocket. Of course, he notices.

"The blue one?" he scoffs, frowning. "What are you, a smurf? The red one is clearly the people's favourite." He snatches the pack back from me and we walk down the

130

driveway towards the sidewalk as he shovels red Skittles in his mouth. I scowl at him; the red ones taste amazing, but the blue ones dye your tongue. So much more fun, let's be honest.

"I beg to differ," I chime, shoving a few more carefully selected blue Skittles into my mouth. "Blue is underrated. I'm like a Skittle hipster – I don't go for the mainstream flavours."

Millie looks back from her place skipping ahead in front of us, nodding in agreement. I offer her a high five.

"I've got red, you've got blue . . . Wanna make purple?" Alec winks, leaning in to make kissy noises in my ear.

I squeal a little bit and shift away, throwing a sweet at him in defence. I have incredibly sensitive ears. It's my weak spot. I watch sadly as the poor defenceless green Skittle hits him on the nose, before falling to the floor with a clatter.

"You're a waste of Skittles," I huff. "Stop hitting on me, dude."

"Hitting on you?" Alec raises an eyebrow. "I don't need to hit on girls to make them fall at my feet."

"Cocky grasshole," I mutter.

"I'm sorry, what was that, Riley?" Alec says. "Something about my cock? Don't worry, girl. I can assure you that it's in perfect condition."

"I don't want to know!" I yelp, grabbing some Skittles and shoving them into his mouth to block what he's going to say. "There are two pairs of very innocent ears walking beside you," I warn him. "Be aware of that, okay?"

Alec just laughs.

The park in Lindale is only about a minute's walk from our houses. We turn onto the road leading to the entrance, a terraced row of cream houses with black iron railings. The park is located right by the coast, a road away – I can taste the sea breeze on my tongue. Alec clears his throat. "Speaking of falling at someone's feet ... my mom is getting married."

I choke on air. "Are you kidding me? I didn't even know she had a boyfriend."

Alec looks at me, slightly bemused. "Her *girlfriend*-slash-fiancée's name is Fiona, and *she's* a soldier."

"Oh wow, sorry, I shouldn't have assumed –"

"She and Mom have been dating for a couple years now, and she proposed on the visiting day last weekend," Alec says. I guess he thinks my apology is irrelevant. "It's the first time Mom's seen Fiona in a month. They've been meaning to marry for years but wanted to wait until Fiona quit her status as a soldier fully."

"That's romantic." My heart warms, but there's a question I mean to ask Alec which has just been brought to the forefront of my mind. I take in a deep breath, aware this is a slightly risky topic. "So ... is your dad going to go?"

Alec releases a short exhale. "My parents divorced just before Millie was born. I haven't spoken to my dad in years, so no, I assume not."

"Why did they divorce?"

"He's not a nice person." Alec's reply is short and slightly curt, and I'm instantly uncomfortable that I asked. Of all people I know how to respect privacy, and I don't want to push Alec to answer anything he doesn't want to.

"Sorry. Do you want to talk about something else?"

"No, it's okay, it shouldn't exactly be a secret or anything." He runs his hand haphazardly through his hair, and that's how I know that this conversation is stressing him out. "Dad didn't react well when Mom told him she was bisexual."

"Right," I hum, staring at my feet. I'm tentative around him; I don't want to say the wrong thing around such a delicate topic. I can't imagine how hard that must have been for Marie – to have been rejected by the one she loved, because of who she was. Similarly for Alec and Millie, to have their foundations crumble so quickly. When my parents divorced, I'd had time to adjust – there was a slow build-up to the announcement. Millie and Alec must have seen their parents' marriage disintegrate in a matter of days.

"He wasn't a great dad beforehand, but he hasn't wanted anything to do with us since that announcement. Now I don't want anything to do with him either."

"I'm so sorry, Alec. That must have been horrible."

"It was fine," he replies curtly. "We got through."

"And now your mom is getting married to someone she loves," I reply, trying to divert the topic into something more positive again. I can sense any more pushing on the father front might be a little too far for Alec, at this stage in our friendship. "So, will I ever get to meet Fiona? She sounds cool, although I'm not going to lie, the whole soldier thing is kind of intimidating . . . she could shoot me if she doesn't like me."

Alec smiles gorgeously and just like that, the conversation has been swept under the rug. "I'm positive you'll get to meet her. She'll be home for good in a few months, and that's after the engagement party, which your family has been invited to by the way. She's really cool, good with Millie too I guess." Thinking of his younger sister, his eyes lift up from the ground to check on her, skipping along ahead of us. "Millie," he says threateningly, "I'm gonna chase you . . ."

Millie glances back and squeals as she sees Alec approaching.

"You're a pretty adorable big brother you know," I say. "It makes me wish I had an older sibling to play with me when I was younger."

"Don't call me adorable." Alec wrinkles his nose. "Sexy? Yes. Manly? Yes. Rugged? Yes. Adorable? Hell no." He turns back to Millie and wriggles his fingers tauntingly. He'll chase her in a second.

My smile sparks deviously and my voice morphs into an exaggerated coo. "What a cutie you are, Wilde. Adorable. You're like a giant, fluffy teddy –"

Alec interrupts quickly. "I think you better start running."

I grin and jog to catch up with Millie.

"Quick!" I tell her. "Alec is the mean monster and he's trying to catch us! We need to run away!" Millie gasps at the news, abandoning her skipping and grabbing my hand. Together we run (well, jogging for me, running for Millie) down the sidewalk as fast as we can. Alec is making monster noises behind us, playing along, and Millie squeals as she hears him getting closer. After a second of running however, Millie is yanked away from me and "eaten" by Alec. I can hear her giggling loudly as Alec tickles her.

I've reached the park's entrance now. "Run, Riley!" Millie screams, and this time I really do run. It doesn't take long for Alec to catch me, though. He grabs me by the waist, hitting my ticklish spot, and pretends to take a bite out of my shoulder.

"Delicious." He grins, and I swat him on the chest. Millie runs up behind him and hooks her tiny arms round his waist.

"Let's go to the playground!"

"Look at Millie, she's making friends!" I point over at the playground from where we're sitting, watching the little angel talk to a couple of girls her age. She wouldn't let Alec and I stay in the playground, claiming instead that she wanted "freedom", so we're sitting next to the skate ramps instead and keeping our eyes on her from a slight distance.

"Riley, that guy is staring at you."

"What?" I turn to Alec, to find him completely and utterly involved in the skate ramps, more specifically by the boys around our age doing tricks by the fence. Sure enough, one of them is already looking at me as I look up, and he smiles when I meet his gaze. He's cute. Really cute.

And then he starts heading towards us.

Alec stiffens.

"All right, bro?" He grins at Alec before his twinkling green eyes flash back to mine. He's quite good-looking, with dark curly hair and a lip piercing. Not my type but still pretty hot. He throws me a wink, and my immediate response is to look down at my lap.

"Yeah, I'm good cheers," Alec replies coolly, yet he is stiff as a statue on the bench. Then, ever so casually, he throws his arm round the back of the bench, round me. I stare at him, surprised. The boy in front of us watches the action, and I start to feel a little unsettled. What is this, a possessive thing? I glance over at Millie. I'm glad she's okay playing with the other girls. They seem to be getting on well, at least. Maybe I'll escape over there.

"I'm Nick." The boy grins. "You any good at boarding? Want a go?"

"Alec. And no thanks, it's not really my thing, Nat." Alec's voice sounds slightly defensive and cold, and I watch him cautiously. Why is he being so rude? Nick's eyebrows rise a little at his reaction before he turns to me with the twinkle returned to his eyes. What a flirt.

"It's Nick," the boy says. "What about you, babe? Want a go?"

I glance over to Alec before shrugging. Nerves squeeze my windpipe, and it takes all my effort to ignore it. "Yeah, I think I will."

Nick grins, offering me a hand to pull me up. "That's cool." He smirks. "Yo, dude, I think your girlfriend here has bigger nuts than you." He kicks up his skateboard and offers it to me, smiling smugly over at Alec when he thinks I'm not looking. As for Alec, I don't think he's even noticed me leaving; he's too busy glaring at Nick. Boys and their stupid pride. I grab the skateboard and begin to walk towards the ramps. I climb up a medium-sized one in the most dignified way I can, setting the board on the edge and placing my foot on it to steady it. I can sense them all watching me, and I falter. No pressure then.

I place my weight on the board and slide down the ramp towards the jumps. I'm no expert, but I used to skateboard a lot a few years ago. Toby and I used to do it together, and we came here to practise. It's been months since I've even touched my skateboard. The wind rushes in my face, and I feel the familiar rush of adrenaline as I jump down the ramp. Boom! The skateboard spins beneath my feet in an ollie that I've practised many times (usually in my backyard because

136

I'm sad like that), and then I continue to slide up the nearest jump. My skateboard flicks high in the air at the end, and I catch it, landing firmly on my feet.

Still got it.

I turn towards the boys and offer Alec a small curtsey, feeling smug. I've missed skateboarding. Nick is full on grinning, but Alec just looks shocked. Is it really that surprising? I chuck Nick his board back, and he catches it neatly. "Thanks." I smile as I slide not-so-gracefully down the ramp and back onto solid ground. "I needed that."

"You're welcome." Nick steps closer. A little too close for my liking, despite how hot he is. The player vibe is practically dripping off him. "Maybe I could get your number in return?"

Instantly my throat tightens again and I splutter.

I go to reply but Alec beats me to it, interrupting. "I think we should go now, Riley. Nice meeting you, Nash." Alec grabs my arm, purposefully getting Nick's name wrong again. I cock an eyebrow at him as he drags me away from the guys. I can hear them laughing behind us. Alec is either jealous, or those guys have said something really rude to him. He pulls me into the playground, away from the skateboarders. Waves of pure anger pour off him and he avoids my expression entirely.

"Okay, what's up?" I sigh. "Because you're acting like a spoiled brat."

"You should be thanking me," he grunts. "I saved you from that pig." His arms are crossed. The resemblance between him and a pouty kid right now is astonishing.

"Saved me?" *Yeah right.* "Oh, noble Alec, however can I repay you for stealing me away from the cute skateboarding guy who wanted my number?"

"He wasn't good-looking, and he was a pig. You don't need him."

That's true, but still.

"Besides, when you were going down the ramps, all he was talking about was your ass."

"And who can blame him?" I joke, winking at Alec.

He just shoots me a blank stare in reply, and I roll my eyes. "Okay, seriously, Alec? I was kidding, you grouch. And for the record, I don't need you monitoring my social interactions – I actually really liked skating but I guess that's not important to you." Rolling my eyes, I decide to separate from Alec and head over to the swings and slides, where Millie is playing with her newfound friends. All of the girls look up at me when I approach, and Millie offers me a big grin.

"This is Riley," she tells her friend. "She's my babysitter. Alec, my big bro, is her Prince Charming. Aren't you, Alec?"

I spin round. I hadn't realised that Alec was still behind me. He ignores me and looks at Millie instead. "Prince Charming? Oh I don't know about that. Riley isn't the princess type. She's more like a toad or a –"

"A knight," I finish for him, shooting him a glare. "I think you'll find that Alec is the swamp monster, definitely not Prince Charming. Gosh no."

"Swamp monster? I don't think that's very fair."

"Someone's cheered up," I observe.

"I was never grumpy," he mocks.

"Yeah sure," I drawl sarcastically.

Alec ignores my comment. "So, I have something to ask you."

My heart thuds in my chest. "What?"

No, no, no. He's not going to ask you out. Shut up, Riley. Seriously, shut it.

"We're headed to the beach on Saturday. You and Violet up for it?"

Not like I was expecting anything else, was it? Stupid swamp monster.

12

The Beach

When Alec invited us to go to the beach, I wasn't quite sure what to think. It made me feel warm and appreciated – the fact that he wanted us to join them – but I also had my doubts. Being in my swimming costume in front of guys I've only just befriended? That's actually kind of intimidating. I also haven't been on a group trip out with friends for . . . well about a year now. I'm unused to this kind of thing. To make matters worse, there's also the minor detail of me not being able to surf.

Yet somehow, Violet still managed to convince me into saying yes.

"I know you aren't comfortable with them just yet, but they like you, and they want to spend time with you. This is not a scary thing or a bad thing; it's an opportunity to defeat some of your fears and get close to some pretty nice people," Violet had said to me, when I expressed my nerves. "Plus, I'll be there with you if you ever do want to leave, or feel uncomfortable. Come on, Riley, you're great and you can do this."

I said yes. Now my poor unfortunate ears are facing the consequences.

"The wheels on the bus go round and round!" Joe's voice bounces around the car as he belts out the rhyme in quite possibly the worst tune I've ever heard. He clutches his chest dramatically, blissfully unaware of the way the rest of us are wincing at the pitch. "Round and round, round and round!"

"Dude, we're in a car," Alec deadpans from beside me. His warm arm is slung round my shoulders in a casual gesture, which somehow still makes my skin tingle and my heart race. Dylan and Violet are sitting in the back making small talk, with Chase driving and Joe sitting shotgun. We've been on the road for the best part of five minutes and already my ears are bleeding. Luckily for me, we should be there soon, and part of me is actually excited.

Sparking a bright idea, I fish around in my pockets for my phone and my earphones. Joe has moved onto a rendition of "Humpty Dumpty" now. If he doesn't shut up then I'm just going to have to drown him out instead. Alec spots me fumbling and leans closer to speak quietly to me. The hair on the back of my neck rises at our proximity.

"Can I listen too?"

"Sure." I pass him an earbud with a smile. "Taylor Swift or One Direction? I don't have any other music on this phone."

"Nice try," Alec scoffs, elbowing me playfully so as to make more room for himself in the middle seat. "I know you aren't into that kind of music. I practically hear your playlist on repeat, from your bedroom speakers. Put Twenty One Pilots on or something." Impressed by his observation of my music, I do exactly that, chuckling as I elbow Alec back and sling my legs over his as best I can with the seatbelt. I win.

"Guys, can you just date already?" Chase groans from the driving seat. "The sexual tension in this car is unbearable. My boy radar is picking up on it."

Joe stops singing to gape at his best friend.

I inhale sharply at this, fighting the urge to laugh. "Is that your indirect way of saying we're turning you on?"

"Maybe."

"Just think of your grandpa in the shower. Naked." My voice is laced with a daring sense of amusement, and Alec cringes beside me.

"Ahh!" Joe yelps loudly, covering his eyes as though it'll help. "I'm imagining it too!"

I hear Violet snickering behind me, and she pats me supportively on the shoulder.

"You're going to make Chase crash the car," she points out. "He looks horrified enough as it is. In fact, all the boys do."

I glance over at Chase, letting out another dark giggle. At the moment the poor boy is blinking repeatedly, as though he hopes to get rid of the image that way, and his face is coloured a bright red hue. Serves him right.

I wonder briefly what we'll be doing today, but the answer is pretty evident. The surfboards are attached to the roof of Chase's car – a dark truck with the licence plate peeling off at the back. My minimal experience of surfing was noted and ignored, and Violet happily pointed out that we can just go swimming, sunbathe or walk around instead. It's her first real bonding time with Chase, Joe and Dylan and she seems to be fitting in really well. Not that I'd expect any different from my bubbly best friend.

"Can you surf?" Alec asks, as if reading my mind. I shake my head. "Guess I'll have to teach you." He looks oddly pleased by that fact. After the skateboard incident, guess he's just happy that he's better than me at something.

"I'm sure she'll get the hang of it," Joe says, winking at me. "If she doesn't, then it'll be funny to watch her failing, so it's a win-win situation for all of us."

Alec smirks at this, high-fiving Joe. I guess boys will be boys.

"Fail like your last Math test," I mutter under my breath. I don't think Joe heard it, but I can tell that Alec has from the widening of his smile. We turn onto the coast-side road and turn into the little dusty car park. Chase pulls up promptly in the first car parking space, right by the steps down to the beach. The beach in Lindale is small and sandy, a beach for locals rather than tourists. There are a few small stores in the road behind it, but nothing major. I don't even think we have a hotel in a fifty-kilometre radius, that's how lonely this place is.

"The waves look great," Alec says as we all clamber out of Chase's Range Rover. "I call dibs on the red surfboard!"

The sun beats down on the pale skin I have exposed, and I pull my sunglasses over my eyes.

Chase curses. "Dude, you know I love that surfboard!"

"Slim, sexy and gives one hell of a ride," Alec agrees, subtly winking at me. This boy should sell innuendos for a living. Dylan smacks him lightly on the back with a grin, and immediately the three boys scramble to get the surfboards down. I feel like a bit of an awkward lemon, standing watching. I would help, but I'm a bit short.

Chase begins to hand out surfboards as they come down. Alec gets the red one he wanted. Violet's is pale blue, with a rounded top.

"Right, let's roll." Chase shoves a slightly smaller yellow surfboard into my arms, and I mimic the others' positions of holding as we make our way down the steps, me trying my absolute hardest not to fall down. The beach isn't crowded luckily, but there are a few people dotted along the sands because it's a hot day. Usually it would be empty. My flip-flops sink into the hot sand, and Alec's tanned skin does wonders at distracting me.

After laying down the towels and piling up the surfboards in the centre of the beach, I collapse down onto the edge of my towel and fling my beach bag carelessly beside me. Violet, splayed beside me with a pair of dark aviators on, raises her eyebrow.

"Are we going surfing or what?" she asks.

"Yeah, I guess so."

Chase grins at me. "You sure you can handle it?"

"I was born ready."

So not born ready.

At my confirmation, all four of the boys begin to pull their shirts over their heads – leaving them in their swim shorts. I glance at Violet awkwardly, and her eyes are bugged to almost twice the size. *We were also not ready for that hormone-fest.* All the boys are chiselled, tanned and muscular in all the right areas. Leaving me ogling, Dylan, Joe and Chase grab their boards and run down to the sea immediately.

Alec, however, lingers behind, and I snap my jaw shut and try to act cool.

144

"Think you have a bit of drool there," he teases, pointing at my chin.

I stick my tongue out. My cheeks are slightly hot. "We'll meet you down by the water in two minutes."

Truthfully, I need some time to compose myself first. Not just for the surfing, but for the guys seeing me in a swimsuit too. As he runs down the beach, I look to Violet again and she smiles at me, standing up and brushing the sand from her legs. At least I'm not in this alone.

"We're going to do this," she says in a singsong tone, pulling me up by my hand. "It's about time we show them some girl power." Together we begin to get changed in the hot sun, with me glancing dubiously down to the sea every chance I get.

"Very easy for you to say – you've surfed before," I grumble, kicking off my flip-flops.

"You'll be fine, Riley, I promise. It's so much fun."

"I'm scared."

I glower apprehensively down at the waves licking my toes. My surfboard is dug into the sand beside me, ready to be used and disappointed that I can't seem to bring myself to do just that. Alec, standing beside me, grabs my hand reassuringly and tugs gently as he walks deeper into the cold sea. "You have nothing to be scared of, I promise." He tugs again. "What harm can come from trying?" Sparks shoot up my arm, but I ignore them.

"I can do this," I mutter to myself, tightening my grip on Alec's hand and pulling both myself and my board further into the waves. Dylan is waiting, about knee-deep, and I'm hardly ignorant of his eyes straying over my bikini-clad

145

body. Alec made his fair share of remarks too. If my whole body could blush, I would be red all over right now. When we reach about waist-deep into the water, and I'm pretty sure my limbs are going to fall off with the cold temperature, Alec stops and releases my hand.

I can't help but feel a little disappointed.

"What do I do then?" I bite my lip, intimidated by the scenario. I expected Violet to stay and support me, but she's already stomach-deep in the water with Chase and Joe, ready to show off her skills. *So much for girl power, team.*

"You should probably just start off with paddling," Dylan suggests, "so just get on the surfboard and float for a while. There's no real current or anything here, so you don't need to worry about that. Just paddle towards the waves, and when you hit them, lift up the top half of your body. I can help you if you need me." He helps me onto the surfboard after a minute struggle, and I clutch the board with heavy breaths.

"Okay," I say. "Like this?"

Slowly I start to paddle towards the waves, bobbing up and down precariously. I don't get far, though. Alec shakes his head and grabs the board to stop me.

"You need to go faster, or else you'll be dunked on. Here, curve your hands like this," Alec grabs my hand and curves it into the right position, and I pray that he can't see my blush under my wall of hair. I set off as soon as I can, paddling faster this time. "Yeah, that's better!" I can hear the smile in his voice, and after a second or two, he appears beside me on his own board. Dylan bobs up beside us, grinning.

"Okay, aim for a few waves, and lift the top of your board to cross them," Dylan instructs me. I gasp when I'm suddenly pushed forward, before my instinct kicks in and I begin to paddle furiously towards the first gentle wave. I pass it without a hitch, relaxing slightly. The second one however, I tilt sideways, sliding off into the water.

It takes me more than a few attempts to get back on the surfboard each time that I fall off, but gradually I find myself slipping off less and less as my technique improves. Albeit, I'm only facing fairly small waves at the moment, but I'm feeling pretty good about myself.

"I want to try to stand up at least once today," I tell Alec with determination. "Can you teach me to stand up?"

Dylan has left to follow the others, and I long to be with them, riding the bigger waves.

"Okay, but know that you'll probably fall off," Alec says. He slides off his own board to steady mine. "Right, so first lie down in the paddling position." I do as I'm told. "Now keep your knees together – that's important for balance – and slide your legs underneath you so that you're kneeling." I clutch the surfboard so hard that my knuckles turn white, wobbling unsteadily. By some miracle, I don't fall off.

"Now get your balance, and let go of the board," he orders, holding the board steady so that it doesn't bob away. My breathing hitches as I register my next move, but nevertheless I steady myself, my hands flying out either side for balance.

"Now, slide one leg up. Slowly . . . slowly, Riley, *slowly* –"

One minute I'm standing, the next minute I'm engulfed by cold water. The temperature change is a shock to my system, despite slipping in numerous times before, I was never fully under. I emerge with a gasp, my auburn hair stuck to my back as I settle myself on the edge of Alec's surfboard. We both have our arms crossed on the edge, facing each other. I puff out a little bit and Alec cracks a smile that stirs up a feeling in my gut. "Ready to try again?"

I beam at his question, and my heart seems to flutter at the sparkle in his eyes.

Stop that.

"Why the hell not?"

"Riley, we're going back into the water," Chase and Joe announce, clutching their surfboards. I sit up a little bit, squinting at them through the harsh light. They've literally spent most of the day in the water, their skin is sun-baked and they're going back in? Idiots. I nod in acknowledgement of their plan and continue to apply sun cream to my pale limbs. Dylan is lying on the towel next to me, and Alec has disappeared to the shop for some drinks. Throughout the course of the day, I've found myself gaining a bit of confidence around the boys, in exactly the way that Violet said I would.

We're friends. Pretty good ones at that – although my insecurities are screaming at me that something must be dodgy about this. It's so strange that I'm friends with some of the most popular boys in school. It's strange that I'm hanging out with this many people again.

My thoughts are interrupted when Alec arrives back, plonking himself down at the end of my beach towel. I didn't even see him coming.

"I got you a Pepsi," Alec declares, thrusting the bottle into my lap.

"Thanks," I mumble gratefully, holding the cold bottle against my heated skin. I spot something in my peripheral vision. "What's that?" Alec is holding a small brown paper

148

bag, angling himself to shield it from me, which naturally makes me curious. He pushes his hand out of view.

"It's nothing. Hey, will you do my sun cream for me?"

My eyes narrow at his blatant change of topic but nevertheless I grab the bottle. "Okay, turn round and I'll do your back."

"Don't act like you aren't desperate to," Alec teases, spinning on the towel and flicking sand up my legs. "This is your dream come true."

I pour the sun cream into my palm and smack it lightly on his back, before rubbing it in with circular movements. Once I've covered the lower half of his back without any discouragement from Alec, I'm hit with a stroke of genius. I rub the rest of the sun cream into his upper back, and then use a single finger to scrape the word 'smile' out of the sun cream. Alec is being quiet, staring pensively out at the sea.

"You look grumpy," I say. "So I wrote 'smile' on your back. Be happy, Wilde."

Alec turns to look at me, running a hand through his hair. "You're one of a kind, you know that?"

I fight to restrain my blush and fail. Luckily, this is the moment that Dylan decides to sit up, with a strange expression on his face.

"Riley," he says, "do you want to come down to the water with me? I need to speak to you."

I nod enthusiastically at the chance to escape from my awkwardness with Alec, and together Dylan and I stand up and head towards the chilly waves at the bottom of the beach. The wind is getting increasingly bitter as the afternoon draws to a close, and I know we must be leaving soon. In my peripheral vision I can't help but notice the slight scowl on

Alec's face as he watches us leave. My feet sink into the sand and my hair whips back from my face.

"So . . ." I turn to Dylan expectantly. We've reached the damp sand now, just kissed by the sea. We begin to walk along the waterfront. "What is it that you wanted to talk about?"

The expression on his face is almost guilty.

"I like you," Dylan says bluntly.

My throat thickens as I choke out a single word. My feet falter. "What?"

"You heard me," Dylan sighs, stopping too.

"Dylan, you can't –"

"Well I do." His expression has solidified, and I feel small under his intense smoulder. He stares for a few seconds. My heart is thumping heavily inside my chest. I glance back up the beach, towards the cheeky boy with dimples and a past. The boy that has made no moves on me, that flirts with other girls. I look back at Dylan, torn. He's smart and hot and so genuinely sweet. There must be something wrong with me. Should I say yes? I'm sure he could make me happy. He'd treat me really well. The tension is so thick it could be sliced like a hot knife through butter.

"Dylan –"

"I know." He glances down at his feet. "But can you just tell me if there's a shot?"

I stare at him, completely bewildered.

"I-I don't know." I hadn't ever thought about Dylan in that light. My brain was so annoyingly focused on Alec – our heart-to-hearts, the times he touches me. The truth of the matter is, though – he hasn't made a move. He's nice to me, and what we have is special, but does he see it in that way?

Would he *ever* actually make a move? Maybe after all this time I am still just the goofy girl from next door with the Mickey Mouse bra. Meanwhile the boy standing in front of me looks at me as if he's already expecting to be shot down, and I'm so confused.

That's the moment when Dylan chooses to step forward and press his lips against mine.

It's damp and sweet and everything a kiss should be. Lingering for only a second, he steps back and looks at me with melted blue eyes.

"Hey," I say softly, catching his attention. "I'm so sorry, Dylan . . . I just –"

"It's okay," he mumbles. "I know you're confused. I know why."

"I don't want to . . . get into anything," I struggle to find the words, "if I'm not sure about it, you know? I want to be one hundred per cent sure, and I'm not sure I am, with either of you yet. I don't know if I'm even . . . even *ready*."

"That is completely understandable, don't worry."

He nods and offers me a small smile, before turning and heading back towards the beach. I feel numb and shocked. I don't look after him. I can't. My hands are shaking, my breathing is funny and it feels like I don't even know how to walk any more. That's when I notice Alec stalking away from the beach, and I consider how much I'd want *his* lips on mine. More than any boy, even one as funny and smart and attractive as Dylan. Does he want that too, though? A sickening pang hits me in my abdomen.

Riley Greene, you absolute idiot.

13

Time of Year

"Riley, can I speak to you?"

I recognise the voice instantly.

"No," I retort, slamming my locker shut and walking away quickly in the hope that he won't follow. To my displeasure but not surprise, he does. He sticks to me like glue as I wind my way through the corridors towards the library. It's Monday, I have a free period and I *really* hope he doesn't have one too.

"Come on, Riley, give me two minutes?" Toby pleads from behind me.

"No. Believe it or not I was having an okay day until you showed up," I peer back over my shoulder to hiss at the boy who broke my heart. In actual fact, since Saturday I have done nothing but work and stress over my social situation. Alec has been suspiciously absent from his bedroom, although admittedly I was somewhat grateful about that. Everything is confusing right now, and his gorgeous face and mischievous nature do absolutely nothing to alleviate that. I don't know if he's even interested at all. I don't know if that means I should give Dylan a chance.

"Riley," Toby repeats desperately.

"If you have any kind of respect for me at all, you'll leave *now*." Shaking my head to dispense my worries, I increase my pace.

"Jeez, that's a bit harsh, isn't it?" Toby says, grabbing my arm to prevent me from storming away from him again. Where I used to get happy tingles, my skin feels cold and if anything repulsed by his contact. I tear my arm away from him quickly, and I don't miss the hurt that flashes in his eyes. Like he has any right to be hurt. Toby sighs in resignation and doesn't reach out again. "I just want to talk to you."

"Talk, and make it quick," I say icily. "I'm not wasting any more time on you than absolutely necessary."

I don't know why I'm even giving him a chance to talk, after what he's done to me.

"Well . . ." Toby clears his throat and glances around the corridor at the dwindling students. He's checking people aren't in earshot – but why? His mannerisms are shifty, sheepish. "Well I know what time of year it is . . . I just wanted to, um, offer my condolences I guess." His eyes flicker to me for the first time since he started talking, to judge my reaction.

I freeze, melt and boil all in the space of a second.

"Your *condolences*?"

"For your family," Toby says. "I know this must be difficult for you."

"You sicken me." I step back, and my face is a mask of disgust to shield the throbbing I feel inside. His words are rubbing salt in a wound. Salt. Alcohol. *Bleach*. He's rubbing bleach into my open chest. "Do you honestly think I want your condolences, after what you put me and Kaitlin through? I

153

cannot believe you've just said that. Like she wasn't anything to you at all. Like she wasn't your best friend, as well as my cousin. You know how much you meant to her." Tears bead in the corner of my eyes.

Toby curses and tugs his hair in angst. "I know how –"

"You don't know anything," I interrupt with a broken voice. "Thank you for your condolences, Toby, but I don't want them. This time of year is hard enough for me already without you pretending to care about her."

"Hey," Toby snaps, "I cared about her!"

He draws a few passing eyes with his volume.

"Cared. Past tense," I hiss quietly. "Just leave me alone, Toby. I am a spark you *really* don't want to fan into a flame."

Toby watches, stone faced, as I turn and storm away, and for once I am grateful to him. Grateful that he has the sense not to follow me this time.

"You look lonely," Joe's voice says from behind me.

I glance up from my half-eaten sandwich to see Joe, Chase, Dylan and Alec standing nearby with their lunch trays. My chest twists with anxiety as I remember my situation. Chase is observing me with amusement. I'm sitting alone at a table, on the edge of the busy cafeteria. I must look incredibly lonely, but Violet hasn't come out of her lesson yet for some reason, so there's not much I can do until she comes. Until now, I've been pretending to text under the façade that I actually have friends. I smile at the sight of the boys, but my gaze lingers on Alec and Dylan.

"I am a bit lonely, to be perfectly honest." I smile weakly.

"Guess we're sitting here today," Chase announces,

154

sliding into the seat next to mine. "I'm sure the football team won't mind *too* much."

The other boys sit down without question, and I feel oddly flattered to have them sit with me, despite the shocked looks I'm getting from surrounding students. Alec sits down next to me without speaking, and my breathing flutters. Oddly, we haven't spoken to each other since the other day, and I have no idea how to act around him. What do I say?

As for Dylan, I have no idea how to act around him either. *Awkward.*

"So where's Violet?" Joe asks with his mouth full, holding a greasy burger with two hands. How he can afford to eat the way he does and maintain his chiselled body is a mystery to me. Whatever it is, I want it.

"Right here," Violet interrupts and we all suddenly notice her standing by the table with her eyebrows raised. "Riley," she says, turning to me with a feigned nervous expression, "I think our table has been invaded by *populars*."

"Heaven forbid!" I play along, putting a hand to my forehead and pretending to faint.

"You two are weird," Chase states bluntly, observing us like creatures under a microscope as he looks up from his milkshake. "But funny."

"Thanks, I guess." Violet laughs, taking a seat beside Joe.

All of the other boys greet Violet except Alec, who merely prods at his food with his fork. Luckily, Violet doesn't seem to notice.

"Hey." I suck in my nerves and lean closer to him. "Are you okay?"

Alec grunts a little. "Yeah I'm fine."

"No you're not." My eyes narrow. "What's wrong?"

"Nothing."

"You're lying."

"I said *nothing*," Alec snaps, suddenly shifting his weight away from me.

"Hey, don't snap at me!" I retort, eyes narrowing. "You and I both know I've done nothing wrong. What's got you like this?"

Alec gives me a look of disgust. "Nothing. I said *drop it.*"

"Fine, I will."

There's awkward silence for a few minutes between us – foreign territory in our friendship. If the others picked up on it, they draw no attention and carry on in their blissfully happy world of bonding. Violet is chatting away contentedly. She seems to be fitting in really well. It's nice that she feels welcome, although it would be even nicer if Alec could be bothered to chip in and greet her. He needs to pull that stick out from his ass and stop manstruating.

"Look." He clears his throat and sits up a little but his voice is low. "I'm sorry, I just don't want to talk about it. I'm not really in the mood to fight."

"And you think I am?"

"No," Alec chooses his words. "I just . . . I'm a little frustrated."

"Are you going to tell me why?"

Alec looks at me for a long second. "What's going on between you and Dylan?"

"What do you mean?" I ask, startled by the blunt question. How does he know? Unless, when I saw him storming at the beach it was because . . . "Wait – you saw, didn't you? You saw what happened at the beach?" I say with trepidation.

"I saw," Alec confirms. I note that he doesn't exactly sound overjoyed, which stirs up the butterflies in my stomach.

"I don't think anything will happen," I tell Alec quietly. *I like you.*

"Really?" Alec sounds disbelieving. "You seemed pretty happy with his tongue down your throat." *He's jealous.* My heart surges with hope, but it's quickly extinguished by the reality of my situation. Even if he is jealous, it shouldn't *matter.* I don't know if I'm even ready for a relationship; I said no to Dylan for precisely that reason. There's also the rather substantial factor that Alec may not be ready, and may not want one.

"I don't like him," I say softly, hedging my chances. "He knows that."

Why can't you just make a move if you're interested? Tell me if you are!

I prod his arm, and when he looks up he seems less moody. His face is a few inches from mine, and from here I can see every detail about his face from the gold specks in his eyes to the faint freckles dotting his forehead. My toes curl.

Riley, you have it so bad for him.

"Riley, there's this thing," Alec begins vaguely.

"A thing?"

"Yes, a thing," Alec says. "My mom's engagement party tomorrow night."

"I am aware of that event."

"Well . . . because both our families are going, and my mom wants me to take a date . . . she told me to ask you. So, um, do you want to be my non-official date to this party?"

Don't scream yes. Say it calmly. He's not asking you out; he's just being forced into going to an event with you. One which you were going to anyway. Be chill.

157

"That sounds calm! I mean, um, good. Yeah, good."

Alec gives me a strange look, but he's smiling. "Cool."

Feeling eyes on my back, I go rigid before turning round to survey the scene. Toby walks past us a few metres behind, and his eyes are locked onto mine. Not this again.

Alec grumbles beside me, so I'm guessing he's seen too, and then he slowly intertwines his fingers with my own. I can't help but notice that, again, it is only for the sole purpose of keeping another guy away. Toby's eyes narrow. Another dominance fight. I turn back to face the table, glad to see that Violet and the boys are too busy debating werewolves versus vampires to notice the focus of mine and Alec's attention. After a second, Alec turns back to face the front as well, although his demeanour has definitely changed. His hand slides slowly from my own, and I miss the warm buzz of comfort that it brought.

"Are you kidding me? Werewolves are so much better!" Violet argues. "I mean take Edward Cullen as an example. He sparkles. That's hardly big bad vampire material is it? That dude has ruined the reputation of vampires. Werewolves are so much hotter, plus the whole full moon thing just makes them so much cooler too."

I agree. I mean, have these guys not seen the *Teen Wolf* actors? Drool.

"What about Dracula?" Dylan retorts, shaking his head. "Dracula is a legend, one of the classics. You don't see any classic werewolf stories, do you? Vampires have been around so much longer."

"Exactly!" Chase says. "Vampires are old, man. Werewolves are fresh." He slaps the table to emphasise his point, as though he's just ended the debate, which makes me laugh. I glance at Violet, feeling a small buzz of happiness in

158

my chest. We're sitting with people at lunch, and it's fun. It feels like I haven't had anything like this in so long.

"Excuse me." A voice interrupts our debate, and I look to the side to see a pretty brunette girl standing there, hand on her hip and flanked by a petite blonde. She wears a slightly too short dress, and her eyes are bright. Not one of Tiana's minions, I don't think. "Hi." She smiles at Alec, fluttering her eyelashes. "I just wanted to give you my number, because you seem like a really nice guy."

What? That's the stupidest thing I've ever heard. No way does she want to give Alec her number because *he seems like a nice guy*.

She pauses to flick her hair behind her shoulder, leaning in towards him seductively, "I'm free tonight if you want to come round?" she murmurs quietly.

I snort quietly to restrain my sarcastic remark. I'm sorry, but just how obvious can you get? We all know what she said, judging by Joe's eye roll and Chase's impressed stare. Alec must get this a lot. Still, my laugh has a tone of bitterness to it and I wonder if anyone notices.

"Er, no thanks," Alec coughs, blushing a little, and I think we all turn to stop and stare. Alec Wilde is rejecting a girl?

"Your loss." The girl leans back, her flirty aura turning cold and hostile as she flounces away with the blonde girl in tow.

Meanwhile, I'm still choking on my saliva from what Alec said. He's probably already seeing someone tonight – that's got to be it, right?

"I'm sorry but did I just hear that right?" Joe questions him, mouth agape. "You're denying a hook-up?"

Well at least I know I wasn't imagining things now, and

that Alec actually did just totally reject a hot girl.

"Dude." Chase coughs out a laugh, leaning over the table to slap Alec on the forearm. "When was the last time you got laid?"

Do I really want to know this? I share a look with Violet, wrinkling my nose.

"Alec's not getting any," Joe sings, laughing, and I chuckle quietly along with him.

"Shut up," Alec mutters, blushing the tiniest bit. "I got laid last night for your information."

Lie. Last night Alec was at home studying. I saw him through the window.

"Well I don't know about you guys," Dylan says with a smirk, "but I don't believe him."

And I definitely don't.

"Hey, Riley."

"What?" I look across the window at Alec, frowning. He's lying on his side on his window seat, wriggling his eyebrows at me mischievously. In all honesty, he looks like a complete and utter weirdo, but it's quite endearing at least. Not every guy would do this.

"You know what I've been thinking?"

"Enlighten me."

"You and I are like butt cheeks," Alec drawls. "Although there's crap between us, we always stick together."

"Oh my God." I face palm, placing my pen back down on my desk. These keep getting better and better. I'm supposed to be studying, sitting here in my sweats with my hair pinned into a pile on top of my head, but Alec is a huge, gorgeous distraction. I can't say I'm complaining.

160

"Can I borrow a kiss? I promise I'll give it back."

"Shut up, Alec." I laugh. "Give me my *bra* back and then we can talk."

"Do you work in Subway? Because you just gave me a footlong."

"I really hope you mean a sandwich. Seriously, where do you come up with these lines? Do I need to check your search history?" My voice is weary, but I can't deny that I love the little conversations Alec and I have over our windows, even if they do revolve around some quite dirty pickup lines. They make me laugh, at least.

"Tumblr," Alec admits sheepishly. Then, unwilling to give up on his fun and games, he continues with another stupid and clichéd line. "Are you from Jamaica? Because Jamaican me horny."

"Nope." I shake my head with a confident smile playing on my lips. "But you must be from Yukon, because Yukon go screw yourself."

He's not the only Tumblr fan.

"Ouch!" Alec clutches his heart dramatically. "You wound me."

I smile, and Alec goes back to his studying like I go back to mine. My head doesn't seem to want to shut up, though. Thoughts of Alec, memories of today, overanalysing every possible detail to the extreme. I thought it was weird when he denied that hook-up, and yet he shows up at my window playing bad pickup lines like an old guitar.

I think that's a good sign.

I can't be with Dylan. I just can't.

14

Dancing Hurts

"Why do I have to wear a tux?"

I glance up at Alec from my place in front of the mirror, smirking a little at his disgruntled face. "Why? Don't you like it?"

He shakes his head and pulls a face in reply, making me laugh even though I completely disagree with his judgement. Alec in a tux is just too much for me. He looks annoyingly perfect; the suit hugs him in all the right places, emphasising his defined figure and his hair is styled into that effortless tousle he always seems to achieve. Although he might be uncomfortable, he looks like a frigging angel. That has to be some consolation, right?

"Well you have to wear it," I say. "It's your mother's engagement party, and you are the son of the brides-to-be." Saturday night has arrived, and we're almost ready to go.

Once again, my eyes scour my appearance in the mirror. My dress is a soft gold colour, strapless and satin, with matching heels. I've been ordered to wear them both with no objections, by my darling mother who bought them for me. I'm just trying to figure out whether I look like a princess or a marshmallow.

"Okay, Riley," I mumble. "We can work with this."

"You know that mirrors can't talk, right?"

"Luckily for you, they can't laugh either," I retort, sticking my tongue out at him.

Alec, noticing my attire for the first time after scrutinising his own, wolf whistles as he steps behind me. "Hot damn, Riley." Our eyes meet in the mirror, and I hope and pray that he thinks the red tinge in my cheeks is purposeful. "Nice dress," he compliments, then he grabs a lock of my hair and twirls the freshly curled ringlet round his finger. "You should have your hair like this more often."

My heart jumps a little, and I have to swallow down my hope.

"If I did, my hair would be dead." I pull a face. "Anyway, how come you're here instead of with your mom at your house getting ready?"

"Because I wanted to let my date know to hurry the hell up," Alec says, throwing himself on my bed. "We're cab-sharing, and our families are waiting downstairs, so get your ass into gear." Alec pauses for a moment, distracted by something on my bedside table. It's only when I crane my neck that I discover it's the photo of Kaitlin and me. I turn stiff as I stare at him for his reaction.

He notices the resemblance. "Hey, this is the girl from your phone."

"My cousin." I manage to get the two words out. I must have done it calmly enough that Alec didn't suspect anything, because he has no real reaction to the words.

"You know," he begins, "you'd get along really well with

163

my cousin Natasha actually. She'll be there tonight; I'll introduce you two. She'll love you."

"Definitely, sounds good. Let's go then," I say hurriedly, grabbing my clutch and targeting the door. "I can't keep them waiting any longer." All I want is for Alec to get the hell away from that picture as soon as possible. Although I'm glad that he knows about Kaitlin's existence now, I don't think I'm quite ready yet to tell him everything.

I know it shouldn't be a secret that she's gone, but I don't want people to know. Because she didn't live in Lindale, it's easier for me to pretend that she never existed, because nobody ever knows she did. I don't want the sympathy and the pats on the back and the questions. My only form of closure is if people don't talk about her. That's how we cope as a family. It's coming up to the anniversary in a little under a week and now is not the time to open that can of worms.

Maybe I'll tell Alec at some point, but not just yet. Not now.

We walk down the stairs and I manage to somewhat compose myself before we see our families waiting. Both of our moms are wearing gorgeous cocktail dresses, but there's something about the happy glow around Marie that makes her the most beautiful of us all. Her fiancée is arriving about halfway through their party, after something she has to attend first. Marie looks like a bride-to-be, and it's amazing to see. Jack is wearing a tux, with his head in his iPad as per usual. Millie beams as we come down.

"Riley, you look beautiful!" Marie gushes, coming forward to meet me at the bottom of the stairs. "I knew you'd look a bombshell in that dress."

"Thanks." I curtsey jokingly. "You both look stunning.

Is the cab here yet? Are we ready to go?" *Don't think about Kaitlin. Forget about it, just for one night.*

"Yes, but they can hold on a minute while we take a few photos of you two. You look like such an adorable couple," Mom says, pulling her camera from her bag.

I don't dare to see Alec's response to this. As the camera is directed at us, I stare into it like a deer in front of headlights. A warm arm slides round my waist.

"Go along with it, Greene," Alec whispers in my ear.

The camera flashes. I smile my way through, and somehow the brittleness of my lips dissolves as he pokes my sides and whispers nonsense pickup lines in my ears. I like the boy standing next to me so much that it hurts.

And by the end of the photographs, my smile isn't fake at all.

Alec doesn't remove his arm from my waist until we get into the cab.

When we finally arrive at the country club where the engagement party is being held, I'm more than a little impressed.

It's a vintage building with huge decorated columns and arches, surrounded by fields. Vines lace up the side of the old stone, and the gardens are immaculate. Based up in the cliffs, in the richer part of town, I have only ever heard about this place.

"Whoa," I breathe out. "This is amazing."

We're standing at the entrance, a pair of glass double doors that lead straight onto the balcony of the ground floor. The balcony wraps round the exterior of the building, framed with a gold fence covered in vines. A sweeping staircase leads down to the dance floor and a fancy café with a bar, which is currently brimming with people. People begin cheering as they recognise Marie coming down the staircase.

"Can I accompany you down the stairs, *princesa*?" Alec holds out his arm, and I take it without hesitation. We make our way down the stairway as elegantly as possible, and I try my very hardest not to slip in my shoes on the polished marble.

"*Princesa* huh?" I tease Alec. "Look at you, Chico, speaking sexy."

"Are you calling me sexy, Riley?" Alec's lips twitch into a cocky grin.

"Nope." I shake my head. "I'm saying Spanish is a very sexy language."

"Ah, but I am part Spanish. Therefore you are calling me sexy by default."

"You're about as sexy as a dog's behind."

We reach the bottom of the stairs, without me tripping (achievement unlocked!), and head straight over to the bar area. Millie is already over speaking to a couple of other kids her age, who I assume she knows. Jack is standing, looking about as awkward as I feel, right at Mom's side as Marie introduces her to the guests. I know no one at this party, and it's quite intimidating as I feel the weight of stares from strangers. The eyes on our linked arms.

"Alec, who's this hottie you brought with you?"

Alec and I spin round to see a tall girl with short raven-black hair, curled around her face. Her features are delicate and feminine, and she's freckled intensely in an adorable way.

"Hi," she greets as she looks at me. "I'm Natasha."

"My cousin," Alec explains.

"Oh right!" I realise, smiling at her. She's absolutely

gorgeous – evidently it runs in Alec's family. "It's nice to meet you. I'm Riley Greene, Alec's friend."

"He didn't do you justice when he told me how pretty you are." Natasha's eyes glint deviously as she glances at Alec, and I'm suddenly hit by the resemblance of the two cousins. Alec grumbles something next to me, and she turns her attention back. "I know who you are anyway," she continues. "You're the one who drew on his face, am I right?"

Well that makes me seem like a right bitch.

I open my mouth to protest but she beats me to it, with a mischievous laugh. "No need to explain; I've heard all the details. You're basically a legend." She lifts her hand up for a high five, and I stare at it for half a second before slapping it enthusiastically, slightly dazed that I really do seem to like this girl as much as Alec said. Damn him, why does he have to be so right all the time? Alec's hand tightens round mine, and Natasha doesn't fail to notice. "So, Alec, how did you manage to grab yourself a girl like this?"

"I didn't grab anything," he mutters uncomfortably. "Shut up."

"Well I can't believe that he hasn't introduced us until now." Natasha smiles warmly, tucking a curl behind her ear. "Boys huh? Hey, you should come with Alec to my mom's barbecue in a few weeks. I think a few of Alec's friends are coming too, so you can help me increase the girl population in the house. I'm sure Alec wants you to come," she says, elbowing him.

"I'd love to," I say, glancing at Alec for his approval. He just shrugs, which I'm not sure whether to take as a subtle hint for a no.

"Anyway, I have to go and help my mom in the kitchen,"

Natasha apologises. "I was on my way there when I saw you two, and I couldn't resist coming over to say hi. She's making the cake for the party, and I'm second in command. It was so nice meeting you, Riley. I hope I'll see you again soon." She offers me a somewhat dorky and endearing wave, before heading off in the opposite direction, her elegant silver dress flowing behind her. She looks like a model, yet she's only our age.

Alec's family has a pretty damn amazing gene pool.

"So." Alec's voice snaps me out of my reverie, and he sounds sheepish. "Do you want to dance? That's what everyone else is doing. Might as well do it now, before Fiona arrives and the food is served . . ."

I spin round to look and sure enough, the adults are pairing up and making their way to the dance floor together. I don't recognise the song playing, but I nod to Alec anyway, a small smile making its way onto my lips. *Now don't go thinking this will be all romantic, because it probably won't. I bet he'll step on your feet or something.*

I shake my head to clear my thoughts, letting Alec lead me to the dance floor. "Can you dance?" he whispers to me as we stop, and he puts a hand on my waist. The skin under my dress tingles like it's alive with electricity at his mere touch. He stares down at me, and I'm struggling to breathe.

"Not a clue," I whisper back, breathing in his musky vanilla scent. "You?"

"Not really."

"Remind me why we're dancing then?"

Alec doesn't reply, but I can tell he's amused. Slowly he begins to bring us into a basic box waltz, about the limit for me in the dancing area. I raise my eyebrows at him in

168

question as we bob from side to side, before he raises my arm above my head, pushing me lightly into a spin under his bicep.

"I can dance a little bit," he admits with a grin.

"That dance move is old, Wilde. I did that with boys at elementary."

"But it wins you over anyway, doesn't it?"

Crunch.

Pain swells in my foot and I wince, breathing in sharply. "Well standing on my foot certainly doesn't win me over."

"Er – well, yeah." Alec glances away gracelessly, as I try to suppress the pain. Still it's not all bad. Mr Smooth just stood on my toe.

"Oh my goodness." I laugh.

Alec opens his mouth to protest but is swiftly interrupted by a woman beside us.

"What a cute couple you two are." She smiles, held in the arms of a slightly older bearded man.

I have no idea who they are, but I think Alec might judging by his gracious thanks. I stand there and blush as they walk away, and Alec laughs at my bashfulness.

"I knew I had an effect on you, Greene." I can hear his smug happiness in that fact.

"Oh shut up. I blush easily." I flick my hair over my shoulder. The pace of our dancing changes to meet the ever so slightly faster music which has just come on. He spins me again, but only halfway this time, wrapping his arms round my waist so that my back is to his chest and his head rests on my shoulder intimately, as we bob awkwardly to the music.

"What are you doing, Alec?" I ask him suspiciously, and he blows lightly in my ear in reply.

169

Being annoyingly ticklish, I let out a small squeak and squirm away from him, spinning the rest of the way so that I face him and his self-satisfied little face again.

What a douche he is.

"I need to go to the restroom." I roll my eyes. "Don't miss me too much."

After asking for directions twice, I finally make it to the restrooms and in here it is just as gorgeous. There's a large window to the side showing a view onto the activity fields, and the sky is dark now. The whole counter for the sinks is made of polished marble, and instead of having faucets like a normal bathroom, they have mini waterfall things that look really cool. Maybe I should ask Mom if we can have those at home. I stare at my flushed face in the mirror before fishing my phone from my pocket to call Violet for some much needed dancing advice.

She picks up after three rings.

"Nashville Sperm Bank. You squeeze it, we freeze it – how may I assist you?" I can't help but chuckle at Violet's pickup. Our traditions are so cool.

"Hi, Violet," I say. "Great line."

"I'm pretty proud of that one if I do say so myself," she replies cockily. "If you don't mind me asking, what are you calling for? Aren't you supposed to be at the party?"

"Yeah. I'm in the restroom at the moment."

"So why are you not flirting your ass off with that lovely slice of man cake?"

"Man cake?"

"Alec Wilde of course. You need him to make a move."

"I just wanted some advice . . . how do you dance? And make it, y'know, look good?" I frown at myself in the mirror.

170

"Alec and I are having some trouble, you see." I know Violet will have at least one tip on how we can dance effectively – she was forced to go to ballroom dancing classes for six years with her mother. Okay, she was only thirteen when she stopped, but she's got to remember something, right?

"Dancing is simple. Stick to a box waltz, and then every now and then, you step to the left, and he steps to the right, so your arms are stretched against each other's body, okay?" she clarifies. "That move looks good, but it's easy too. You can add in a spin every now and then, and maybe even a dip? All Alec has to do for that is support the back of your waist whilst you lean backwards. You don't need to do anything too difficult for it to look decent. Try that sort of stuff."

"Okay, that sounds manageable I guess . . ."

"Yup, now get back on that date sharpish."

"I will, thank you. I'll call you later – bye!" I shove my phone back into my clutch and head back out of the restroom, now eager to get back out there to Alec and show him some moves. I'm surprised to find, however, when I step back out on the dance floor, Alec is standing with someone else.

An older woman, flirting with him.

He looks more than a little uncomfortable, leaning awkwardly away and scratching the back of his neck. Alec just can't go anywhere without being hit on, can he? Suffice to say, that dress does her no favours.

"Hi honey," I say, coming to step by his side.

I'm going to pull an "Alec": pretend that we're a couple.

He obviously catches my drift, because his arm wraps tentatively round my waist.

"And who is this?" I turn to the woman with an elasticated smile, which she begrudgingly returns. I think even Alec

171

would draw the line with cougars, thank goodness. I can't help but feel a little bemused by this situation. The woman looks about thirty, with dark hair and smoky eyeshadow.

"I'm Megan," she says. "Excuse me, I'm going to go and grab a drink. Lovely to meet you." And with that, she scurries off. I turn to Alec and wriggle my eyebrows suggestively at his antics.

"You like the older women then, Alec?"

"Shut up," he grumbles. "She was terrifying. I'll have nightmares."

"C'mon." I grab his arm and lead him back onto the dance floor. "Let's go and dance. I called Violet and she's given us some tips."

Alec gives me a dubious look but takes my hand anyway as we return to the simple box step.

"Okay, you step to the right and I'll step to the left," I instruct. "One, two and three, go."

I step to the left and Alec steps in the opposite direction, pulling my arm taut against his chest so that it's uncomfortable, but not quite painful. He grins, and then pulls me into another one of his favourite spins, ending with a flourish.

"Well done," I say breathlessly. "Now for the dip. Put your hand on the small of my back, and I'll lean backwards, okay?" He does as I instruct, and I begin to dip. I've always had issues with trust, but call it a gut feeling, I just know that Alec isn't going to drop me.

"Well done!" a voice calls nearby, applauding.

Thud.

"Ow, Alec, what was that for?" I groan, dusting off my dress as he apologetically offers me a hand up. My butt is aching from this stupid hardwood dance floor.

"Sorry. Fiona scared me." His voice is sincere but with an underlying sense of amusement. He helps me back up and sure enough, as I glance over, a woman stands nearby watching. She mouths an "oops" at me and cautiously approaches, tugging Marie by the hand. Fiona is everything that I expected and more. She's tall, taller than Marie, and she walks with an air of assertiveness that I think only years in the army must have provided her with. Her skin, dark as treacle, is flawless aside from the glint of a blue stud in her right eyebrow. Her smile is wide, and her bright eyes are smouldering with curiosity. She's by far one of the most entrancing women I've ever seen.

"I think we should give the dancing a miss from now on." Alec scratches the back of his neck, oblivious to my fascination. "We don't seem to be doing very well."

"I agree," I murmur absent-mindedly, suddenly faced with the nerves of meeting this woman. What if she doesn't like me? I know how highly Alec thinks of her.

"Alec," Fiona says as she stops in front of us. For a second I think she's upset with him, but suddenly her mouth breaks into a smile and she tugs him towards her in an understated and somewhat awkward hug. "I've missed you."

"I missed you too." Alec chuckles, pulling away.

"Good, because if you miss me, you haven't forgotten me. And the chances *are* if you haven't forgotten me, you shouldn't have forgotten your manners." Fiona raises a sassy eyebrow. "Aren't you going to introduce me to your friend?" Finally she looks at me with curiosity.

"Right." Alec shakes his head. "Riley this is my soon-to-be stepmom Fiona. Fiona, this is my Rile – I mean, just Riley."

"It's nice to meet you at last," I say. "This is such an amazing party."

"It's nice to meet you too. I've heard a lot about you," Fiona replies charmingly. She gestures around with her hand. "Unfortunately, I can't steal credit for the party. Marie is the party planner in this relationship; I just show up and eat the food." Fiona glances back at her future spouse with a small smile, her eyes sparkling. Behind her, the extravagance and elegance of the party seems to pause for a second as people glance over. The happy couple are the nucleus of this social gathering; every movement they make is hard not to notice.

"Don't forget drinking all the alcohol," Marie scoffs.

"Of course, I do that too." Fiona laughs sheepishly, swilling the drink she holds in her free hand. "Anyway, Riley, I hear you live next door? Are you in Alec's year at school?"

"Yup, I'm in his Physics class." I glance over at Alec, surprised to see that he's already looking at me. "I think we classify as friends, don't we?" I tease him.

"Easy there." He grins. "We're taking it slow, Greene. Acquaintances, I think."

"Are you kidding?" Marie drawls, not comprehending our sarcasm. "These two have been inseparable since we moved."

Awkward.

"Interesting." Fiona's eyes sparkle. "Well I'm rooting for it."

"Thanks," Alec grunts, scratching the back of his neck. I'm finding it hard to contain my laughter. "Say, haven't you two got somewhere to be?"

"Sure, let's leave them be and check on the drinks." Marie tugs at a reluctant Fiona's arm.

"But I want to make them even more uncomfortable!" Fiona whines playfully as Marie tugs her away. "It was so nice meeting you, Riley! Don't hurt my boy!" They disappear into the crowd standing near the bar, leaving Alec and I in an uncomfortable and amusing silence.

"Well . . ." I begin, "she was not what I was expecting."

"She surprised me too. Although she wasn't as embarrassing as some of the relatives that came up to me while you were in the restroom." Alec grimaces. "It was so bad, Greene. They were asking about our 'relationship'."

"Oh."

"Yep," he says. "And Riley?"

"What?"

"If my mom's friends ever ask how we met . . . You snuck into my room one night and stole my boxers for a dare. Completely unprovoked."

"What?"

"I'm joking, jeez!"

"Don't joke about something like that!"

"I think it's about time I stifle your fuse, Greene. I don't think the world could handle the explosion of bitchiness. You might just be the end of us all."

"Alec?" I say in the sweetest possible voice.

"Yes?"

I stamp down hard on his foot, making sure the heel digs in. "You're a grasshole."

15

The Whole Story

"Riley!" I hear Alec calling from his window for what seems like the hundredth time since he came home from school. Once again, I ignore it. You'd think he would have got the hint that I don't want to talk to him: my drapes are firmly shut, my phone has been turned off for the last few days and my window is only ever so slightly ajar. I don't want to see people right now. "Riley!" he persists, calling again. "I know you can hear me! Your light is on!"

"Please just leave me alone," I shout back, begging internally that my voice doesn't convey my inner turmoil. I can't do this today. I am not able. "Please, Alec. I'll talk to you tomorrow, I promise. Any other day but this. *Every* other day but this one." I walk away from the window and lie down on my bed. I haven't really moved from there since this morning's visit. I must look horrific.

Evidently, Alec ignores my words again, because it isn't long until I hear the huff of effort and the loud thud of Alec landing on my windowsill. It takes him a good while to push himself over the window, but it's not long enough. Alec emerges from my drapes and drops onto my bedroom floor almost proudly. His face tells another story, though.

Alec is concerned about me.

"Alec," I mumble weakly, and I can already feel the fight draining from my body. I'm too emotionally purged to resist his advance. Maybe this is what I need. Maybe I need to talk to him. What if he is exactly the thing that makes these last few hours of today bearable?

"Riley," Alec sighs, "I've been worried sick about you. Both you and Violet have avoided us for the past few days. Today, when you weren't in school, I figured something had happened to you. What's wrong?" His voice evolves into a soft murmur, which I would not be able to hear if I wasn't listening closely.

Where would I even begin?

My bottom lip begins to quiver, and I feel the lump rise in my throat. Alec is seeing me at my most vulnerable, and all I want to do is to shield myself away from him. To hide, to put my walls up and never let anyone in. Yet, there's another part of me. A part of me which yearns to spill everything out onto him. To smash the bottle of my feelings and feel the release that would come from telling someone other than Violet. Telling Alec. It's this option that is simultaneously the most appealing and the most dangerous to me. I can't stand being hurt again.

Alec senses my weakness and sits down on the bed beside me. Without question, he lies down and wraps his arm underneath my shoulders, pulling me to his warm body. I don't fight it. In fact, curling up next to him is oddly comforting. The dribbling tears stop, and suddenly I can't contain myself any longer. "This is the anniversary of my cousin's death."

Once the words are out, I gasp at the shock, relief and pain of it all. I shouldn't have told him that, but at the same time, I've never felt more relieved. *What will his reaction be? Will he run away from the emotionally damaged girl he's holding, who's been through enough crap and felt enough insecurity for a lifetime?*

Alec stiffens, expectedly. It takes him a couple of seconds of breathing to come out with the words. "You don't know how sorry I am to hear that."

"I think I do." I attempt a laugh, but the sound comes out hollow and sad. "She died a year ago."

"How?" Alec adjusts himself, pulling himself further down the bed and tugging his arm away from me, before spinning to face me. We're both sprawled across my Star Wars sheets, staring at each other, and it's probably the most intimate moment I've ever shared with anyone. I want to tell him everything, I realise. Maybe I need to, for the sake of myself. I wince at his question choice, but there's an indescribable pull from my soul. I want to share myself with him, if he wants to listen.

"Do you remember I told you the story about Toby and the cheating?" I ask weakly. Alec nods in reply and I continue, having already expected that. "Well I told you then that there was much more to the story. I . . . I'm going to tell you everything now."

I look at him and with my eyes try to communicate the warning and dread I feel inside.

If he wants to leave, he should leave now.

"Go on." Alec's voice is raspy. His eyes are beautifully entranced.

"I had a cousin. Her name was Kaitlin."

I let out a breath. *Had.* The word seems to stand out. It bends and warps the sentence around it from something happy, something positive, to a grim reality. There's no going back now.

I knit my fingers together before continuing into the story, lying on my hands to stop them from shaking. "Kaitlin and I grew up as two quite different children. She lived a town over, but we would visit each other constantly. After my uncle's wife left, our families really connected. We were both broken. We depended on each other. She was my best friend; I grew up with her. We spent weekends together, we had sleepovers and I spent all of my summers at her house or vice versa. We were inseparable. People thought we were sisters. We acted like it."

I don't think I can do this.

"Do you remember when I said Toby was my childhood sweetheart? My best friend?"

Alec nods.

No. I can't do this. I can't tell him this part. I can't tell anyone this part.

"Well he wasn't just . . . mine. Toby, Kaitlin, Violet and I were all best friends with each other. Toby had been friends with me and Violet for years, and so he used to come with us to see Kaitlin in the summer, or when she came to our house. We were a little gang. Kaitlin and I both had a crush on him . . ." I try to force myself to say the next part but every part of my brain is fighting it.

A darkness in my chest seems to suck the words back down my throat. So I decide to omit the part of my past I am most ashamed of. The thing that tears me apart inside every day. I don't tell him about how Toby and I *really* came together. I tell him all he needs to know. Not even Violet knows that part.

"In the end, he liked me," I hurry out. "It was Toby and I, and her and Violet."

One look at Alec's balled-up fists, and I know he's thinking of Toby and what he did to me. I grab one of his hands in my shaking one, squeezing on his wrist for comfort. I need to tell someone. I needed to let this much out.

"A few months before her fourteenth birthday, we all went to a party. Toby and I, well we were fifteen years old and this was one of our first experiences with alcohol. We got tipsy, and Kaitlin decided to leave early . . ." I swallow down my sins, choking back the demon growing in my stomach. I feel nauseous with guilt. I hear myself say the next words rather than feel them. I feel detachment from myself, like I'm looking down and watching the girl who's been through so much, done so much, admit her past to the boy she likes. *Don't think, Riley. Don't think too much.* My therapist's voice echoes in my head.

"She got hit by a car outside the party and died instantly."

Alec's small intake of breath alerts me back out of my daze, and I'm suddenly aware of the water that's spilled from my eyes.

"Hey," he murmurs, wrapping his arms round me to enclose me into a firm hug. Telling him has made it more painful, and I let out a strangled sob as I bury myself in his arms. However, I also feel relief. Relief that I've shared my story. That he understands me. He smells like vanilla and cologne, and it's all the comfort I need.

180

"That's why I wasn't in school today," I choke. "We visited the place we scattered her ashes this morning. I saw my uncle for the first time in eleven months and he was a *mess*, Alec, he was broken. She's been gone a year, Alec. A whole *year*."

And it's all my fault.

"I know," Alec mumbles, stroking my hair, "I know it hurts. But it will get better. I promise you, it will get easier." His words are like magic to my ears, or maybe I've just cried myself out today, but I can feel my sobs slowing to splutters. "How's your mom coping?"

"She's just holding on I guess," I breathe. "We're all holding on by our fingernails. Kaitlin was like another daughter to her, and having to lose contact with her brother too . . ."

Alec shoots me a questioning look. I take a breath. I want to get every detail out that I can manage to. Everything but *that*.

"My uncle ... he suffered severe depression for months after Kaitlin died... We thought he might commit suicide, but instead he just disappeared into thin air. Lost contact, aside from the occasional message." I try to slow my breathing, "My mom didn't take it well either, but she coped. She held on, and so did I."

"And Jack?"

It somehow flatters me that he's asking these questions. He wants to know. He cares. My breathing is normal again, and I wipe away the evidence of my breakdown from my cheeks. "Jack has cried too. He doesn't want me to know that, though." I sniff slightly and try to fight away the sinking feeling in my chest. The feeling I get before I get swallowed

181

with anxiety, or wracked with guilt. I'm okay. I'm going to be okay. Alec is here and he cares.

"You can guess the rest." I sit up and turn to face the wall. I daren't look Alec in the eye, I'm so humiliated. "Dad had already left just after Jack was born, but he was notified. He came to the funeral and said his goodbyes to his niece." I grit my teeth as the image enters my head. I hurt so many people with my actions.

"As for Toby . . . he took it hard as well. I think he wished he'd chosen her . . . I guess the guilt and hurt got too much. He cheated on me, and when his mom was offered a new job in Chicago six months ago, he didn't tell me he was leaving. He managed to escape everything." I chuckle bitterly. "Now he's back, and after a year of me, Mom, Violet and Jack trying to avoid the topic because it hurts so much, he's brought all those memories back. He wants another chance," I mutter.

He did choose her. You ruined that for Kaitlin. You ruined that for Toby. You ruin everything.

"Who was the girl?" Alec questions softly.

"Tiana." I glance back at him. The shock in his face is evident. He would never have expected that. Most people don't understand the dynamics of mine and Tiana's relationship . . . other than what they take at face value: she's a generic mean girl and I'm a generic dweeb.

"I . . . I don't know what to say," Alec says quietly. "Thank you for telling me everything. I'm so sorry about Kaitlin, Riley, I really am. You've been through so much crap, and I can't even begin to make up for that."

"Thank you for listening," I reply quietly, chuckling another hollowed laugh. I don't regret telling him, but I feel oddly vulnerable. How is it that I've known this boy only a month or so, and already I'm telling him things about myself that I struggle telling anyone? Am I so needy, so weak, that a boy can break down my barriers so easily? "Sorry for getting tears on your shirt. It's a good job I'm not wearing make-up, isn't it?" My dull attempt at humour sucks, but Alec feigns a laugh anyway.

It was good that I got part of it off my chest, but at the same time so much worse. There's so much I can't tell him, and omitting it from everything has made the guilt fester in my brain. It reminds me that what I did, I can't tell anyone about. It reminds me that I'm the worst person I know. Having someone to tell should make me feel loved. But this? This only reminds me of how unloved I will be if I ever tell him the truth. I don't think I can ever share that part of me with him, as much as I've come to care for him.

There's something inside Alec Wilde . . . a warmth, below the shell of cocky bad boy, that's slowly coming out. Alec's changing as I get to know him better, and slowly I'm getting to see more and more of the sweetheart coming out, not the bad boy. I want him to see the best in me too. I don't want to show him what I did.

"What do we feel like doing?" Alec asks, as though it's assumed that he's staying with me until I feel better. "Do we feel like watching a movie and trying to keep our minds off things? We could go to my railway-bridge spot and talk some more? Or you could kick me out and say you need time alone." He elbows me in the ribs lightly. Believe it or not, it is enough to make me crack a minute smile.

"Movie sounds good," I say. "Let's have a movie night. With lots of gore and violence and blood."

Alec blinks. "You worry me sometimes."

I smile weakly. I miss Kaitlin with all my heart, but if she were here right now, she would be screaming at me to let the cute boy comfort me, to let someone in.

"I know," I say.

16

Beanie Boy

"What have you got first?" I ask Alec conversationally as we walk into school together, clutching my folder to my chest. My hair is thrown up into a braided bun, and a few loose strands tickle my ear. Since when have I made an effort? Since my mom decided she wanted to make me look pretty for Alec. She has turned into a hardcore supporter of our "relationship" since I told her what happened on the anniversary of Kaitlin's death. It's been about a week now, and I came back into school a couple of days ago. Nobody's asked me why I was gone, which I will forever be grateful for. Things are looking up again.

"I have Media," Alec replies smoothly, adjusting his backpack.

A beanie rests on his curls, and honestly? This boy is like the freaking surface of the sun hot wearing that thing. It's making it very hard to concentrate. I love guys in beanies, but I don't think anyone could pull one off like Alec does. Since Kaitlin's death date ... my feelings for Alec have grown a hell of a lot stronger. So much so that

I'm beginning to get very worried. If I were to ever tell him the whole truth, there'd be no chance he could ever feel the same. There are some things in the world that can deem you unlovable. In my eyes, what I did to Kaitlin is one of those things.

I nod, humming a little under my breath as we join the crowd entering the front doors. I got a ride in with Alec today, but I had the common sense not to question him while I was sitting on the back of his bike this time. If he doesn't mind obliterating his reputation for me, then I'm going to take full advantage of that fact. I breathe a sigh of relief as we escape the crowd, and automatically we begin heading to my locker.

Clearly I spend too much time with this guy – he knows my daily schedule better than I do.

As we enter the corridor, Alec suddenly comes to a halt beside me and grabs my forearm in a deathly tight grip. It takes me a few seconds to realise why. Standing by my locker is Toby Charlton, his radiant blonde hair shining above all others in the corridor. I frown. Joe is standing nearby, suspiciously eyeing the figure by my locker.

"C'mon, Riley. Let's sort this once and for all – he can't keep trying to intimidate you," Alec growls under his breath, tugging me forward towards my locker.

I don't want a confrontation, it's too risky, but Alec is seething so it's pretty obvious I'm going to get one.

"Excuse me," I say politely, dodging between the two boys to reach my locker. I'm acting calmly as I get my books for the day, but in all honesty my hands are shaking. I wish Violet were here – she'd have all three guys put in their place and out of my way within the minute.

186

"Alec Wilde," Toby says. "Nice to meet the subject of all the rumours."

What is he doing? Does he have a death wish? Anybody who knows anything about Alec knows that they shouldn't taunt him when he's angry, which he so obviously is.

"Toby Charlton," Alec replies, voice laced with venom. "I'd say it was nice to meet you too, but that would be a lie. So, just moved here from Chicago, huh? Was the Windy City the escape you needed?"

Toby's eyes snap to mine, and I stare defiantly back at him. A flicker of anger crosses his features. He has no right to be angry, though. It was my choice to tell Alec what happened. Toby doesn't deserve a say in what I get to tell my friends about Kaitlin.

"Riley," Toby mutters in a low voice, "please can I talk to you for a second? Alone?" He sounds angry, but I'm not going to react to it. I don't care what he thinks.

"Sorry, but I'm not interested, Toby," I say through gritted teeth. "Get away from me."

"Riley, please. I'm trying, okay? I can't believe you told him!"

He grabs my arm harshly and yanks me towards him, making me stumble. What the hell does he think he's doing? Before I've even had time to blink, Alec rips Toby's hand back from my skin, and the two boys step forward to glare each other in the eye. Their shoulders move in sync as they square up to each other.

"She said to get away from her," Alec hisses. His eyes are stormy and deep now, the angriest I've ever seen, and the muscles prominent in his arms are as taut as live wires. Toby is holding a similar position. One wrong move, and the whole minefield blows up.

"Guys, take a chill pill, okay?" Joe grimaces, attempting to separate the pair. But even his strength makes no difference to the two jerkwads facing each other off right now. Until now, Joe has just been watching the scene, confused, but the testosterone and violence thick in the air must have brought him to his senses. I step up behind Joe, leaning over to pat Alec's arm. His gaze flickers to mine, but he ignores my pleading expression, focusing back on Toby again. Jerk.

"You know nothing about me," Toby spits at Alec, placing his hands on Alec's shoulders and shoving him hard. "You know nothing about her either. Get out of my way."

Alec is back up in his face in an instant.

"I know a hell of a lot more than you think," he growls, shoving back. "I know every little thing you've done to her. Why are you even trying, man? You don't deserve her!"

With that, Toby lunges at him, and Alec is pushed back a few feet with the force of his hands. Their arms scramble and they trip as their feet lock, landing on the floor. They don't stay down even for a second. Toby is on top of Alec swiftly, lifting his fist high before plunging it down onto his chest. Alec punches back; a painful crack on the jaw. Managing to gain stability, he flips to kneel above Toby, yet another hand plummeting into Toby's face.

A crowd begins to form, chanting "fight" at the top of their lungs. I watch in horror as it escalates. Their eyes are focused, their teeth bared in anger. They look like animals. Toby, grabbing Alec by the neck, shoves him back into the lockers. The sound of metal meeting metal echoes down the corridor. I cringe at the sound, my heartbeat escalating.

This cannot be happening. I don't know what to do, how to stop it.

Toby is up on his feet and ready in an instant. Lips curled back and nose bleeding, he kicks forward into Alec's stomach, only to have his foot pulled out from underneath him. Alec pulls Toby harshly off balance, and the boy crashes down onto the floor beside him, landing hard on his arm.

The crowd now begins to look more concerned than entertained, and random cries to break it up emerge. Joe, taking his opportunity, is behind Toby in a second. Pulling his arms behind his back, he jerks the boy up and thrusts him away from Alec. A couple of other boys begin to help restraining him. Alec stands up from the floor, shaking his head as others attempt to grab his arms too. He's calmer already. I release a breath I didn't realise I was holding.

"You made the first hit," Alec sneers. The boys struggle to hold Toby back. The principal's voice shouts in the distance, and teachers begin to clear the crowd as they emerge into the centre of the mass of bodies. Alec is going to get into so much trouble for this. In a surge of anxiety, I rush over and attack him into a hug. His body is warm, and slowly I feel his arms respond to wrap round my back. My whole body is quivering, and my breathing is off. *This all happened because of me. Why is it always me?*

"I'm okay," he says. His nose presses the top of my hair-line, and my arms tighten round his back.

"Clear the way!" Mr Boston, the principal, bellows loudly as he emerges. Most of the crowd has disappeared now, terrified by the presence of authority. I watch from Alec's chest as people disperse left, right and centre to escape his wrath. Toby, Alec and the boys holding Toby back are all that is left. Plus me, of course. Mr Boston's four chins are ruddy, his face scrunched in anger as he examines the scene. He looks like a bullfrog.

"Get to lessons, all of you!" he barks, grabbing Alec and Toby by the arms. His eyes narrow on me. "You three, come with me. I need to have a talk with all of you." Once the hallway has cleared and everybody has gone to lessons, Alec, Toby and I follow Mr Boston to his office. Joe looks after me with a concerned expression, and I nod to confirm that I'll be okay. I'm calming down already. My head is starting to hurt.

Toby looks humiliated, a deep red colour staining his cheeks as he clutches his jaw. He won't meet my eye, but that's a good thing. Maybe he'll finally back off now.

"Take a seat in my office," Mr Boston orders, as we march through reception. He swings his office door open. "Hurry up!"

I sit down on one of the cracked leather seats in the small room, not wanting to get into even more trouble. Alec and Toby sit either side of me, and Mr Boston strolls behind his desk, looking each of us in the eye in turn.

"One of you," he says quietly, "explain exactly what happened." He sits down.

Alec's and Toby's voices instantly begin to clamber over each other in the fight for Mr Boston's attention. I release a breath and focus on the principal, punching both of the boys lightly in the arms to shut them up. We aren't going to get anywhere if they do that.

"Toby grabbed my arm because he was frustrated about something," I explain, and the boys' voices die. "Alec got angry, and one thing led to another. They started fighting. I believe Toby initiated it." I glance down at my lap. I tried to swing that at least a little into Alec's favour, but I'm not sure how much help it'll be.

"And you weren't involved at all other than that?" Mr Boston questions.

"She wasn't," Alec confirms.

Mr Boston stares disapprovingly between us. "Do you understand that fighting on school grounds is completely unacceptable?"

Begrudgingly, both boys nod.

"Both of you are new again here" – Mr Boston's eyes narrow as he lowers himself into his chair – "so I will go over the rules once more so that they are *crystal* clear." He glances at Alec. "This kind of behaviour is absolutely not tolerated. If you have a problem, you deal with it reasonably in a verbal manner, or you consult the guidance counsellor. You do not brawl like a couple of feral children. Do you understand what I am saying?"

Toby and Alec nod again.

"Right, well." Mr Boston leans forward in his chair. "There will be consequences to your actions. A month's detention and school service – you will stay after school for an hour each day to help the maintenance staff with their duties. This is your first and last warning. Do *not* let this kind of thing happen again. Both of your parents will be notified, and we shall have to see if they want to take any further action, but as far as I'm concerned you're both as guilty – and as stupid – as each other." He grumbles under his breath, sitting back and dismissing us with one hand. I notice Toby wince a little at the last line. His parents always have been especially strict.

I stand up from my seat meekly, with Alec following suit. Next to me, Toby is shaking, still sitting down with his hands gripping the arms of the chair.

"You don't understand, sir!" he protests. "Alec has stuck his nose in where it doesn't belong!"

What does he think he's going to achieve by arguing, other than more detention?

"Cool story, bro," Alec snarls. "Wanna hear mine? Once upon a time, nobody gave a fu–"

"Alec Wilde, please exit the office! I will deal with Toby!"

I nod in apology to Mr Boston and grab Alec's arm, tugging him out of the office before he can get himself in even more trouble. A month's school service is enough to be getting on with. I march out of there quickly, hearing Alec chuckle behind me.

"Whoa, easy there. I mean, I know you can't wait to get me alone but calm down."

"You wish." I let go of his arm and turn round to face him. "Are you okay?" I say, not knowing whether I feel relieved or angry with him. His fingers run over his torso and he grimaces.

"Bit uncomfortable but nothing horrific, don't worry."

"You're a jerk," I sigh. "You shouldn't have fought him."

"A sexy, charming, debonair jerk," Alec says. "And yes I should have – the guy had it coming, Riley."

The beanie, the dimple . . . it's just too much. Too much. Then I glance to the side, feeling a gaze on my face.

Tiana stands outside of reception, a cold and icy glare focused on me. She's angry that I didn't follow her orders, no doubt. Well, you know what?

She can kiss my grass.

I speak from experience – nothing can cheer you up like a trip to the beach straight after school. Alec starts his service tomorrow, so we figured we'd celebrate his last afternoon of freedom for a while.

As part of Alec's mission to cheer me up, he claimed that there is a milkshake stand on Lindale beach that I just had to get a milkshake from. Seeing as the beach is only a short distance from the school, we decided to go on a spontaneous trip. No swimming costumes or anything; we're just going for the milkshakes. I'm not going to lie, with the sun slowly heading towards the horizon and the temperature not too hot, I am pretty content.

Alec seems to be the only person who is able to distract me from Kaitlin, and that worries me a lot. I notice the sand on the concrete as we walk along the last string of sidewalk to the beach at the end. Being with Alec has become almost natural, which is no mean feat given how our relationship started out. I didn't expect him to ever see me as anyone but the loser next door. Then again, I never expected to see him as anything but an arrogant attention-seeker. I guess things can change after all.

"Wait, Riley," Alec interrupts my train of thought. "I've thought of another one."

"Shoot."

Alec has once again been hitting me with really bad pickup lines for the entire walk down here. I think I'm too amused by how terrible they are to actually get annoyed by his persistence. Despite his punishment earlier today, he's in a surprisingly good mood.

"Okay, okay." Alec grins. "Do you run track? Because I heard you *relay* want this di–"

"You're disgusting," I interrupt, laughing. "Seriously all of your pickup lines revolve around male and female genitalia."

"Not all of them," Alec argues. "Hey did you get those pants on sale?"

His voice is incredibly serious. I look at him to check if he's joking, before glancing down at my jeans. "Um no, I don't think –"

"Because they're one hundred per cent off at my place," Alec cuts me off, smirking.

As realisation dawns on me, I bite my lip to contain my laughter and just shake my head at him.

"You know, technically, that still revolves around sex, so you haven't proved any point."

Alec ignores my jibe. "What has one hundred and forty-two teeth and holds back the Incredible Hulk?"

"I don't know."

We're right at the edge of the beach now. It looks empty enough – due to the lack of tourists, and the dying sun. This is probably my favourite time to visit the beach.

"My zipper."

"Ew!" I shout as soon as I grasp the joke, before feigning a gag. "That was disgusting, and *still* about male genitalia."

A large wooden hut sits on the sands in front of us. It's a beach milkshake hut, which I have never actually bought anything from, despite seeing it all the time. It's the sort of place that is normally buzzing with activity, judging by the expanded decking at the back and the rows of picnic tables. I assume it's only quiet because we're here at this time, so I guess we're lucky. "This is the milkshake bar, isn't it?" I check with Alec.

"Oh yes." He nods. "Prepare yourself." Alec grins,

pulling me up to the counter where a lady waits, smiling at us. "We'll have one large Nutella cookies-and-cream milkshake please."

My eyes widen at the sound of it. This boy knows me way too well. There must be over one hundred flavour choices on the blackboards. There's no way that Alec can have had them all, right? The woman nods and accepts Alec's money, before heading over to one of the blenders that I can just about see over the counter.

I glimpse at Alec with an awed expression. "Nutella cookie dough? Best thing ever."

"It's orgasmic," Alec agrees.

"Does everything you say revolve around sex?" I laugh. "Control yourself."

Alec just gives me a cheeky grin.

I watch as the woman throws various ingredients and powders into the blender. It begins to buzz, and after half a minute she stops it. She grabs a tall plastic cup and straw and pours out the thick chocolate liquid. I'm looking forward to this. I'm practically frothing at the sight. Yep, my mouth is even frothier than imagining Alec in his swim shorts, after that day at the beach.

Not that I do that, obviously.

"Enjoy, sweethearts." The woman, whose name tag reads Izzy, smiles at us as she hands over the milkshake. I clutch it firmly in my grasp, breathing in the tantalising scent. *Holy macaroni, this smells good.* "Y'all have a nice day now."

"We will, thank you!" Alec says. I tighten my hold on the milkshake as we walk away from the café, watching my feet descend on the sand. I never realised . . . but Alec only bought one. Did he buy that for me or him? Or is it to share?

My cheeks tinge pink at the thought, and Alec doesn't fail to notice.

"Why are you blushing?" Alec immediately stops, as he pokes my rosy cheek. "Are you having naughty thoughts, Riley? Tell me!" I shake my head, laughing at the mere suggestion. "I bet you're having bad thoughts!"

"Get off, grasshole." I laugh, batting his grabbing hands away as he tries to look me in the eye. "Your ass must get jealous of all the crap that comes out of your mouth," I say, putting the straw into my mouth as I take a sip of the drink. A small moan escapes my lips as I do, and I hear Alec snicker beside me. Damn, that is one amazing milkshake. Gosh, why did Alec only buy one of these? I could drink this constantly. I take another gulp of pure heaven, flipping off Alec and his knowing expression as I smile into the straw. "Shut up."

"I didn't say anything," Alec says with another filthy chuckle.

"You looked at me weirdly," I say, slipping my pumps off and holding them in one hand as we walk down the beach together towards the waves. The cold water laps onto my toes like icy velvet, and my feet sink into the damp sand. I love the beach; it's by far my favourite place to go. It's also a great place to think things through as well, and I've done my fair share of that in my time. I relax here.

I take a long slurp from the milkshake, and Alec glances over at me with a pout, reaching out to grab the cup. I step backwards, dodging his clutching fingers. No way.

"Can I have some now? I bought it."

"Not a chance," I sneer wickedly at him, backing away. "You bought this for me, and I'm not sharing. Plus, my

196

mouth has been all over it. I am not swapping saliva with you, pretty boy."

"Aw, is Riley scared of catching cooties from a pretty boy?" Alec teases, darting forward and instantly backing me up into the damp sand and away from the sea. No way is he getting a hold of this. I dance lightly away from him, but he continues to stride towards me with a mischievous spark in his eye. Like a predator stalking his prey. I gulp down some more of the milkshake as I jog away from him, and he darts then. In less than a second, he catapults into me as he grabs the cup, pulling the straw from my mouth to put it in between his own lips. My jaw slacks, and my fists begin to pummel his chest.

Oh no he didn't.

"Thief! That's my milkshake – give it back!" My eyes narrow onto Alec's playful smirk, and I step closer menacingly. "Don't you dare get your germy mouth on my straw, Wilde!"

"Germy? How old are you?" Alec's mouth opens to protest, releasing the straw, and I take my opportunity wisely. With a small squeak, I launch myself into him and grab the milkshake in my hold, feeling victorious that I managed to catch him by surprise. Unfortunately, being my clumsy self, my foot hooks round his leg, which causes him to lose his balance. He slips out from in front of me, and because my leg is attached to his, it's inevitable that I go down with him.

"Ah!" I squeak again as we both come crashing down. I land quite uncomfortably on top of him. Of course I'd somehow manage to do this. As soon as my mind registers the position, my cheeks flame red. Our legs are still wrapped together from my clumsy pounce, and my face is in line with his chin.

Don't look him in the eye. Don't, Riley, don't.

Unfortunately, I can't help it. My eyes meet his, and this suddenly gets a lot more awkward.

I'm lying on top of Alec Wilde. I hope the ground swallows me whole. Right. Now.

Not knowing how to eliminate the tension, I take another slurp of the milkshake and beam, hoping he'll laugh it off and push me away from him. Instead Alec watches me with a perplexed expression on his face. It's scaring me that he's not saying anything. Why isn't he saying anything? I should say something. "I should, um, just –" I clamber off him as quickly as I can. "Sorry about that. But hey – I won the milkshake."

"Yeah." Alec appears a bit dazed, and he shakes his head. His beanie fell off, and he pulls it firmly back on. "You did."

"Come on." I desperately try to act like things didn't just get weird. "Let's go home. You said yourself that you need to talk to your mom about what happened today."

"Oh." Alec's eyes snap to mine, a swirling vortex of indescribable emotions. "Okay. Let's go."

17

Intoxicated

"Good afternoon, buddies! Your little sarcastic ray of sunshine has arrived!" Violet chuckles as she takes a seat beside us.

"I think there's a dead slug in your sandwich," Joe comments, frowning at Violet's lunch as she sits, "but it's been run over by a bulldozer or something. That is definitely not ham."

"It's called Quorn." She rolls her eyes. "Artificial meat. I'm a vegetarian. Funnily enough, I don't even eat dead slugs."

"What can I say? I'm not a chef." Joe flashes her an innocent grin. I watch the affair through my actual ham sandwich – I love my meat – but in silence. I can't seem to shut my mind up about the bloody beach thing yesterday. Alec and I shared a moment there, and I have no way of telling if I'm the only one who felt it or not. Things have been so much more intimate since the night of Kaitlin's anniversary, and I'm not sure if it'll ever go back to normal now that I've put myself in such a vulnerable position. I opened up to him, and thanks to yesterday, our friendship is on a whole new territory. We haven't really spoken since we both arrived home last night. I'm just praying it won't be awkward between us; my moments with him are fast becoming my favourite parts of the day.

I can sense Dylan's stare boring into the side of my face, but I daren't turn and meet his eye. Although things have more or less returned to normal between us, we're not quite there yet. There is an unspoken tension. I still catch him staring at me when we're in the same room, or blushing or talking about me to his friends. It makes me uncomfortable and a bit embarrassed.

I think it's best for me to just act like I don't notice him staring at me.

Alec is sitting next to Joe on the opposite side of the table, and Violet and I are paired together. Chase is apparently ditching to go on a date or something, according to rumour. To be honest I wouldn't put it past him, but at least he's a lovable player. If such a thing exists, that is.

"Riley." Dylan's voice interrupts my thoughts and I look up at last. I feel uneasy, but I'm not the only one judging by Dylan's rosy cheeks and awkward posture. What's up with him?

"Yeah?" I ask.

"I need to talk to you. Can we go and speak alone for a second?"

He's going to bring it up again.

Alec tenses next to me, and I jerk backwards as though someone's touched white-hot metal to my skin. *I don't want to go anywhere.* I have that foreshadowing stir of nervousness in the pit of my stomach. I shoot a vaguely

200

panicked look at Violet, and her expression mirrors mine.

"Er, um, no!" I blurt out before I can stop myself, and my hand slaps over my mouth. Oh crap, why did I just say that? Everyone on the table turns to look at me now. Whereas Dylan looks a little shell-shocked, Violet looks relieved and Joe looks curious. As for Alec, he just appears lost in thought.

"Oh, okay." Dylan swallows. "So you want me to talk here then?" To say he looks hesitant would be a huge understatement. He's flushed bright red now, and he's swallowing as though there's no saliva left in his mouth. I feel really bad for making him feel like that. Why did I have to make such a big deal out of an innocent private conversation?

"No, no, of course not," I say, standing up. "We can go somewhere, sorry."

Judging by the daring expression on Alec's face though, as he stares at Dylan, that isn't the case. A look of realisation dawns on Joe, and then ever so subtly, Joe mutters out what sounds suspiciously like, "Dylan, let's talk this out first."

"Did you maybe want to go out on Saturday night?" Dylan finally blurts.

Before I've even had time to register Dylan's question, Alec's palms slap down on the table, and a loud smacking noise ricochets around the room. That had to have hurt, but funnily enough Alec doesn't seem to mind. A lot of people are staring at us now, and my jaw has dropped to the floor, but I snap it shut as I watch Alec climb out of the booth angrily. His jaw is set in annoyance, and he looks like he's gritting his teeth behind his closed lips.

He was expecting this, I realise.

What the hell am I supposed to do now? I watch, conflicted,

as Alec jogs away from the scene. Should I go after him? Or should I talk to Dylan?

"I'm so sorry, Dylan," I plead, "I can't. I really can't. I can't do it to you."

As I stand up from the table, he grabs my arm. "Wait," he protests.

"I would be leading you on," I reply softly. "I like him, Dylan. It wouldn't be fair to you, if I said yes. I wish sometimes that I didn't, but I do."

Dylan sighs but nods stiffly before staring straight ahead, ignoring Joe's glare directed at him. I feel terrible, but I know I've done the right thing. I tug away from Dylan's defeated grip and following the direction of Violet's urgent pointing, I chase after Alec.

God knows I've hurt enough people. I can't hurt him too.

As I turn the corner, I spot him up ahead, pacing up and down. He still looks furious, and I'm a little hesitant to approach him when steam is practically exploding from his ears. I guess I'd just like to think that he'd do the same for me, so I'm going to approach him and fix this as best I can.

"Alec." My voice is kind of hoarse as I step closer, and his head snaps up to look at me. The ocean depths of his eyes are stormy and grey with anger. They soften slightly as they see me, but it doesn't last long. After a short second of sweetness, the walls go up again, and he looks even angrier than he did before.

"What is it, Riley?" he sighs, features creased in exasperation and annoyance.

"I said no."

An unexplainable emotion crosses his features, but then we lose eye contact and he shakes his head as though trying to erase some thoughts from his mind. "Whatever." He shrugs. "Why should I even care?"

I step backwards at the hurt of his words. After storming out, and after Joe's not-so-subtle mention of talking it out, he's still going to act aloof? Like he doesn't care one bit? I opened myself up to him. I've put myself at my most vulnerable, telling him things I never dreamed I would and making it clear just how much I care about him. After storming out of the room in anger, I'm disappointed that he still feels the need to pretend like he doesn't care. Be that as a friend or something more, I know he cares about me. I've seen it.

"You're right," I mutter. "I guess you shouldn't." Without looking back up at him, I turn round and walk away.

"Riley, what's the matter?" Mom's worried voice comes from the hallway as she watches me enter my bedroom and drop my rucksack to the floor. I didn't shout hello to her when I got back home – that's why she paid attention to me. Mistake on my part. I don't look over at her, but I know she's staring. There's nothing wrong. I'm just numb.

I suppose that's better than feeling pain, which is what I felt initially.

I mean, was I stupid to think maybe something might happen with us? Little things, like our milkshake moment at the beach, like the way he held me when I told him my past, like how Joe mentioned Alec and Dylan *talking it out* and how his friends all tease me about him. Was I stupid to think that I would be the girl who could make Alec Wilde feel something, and overlook his commitment issues? That maybe he returned my feelings? All of that hope, all of that belief, was demolished in a second. If he does care, he's definitely not ready to show it. It stung at first, but now I can't feel anything.

I'm a shadow. The shell of a bullet. I consist of nothing.

Nothing is wrong. Nothing should be wrong.

"Riley, tell me." Mom appears in the doorway, with soft, comforting eyes watching me. "I know something's the matter, baby. Tell me what's wrong."

She steps closer, but I daren't meet her eye, otherwise the numbness might break down again and the hurt flood back in. I like being numb; I don't want to feel. Out of the corner of my eye, I notice that the window is open, and in a sudden burst of anger I pull it shut with a slam.

Of course, he probably doesn't know that he's even hurt me. I walked away in anger, not in pain. The pain came after, when I realised how stupid I was to allow myself to get so close to someone so turbulent. Someone who could so easily hurt me. Alec is in the opposite room, and his head snaps up at the noise, but I pull the curtain closed before he can see my face. Yeah, I know I'm a coward, but I can't stomach facing him yet.

"Riley Jessica Greene." Mom's voice comes softly from behind me and her arms wrap round me, tugging me back into her. "Tell your mama what's up."

"Dylan asked me if I was free Saturday night." I sigh. I'm not quite sure what to feel about that. Evidently, he hadn't discussed it with his friends first, and Alec was not too happy. I've quite possibly ruined my relationship with both of them now. "Alec got angry and stalked away before I could refuse. Then when I went after him and told him I said no, he asked why he should care. I'm annoyed, but I can deal."

"Really?" Mom says dubiously. "I don't believe you. I don't think you can deal."

She squeezes me tight and kisses my hair. "You know that he's jealous, right? He's jealous that Dylan asked you out – that's why he's upset." That's what I thought too, originally, but surely if he cared then he'd show it more often? Why do I keep feeling like he's going hot and cold on me – one minute that distant player and the next back into a lovable boy next door? He can't be both. He needs to choose.

"I thought that too." I pull back and look her in the eye. "But I'm fed up of how he pretends he doesn't care even the slightest bit. He turns into such a jerk sometimes."

Mom stares blankly at me. "You can be one oblivious girl, you know that?"

"What's that supposed to mean?"

"Well, I'm no expert, but it sounds like he likes you back but he has some issues with trust. I bet that boy has some insecurity things going on, and he's not ready for you to know that he cares about you yet, so he pushes you away. That doesn't make it good, but it's up to you to decide whether his commitment issues mean you should get over him." The way she describes it makes so much sense. She sighs. "I've got some paperwork to do. Things will sort themselves out, okay?"

"Okay, thanks, Mama." I pick at a loose thread on my bed sheets.

"Riley," she says, "just…just do me a favour and remember that people tend to put up walls to protect themselves from getting hurt. It's what you and I did for a very long time, and God knows it's what your uncle has done, so try to put yourself in Alec's shoes. He's a lot more insecure than he likes people to see, and I think the problem is that you're breaking down his wall a lot faster than he can build it back up again.

Just make sure to remember that he may not find this whole crush thing easy either."

She pecks me on the cheek and walks out of the room, leaving me looking thoughtfully after her. After deliberating over it for a second, I peel back the curtain and stare into the opposite room. All clear. As quickly as possible, I pull the curtain back and open up the window as far as it can go. My mom has a point, and I know it.

I'm not quite ready to shut Alec Wilde out yet, despite what he said.

"Angel with a shotgun," I murmur under my breath as I focus my gaze on the laptop, trying my very hardest to concentrate on the text in front of me. My music is playing on full volume, so that's not really helping, and I squint at the screen until the words blur into nonsense, impossible to understand. So much for writing my History assessment; if I can't find the will to research for it then I guess I'm going to have to leave it until tomorrow.

Those are the words of a true queen of procrastination.

Just as I select the Tumblr app on my phone, preparing for a few hours of internet scrolling bliss, something sharp hits me on the side of my shin.

"Ow!" I wince and drop my hand to my leg, eyes scanning the duvet for a sign of the culprit. A small white paper aeroplane waits on the covers beside me. My heart rate picks up as I register who it's from, and I resist looking up at the window to unfold the paper aeroplane. Written in large font in the centre of the paper is a short sentence.

I'm sorry for being a jerk.

A small smile spreads on my lips and I look up at the

window to see, as I expected, Alec watching me with shame on his face. What a cutie pie. I drop the aeroplane and saunter up to the window, making sure to take my time so that I can absorb his reaction to the full. It's priceless. He's blushing and scratching the back of his neck awkwardly, which is unknown territory for Alec. He's embarrassed.

Probably because that was one of the most cliché, hopelessly romantic ways of apologising ever. But hey, I'll take what I can get.

"You're sorry?" I ask him, leaning over the window. "It's okay. I'm sorry too." I'm saying that like some kind of saint, like I'm being the better person by letting him off. In all honesty though, I forgave him before I even spoke to him.

"But I hurt you, and it wasn't even legitimate. It was a complete lie. If I had a drink for every crap I gave about you, Riley Greene, I'd be intoxicated. Of course I care." He lets out a breath, gesturing down at the space in-between our two houses. "The number of paper aeroplanes I tried to throw in through that goddamn window just proves it."

I glance down to see what must be about twenty paper aeroplanes littering the grass. I let out a laugh at this. Not so perfect after all, is he?

A happy grin slides onto my face, and I climb out of my window carefully. I know I'm acting like a lovesick puppy right now, but I can't help it. I do mean something to him, and while he's showing me that, I won't reject him.

I manage to climb in through his window, and I hug him tightly as soon as I reach the floor. His warm arms wrap round me, shooting sparks over my skin and causing every hair to stand up on end. He is a really good hugger. He sighs and rests his chin on top of my head. My heart is thudding faster than a hummingbird's on steroids. I don't know how I can possibly stay away from him.

"I have something for you," he mumbles.

I pull away instantly, curiosity getting the better of me. "Is it a bomb? Poison? A bullet to the head? Body spray to the eye?"

He rolls his eyes at my reference back to the body-spray incident. "No, it isn't going to damage you. Shocking, I know." He reaches into his back pocket and pulls out a small brown paper bag. "Do you remember the first time we went to the beach with all the others? We were lying on the sand, and you saw I had this bag, and asked what it was?"

"I remember."

"I couldn't tell you at the time . . . but open it." He presses it into my awaiting fingers. "It's not huge, and it's not overly sensitive. I just kind of saw it and bought it impulsively. I've been putting off actually giving it to you . . . but I guess there's no better time than the present, so just open it."

I open up the bag with attentive, delicate fingers and a bracelet slides onto my palm. A thin piece of string contains a collection of hand-painted wooden beads. A copper anchor charm, and a copper surfboard charm also decorate the bracelet, and in the centre is a shark's tooth. It's small but beautiful. A simple kind of perfection.

I smile and immediately attempt to put the bracelet round my wrist one-handed. I manage for only a brief moment before a second pair of tanned, assured hands clasp it together for me. His skin is warm, and I tingle all over from the contact. Alec is standing close to me. My heart yearns for moments like this, and I hate that I want to repress that yearning.

"Thank you," I mumble, finally bracing myself enough to meet his oceanic gaze. It burns with some deep emotion that I can't explain. "It's gorgeous."

Alec takes a step closer.

My heart goes into overdrive, and I'm positive he can hear the accelerated thuds. He stares at me for a moment, and I drop my gaze to the floor, knowing that with a second more of this intensity, I may just lose my composure and start having a full-on heart attack. His lips. Oh fudge.

"Stop that," Alec growls quietly. I look up, shocked to see how close his face is to mine.

"W-what?" I stutter.

"The stuttering, the blushing," he mutters, and his scent fans my face – vanilla and cologne, a delicious combination. "It's driving me insane."

My heart is threatening to explode out of my chest now, my face flooding even more red and my palms becoming slick with sweat. I wipe them on my skirt quickly, not wanting to break eye contact. From this closeness, I can see a faint scattering of freckles across his nose, just fainter than Millie's. I can see the gold flecks in his cobalt eyes, which are watching me intently as my own gaze examines each square centimetre of his face. It's like we're staring straight into each other's souls, and my heart aches for him to make that tiny step closer.

"Alec," I breathe. "I can't help it when you're standing this close to me. If you're just doing this to embarrass me, then you're a jerk and I'm going to hit you damn hard."

"I'm not doing it to embarrass you."

I may have a heart attack. I'm not even joking; please can someone call 911?

"I told Dylan that I didn't want to be with him," I say quietly. I need him to know that.

"Good."

"Why is that good?" *I can't breathe.* My skin is tingling with goosebumps.

"Because I care about you."

I can't help but stare at him in shock. This is it – this is what I've been waiting for. His lips curve into what is possibly the most irresistible smile I've ever seen on his face, and he looks down at me coyly.

"I care about you too," I say softly. Stay cool. Don't ruin this – don't be awkward. My fists clench in anticipation.

Kiss me. Please, please kiss me.

"I'm so freaking glad I stole your bra." He smiles, before he finally does what I've been yearning for since that taunting moment on the beach. He closes the tiny gap between us, and his soft lips meet mine, stealing away my last breath of surprise.

Alec Wilde is kissing me. Alec, the jerk from next door with the crappy pickup lines, and the innuendos hidden behind every sentence, is kissing me. His lips are on mine with a soft but passionate urgency, his hands lifting to rest on my hips. I can't think properly; my head is swirling. This is so surreal.

I squeeze my eyelids shut and step towards him, my lips finally bursting into action and moving in synchronisation with his. I can't bring myself to think through whatever this means for us, the risks and the dangers. I can't bring myself to focus on anything but how amazing this is, and how I never could have dreamed it would feel like this. My arms automatically loop round his neck to draw us closer, and I run my hands through his thick hair.

210

Butterflies explode in my stomach and attack the lining with their breathy wings, and my skin is on fire wherever our skin brushes. I guess this is what everyone is on about when they talk about sparks, or fireworks igniting in your belly, but that's not the way I'd describe it. Sparks and fireworks don't seem to cover the unbelievable joy I'm feeling right now. In fact, it's more like my insides are alight with warmth, and I can feel myself glowing, radiating happiness.

I'm the freaking sunshine.

Of course, the time comes when we have to break away for oxygen, and my eyes fly open as our lips lose their delicious contact, leaving us panting. The kiss wasn't even that long, but it's left me breathless in the same way that a full-on make-out would, because it was somehow the strongest kiss I've ever had. I curiously glance up to see Alec, and he's staring down at me with wide eyes – I'm not sure if that's a good sign or not. I'm praying in my mind that this isn't an evil dream, that life can actually be this good and my subconscious wouldn't play such tricks on me. It has to be real, though. With my tingling red lips, I crack a smile. It doesn't take Alec long to return it.

"Do you want to go down to the train line?" he asks me, and the answer shines prominently in my eyes. Still, I decide to tease him. It's just in my nature.

"No." I shake my head defiantly, biting my lip to hold in my chuckles.

"No?"

"Yes."

"Yes to the no or yes as in yes? The second one, right?" Alec frowns and his eyes cross as he tries to figure it out. I think it's the ugliest face that I've ever seen him pull, and he still looks frigging adorable. He and his cuteness disgust me.

"Yes."

"You're a weird one, Riley."

I beam up at him. My arms are still looped tightly round his neck, my body flush against his. I don't want to worry in this moment. I want to take this for what it is: something that I wanted to happen, despite the odds. I won't think about all the logical reasons that we shouldn't have kissed. I won't think about all the ways this could be ruined. I will think about how happy I am, in this moment, and pray that it's worth it.

"You wouldn't have me any other way."

He doesn't even bother denying it.

18

Gotcha

"Alec, I'm not so sure about this." I bite my lip for what must be the millionth time today, and the familiar metallic taste of blood fills my mouth. "What if they don't like me?"

The stupid ass decided today was the day; he's finally going to take me to see his cousin Natasha again today, and meet her mother (Marie's sister) Rosa. I'm currently sitting in the back seat of Marie's car with Alec, and I think I've run out of nails to chew with nerves. I'll be chewing off my fingers next.

"You'll be fine, Riley." Alec rolls his eyes. "Honestly, you have nothing to worry about. Mom already rang Rosa up, and she's really looking forward to meeting you. Natasha loved you when you two met. Plus, Joe and possibly Chase will be meeting us there too, so you won't be alone."

That should be some consolation to me, but I'm still nervous, although I can't pinpoint why. Meeting Alec's family? Screwing up and embarrassing myself? It's a mystery to me. Alec seems to be under the impression that me and Natasha already get along really well, but the truth is we only spoke for a few minutes at Marie's engagement party. How do I know that it'll be as good as last time? Or what if she stops pretending to like me the moment Alec's back is turned?

I'm not exactly the most skilled of socialisers.

"Joe is going to be there?" I echo, and Alec nods. His hand reaches out slowly, and his fingers touch mine. We haven't had the "what are we" talk yet, but things have definitely not been the same since that kiss.

"Yeah, we went to my aunt's house a lot when we were kids. He wanted to see her again," Alec informs me. He's sitting in the back seat with me, and Marie is driving. I'm not sure how long it takes to get to his aunt's house, but we're at the edge of Lindale now so it can't be much further. All the larger houses are located here, and I can't help but feel a little intimidated. Are they going to be really snobby and wealthy? No, surely not. Alec would let me know, right?

"Chase wants to see her too, but he might be held up with some kind of event," Alec says after a pause, and I glance over at him. That doesn't sound fishy at all.

"What about Dylan?" I try to act nonchalant about the question, but the truth is that my throat is dry. I want to know if the boys still aren't speaking.

"He was never that close with Nat and Aunt Rosa anyway," Alec replies curtly.

Well, there's the answer to my question.

"Riley, you're going to love it," Marie reassures me. "My sister is so lovely, and I can already tell that you and Natasha will get along like a house on fire. There's no need to worry, sweetheart."

I nod mutely and stare out of the window again. We're

214

turning into a thin road with giant houses and swooping gravel driveways on either side. Intimidating would be an understatement for this. I suddenly feel incredibly under-dressed in my skinny jeans and Converse. Should I have dressed up a bit more? Alec isn't dressed up . . . but then again, this is his family we're talking about. He probably does dress casually in front of them – he has no need to impress them.

Fudge. I should have worn a frigging prom dress or something.

"Here we are!" Marie chirps as we turn in to a stone driveway. I stare at the house in front of me. It's big, just a step smaller than a mansion, and it's painted a pale yellow colour that has faded with years and years of the Oregon sun, I expect. Ivy climbs the wall in an unkempt but kind of homely fashion. It's probably the least intimidating house on the street of clifftop mansions, but I'm still not exactly in my comfort zone.

"You'll love it here, Riley," Marie gushes as we clamber out of the car. "We're going to have a picnic and you kids can play in the yard; it will be amazing I promise you. If you're not enjoying it though or you want to leave at any point, just let me know. I'll take you home, okay?" She offers me a reassuring smile, and I give her a grateful one back.

"Why isn't Millie here again?" I murmur to Alec. At least if she was here, I could have held her hand for comfort or something. I'm not quite sure what the policy is yet for holding Alec's hand.

"She's staying at her friend's house for a playdate today," Alec replies.

So cute.

215

"We can't bring her here very often with the dog," Alec continues. "The thing is just way too excited, not to mention bigger than her. She gets hurt."

Whoa, big dog?

"Marie!" a voice calls excitedly from the doorway, and I turn to see a curvy woman standing in the entrance to the house. She has the same curly hair as Marie, but it's a lighter shade of brown, and she has the same friendly face. She's dressed in a white shirt with a brown belt and some jean capris, her hair pulled back into a bandana.

"Come in, come in," Rosa chirps. "How was your drive over?" Marie places a reassuring hand on my back and guides me to the large door, smiling at her sister.

"It was okay, thanks. Where are Natasha and Percy?"

"Right here." Natasha steps out from behind Rosa, and I get my second glimpse of the cousin that Alec raves about to me. She's as gorgeous as I remember, only this time with a little less make-up on and wearing a simple checked shirt and jean capris. She looks even prettier this way, in my opinion. "We haven't released Percy yet. Don't want to scare off our visitor halfway through the door, do we?" She offers me an infectious smile. "Nice to see you again, stranger."

"You too," I say, glad to see that the tension I imagined is non-existent.

"It's lovely to meet you, Riley." Rosa nods with a wide smile. "Let's head to the living room, shall we? Drinks anyone?"

There's a murmur of approval among our group, and Rosa puts a delicate hand on my back to guide me into the house. Despite the scale of it, the interior shockingly makes me feel really at ease, and I gaze around in wonder.

216

The hallway is wide, painted beige with a driftwood flooring that is partly covered by a patchwork rug. Photographs line the wall and the open-plan layout means that I can see directly into both the kitchen and living room. Both rooms are equally cosy. Warm coloured, with mismatched furniture that just seems to go together perfectly despite clashing patterns and textures. It's gorgeous.

I think the large stone fireplace is my favourite part – you never see those any more, and it looks so beautiful with the candles on the mantelpiece. Honestly? I'm already jealous of Natasha; I'd love to live in a house like this. The others are following close behind us, but no one else is quite as in awe as I am of my surroundings. They must have grown used to it, although I don't think I could ever get used to this.

I gaze around for a while but snap out of it when I sense Alec coming up next to me. He leans in and I stiffen, his breath tickling my earlobe.

"Wait until you see the yard. It's the best part," he whispers.

I think I've melted. My knees shudder, but I straighten and walk away hastily, not wanting him to know the effect he has on me.

But if his smirk is anything to go by, I'd say he's pretty damn aware.

We walk into the living room, and Rosa spins on her heel.

"Let me go and fetch a jug of lemonade, and then we can go outside," she says. "Is it okay with everyone if I let Percy out?"

I'm assuming that Percy is the dog that Alec was talking about earlier . . . otherwise I should probably be calling the cops right now. I nod, and Rosa beams before disappearing out of the room.

Marie, after realising she's been left in a room with three teenagers, escapes just after her. I perch on the edge of a russet leather armchair and smile at Natasha. "So, what are we going to be doing today?"

She shrugs. "We'll have a picnic for lunch, and maybe a barbeque later . . . Until then, it's up to you. We can watch movies, play on the Xbox or whatever. We'll have to squeeze in a water balloon fight when Chase and Joe arrive though; that is mandatory."

I laugh at her enthusiasm.

At that moment, I hear a distinct bark and the thudding of feet coming down stairs. Percy. He bursts in through the door, a giant woollen sheepdog with a pink tongue dripping from his mouth. Fur bouncing, he leaps straight for Alec and stretches until his paws are on Alec's shoulders. I can't help but let a laugh escape my lips as I watch the pair wrestle. That is a beautiful dog. I let out a low whistle and open my arms.

That's all it takes, and in less than a second Percy's bounding towards me, fur flying all over the place. He barrels into me, pushing me backwards and causing me to stumble a little to keep my balance. His tongue is all over my face, paws on my shoulders. Heck, Percy is taller than me. I should be worried.

"Ew!" I laugh, running my fingers through his fur and craning my neck so that he'll stop licking my face. I can sense Alec and Natasha watching me and laughing, but I'm too wrapped up in Percy, quite literally, to retort or say a smartass comment like I usually would.

"So Chase is definitely coming then? How do you know?" Alec questions Natasha, as I finally manage to put Percy back down. I scratch tenderly behind his ears and bend down to look him in the eye as I stroke and coo at him. He's lapping it up.

A faint blush appears on Natasha's cheeks, and she drops eye contact with Alec. "Joe texted me earlier saying they were on their way."

I'm sensing something here. Is it just me?

"Cool," Alec replies nonchalantly, but his eyes catch mine and glint with humour. We're both thinking the same thing; I can see it from his face. She likes Joe. There's no doubt about it. That blush gave her away completely.

Seems Alec and I have some matchmaking to do.

"Let's play truth or dare."

I glance up from my sandwich. Chase is lounging across the picnic blanket, taking up most of the room, and a smug smile is curving his lips.

"Come on, let's play. It's something to do, right?"

He has a point there. Our morning has mainly consisted of lounging around in the backyard, or watching Alec and Joe battle it out in foosball. Mainly because Natasha has gone goocy eyed over Joe, plus Marie and Rosa keep checking on us so we can't do anything too exciting. I glance over at the others to see what they think of Chase's proposal. They all seem to be deliberating, like me, until Natasha finally breaks the silence with an agreement.

"Really?" Chase echoes. "Cool! Okay, I'll go first. Have you guys got a bottle?"

I hand Chase my iced-tea bottle, and he sets it in the middle ready to spin. I have to admit, I'm a little apprehensive of this. Who knows what the dares flung my way will be like? Chase grins at us all as we continue to eat our lunch, his teeth glinting wickedly as he sets his hand on the bottle, flicking his wrist to begin the game. It spins quickly, so much so that it's making me dizzy just watching it. It slides past me a few times as it finally slows, before eventually landing on Natasha.

"Truth or dare?"

"Truth," Natasha replies through a mouthful of sandwich, dusting off her jeans.

"Coward."

"Just give me the damn truth."

"Okay, what's your bra size?" Chase smirks like he's thirteen years old.

I catch sight of Alec's disgusted face – disgusted because it's his cousin. Natasha, however, looks eerily calm. I don't know how she's not blushing right now – if I were her I would have turned into a tomato. Heck, I'm blushing even when I'm not the one being asked.

"It's 34C," she replies smoothly. "My turn."

I watch as the bottle spins again, and this time it slides to Joe. Ooh, tension.

"Truth or dare?" she asks him.

"Dare," Joe grins cockily.

"I dare you to make out with Alec's leg."

What? Joe's jaw drops and I burst out laughing at his and Alec's faces, fishing my phone out quickly so that I can record the event. Best dare ever. Natasha looks so smug, and I don't blame her. This dare is great. Alec tries to grab the phone from my grasp, but I lean away from his reach, grinning as I press record. There's no way I'm not recording this; it's an event to remember. Joe finally lets out a groan and Alec begins rolling up his jeans. With one last glare at us, Joe presses his lips to Alec's shin.

"For ten seconds," Natasha adds, much to Alec's distaste.

"Make sure to use some tongue," I call playfully, and Joe raises a hand to give me the middle finger, not moving his lips from Alec's leg. After ten seconds of Alec pulling faces, Joe finally lets go and wipes his mouth, shooting a glare at Natasha.

He sets his hand on the bottle and spins it, but it lands on himself. Nothing is going his way today, I chuckle. He spins it again and this time, the bottle lands on Alec.

"You choose," Alec says before Joe can ask the question.

"Okay." Joe smiles. After a second, his lips carve themselves into a devious smile. "I choose truth for you, and I want to know if anything has happened between you and Riley."

I freeze, and my eyes snap straight to Alec's. I don't know how to act, or what he's going to say. I don't know if the kiss means "anything" or not.

"Nothing," Alec says with a quick roll of his eyes. He doesn't look at me. "That question is getting old."

Despite myself, I can't help but feel a little stung by his dismissal. I know that he has his reasons. He probably doesn't want to talk about it yet, before we've had a chance to talk it through ourselves. I release a breath. We definitely have things we need to talk about.

"It'll happen soon, Alec," Chase butts in. "Now spin."

Alec places his hand on the bottle and flicks his wrist. After a few seconds, the bottle falls to a stop. Pointing at me, go figure. Alec's eyes meet mine.

"Truth or dare?" Joe smirks.

"Dare."

"I dare you to give Natasha a hickey!"

What the actual fudge.

My jaw lapses and I turn to stare at Natasha. What the hell are we going to do? I could bluntly refuse to do the dare, but then I'd be the awkward coward that nobody likes. Unfortunately, before I've even deliberated over the other options, Natasha says something I really wasn't expecting.

"Okay." She grimaces. "But let us do it in private at least. You'll have your evidence."

Chase glances at Joe before nodding, and Natasha stands up while grabbing my hand.

Oh my gosh. Oh my gosh. Oh my motherfreaking gosh. This can't be happening.

"Natasha," I hiss as we begin the quick walk back inside, wolf whistles chasing after us. "Natasha, we aren't actually going to do this are we?"

"Of course not," she scoffs. "We're going to get revenge."

She leads me into the kitchen and hurriedly begins to rifle around in the cupboard underneath the sink. She turns on the faucet furiously, and the cold water splashes me. What is she doing? "Aha!" she exclaims, bringing her hand out to show me the packet of balloons.

I think I'm in love with this girl; she's a genius.

We set to work instantly, knowing that we only have limited time until the boys come to look for us. Do they actually think I'm giving her a hickey? I hope they do – we could use the element of surprise to our advantage when we're running away after launching our attack. No doubt the boys will want revenge if we soak them – it's not like

222

they're incredibly competitive or anything. After we've filled as many balloons as we can hold, we head back outside with them cradled in our arms.

I feel a buzz of excitement in my gut, alongside the anticipation of the aftermath. I can't wait.

We dash to the wall separating the yard, and I rest against it as Natasha peers over. I feel like a fire-trucking ninja. This is awesome.

"They're talking," Natasha whispers. "Now is the time."

She mouths a countdown, and that is it.

We jump out from the shelter of the wall with a strangled yell, and the boys look up, startled by our not-so-subtle approach. I throw the first water balloon as hard as I can, grinning at the satisfaction of hitting Alec solidly in the chest. The boys curse and leap up from the picnic blanket as a few more hit them, and then their glares are fixed on us, hungry for revenge. Joe begins to run towards us, and I clutch the dwindling water balloons close to my chest as I run backwards, laughing.

Throw. *Smash*. Joe's stomach.

Throw. *Smash*. Chase's shoulder.

Throw. *Smash*. Joe's stomach.

Throw. *Smash*. Alec's face.

I release a manic giggle as my last water balloon is thrown, hitting Alec full in the face, before turning and running towards the house as fast as my legs can take me. Just behind me, I can hear Natasha's pants for breath, and I know that they're gaining on us. My legs are beginning to burn, and my eyes are watering at the wind on my face. Just a little further.

A startled scream rings beside me, and I glance back to

see that Natasha has been caught, her laughter filling the air. I can hear footsteps gaining on me, and I push to run faster, but it's just not enough. As my feet just touch the patio, I am jerked backwards into someone's arms, so fast that I fall on the grass with the person landing next to me.

"Gotcha," Alec whispers. His face is inches away from mine.

Oh, Alec. If only you knew how true that statement actually is.

"Who wants a burger?"

Who doesn't want a burger?

"Me please!" I chirp, alongside Natasha and the boys' hums of agreement. Rosa is standing at the old stone barbecue holding a spatula, grinning at us. She nods and begins to place the burgers into bread, and I shiver with anticipation. I'm so hungry. Water balloon fights really take it out of you.

After we were caught at the water balloon fight, the boys tortured us by grabbing the yard hose and spraying us with the freezing-cold water. I managed to escape Alec's arms pretty easily (being small helps sometimes), but I still got so soaked that I had to change into one of Natasha's shirts. Natasha got it worst though – she was drenched from head to toe, and her hair is still dripping even now, in the evening. Remind us never to start a water balloon fight with these boys again. We were outnumbered.

Rosa hands me a paper plate with my burger on it, and I thank her quickly before beginning to gorge on the sacred food. Dear lord, this is so good. I have to restrain my moan as I swallow the burger. "This is amazing, Rosa." I feel quite at ease here now, and it's surprising how quickly I've adapted to this house and its residents. Rosa is so nice, and Natasha and I have exchanged numbers in the hope of staying in contact . . . Honestly? I love it here. I'd come every week if I could.

I take another mouthful of the heavenly burger, giggling as I watch Percy sneak a sausage from Rosa's plate. She scolds him, but she's smiling and the love is evident in her eyes. I want a dog for Christmas, it's decided. That and the motorbike, of course.

"Riley, come over here, sweetheart," Rosa beckons me. "Would you like a hotdog?"

"How can I resist?" I stand up to head towards the barbeque and Rosa. She smiles at me and serves a sausage on my plate but touches my arm as I turn to leave.

"I just wanted to say that I think you and Alec are very cute together. He's a good boy, despite his image, and I'm so glad that he has someone like you. He used to come here every summer, you know. Him and the boys. They're all great kids," Rosa's eyes mist over with nostalgia before she looks up at me with a determined nod. "Anyway, you two lovebirds deserve each other."

"Oh," I murmur awkwardly. "We're not actually dating . . ."

"I'm not so sure about that." A cheeky smile springs onto her lips. "Enjoy your sausage, sweetheart."

I walk away, frowning.

I *really* hope she didn't mean that in the way it sounded.

19

Spider's Web

I arrive home with a drowsy smile on my face and the buzz of happiness in my stomach. I had a surprisingly great time today, and I can honestly say that it's been one of the best days I've had since Kaitlin died. Did that have anything to do with throwing a water balloon into the face of a certain someone? Or watching Joe slobber all over his leg? Yes, yes it definitely had *everything* to do with that. I think this is the first time I've let myself realise just how happy I've been since meeting Alec – the first time I've just *allowed* myself to be happy. I hate to hand it to him, but the boy sure does know how to cheer me up.

"Mom," I call, kicking my shoes off and closing the front door behind me. "I'm home. How was your day?"

Mom emerges from the kitchen, wrapped in baggy leggings and a face mask. "My day has been fabulous, thank you, sweetheart. How was it meeting Alec's family? Did you have a good time?" She leans against the frame and raises a mischievous eyebrow.

Oh ha ha, like I'm meeting the parents. Very funny, Mom.

"It was great," I say, ignoring her smirk and smiling down at the floor. "They're all very friendly. I wrote a five-star review on TripAdvisor."

Mom chuckles. "I'm glad you had fun. I wanted to let you know that your friend stopped by about ten minutes ago. I told her that she could wait in your room until you came home."

"Violet?" I frown, grabbing a lollipop from the jar and unwrapping it slowly.

"No, this was a different girl."

My frown deepens. I don't have any female friends beside Violet. Definitely not ones I know well enough that they would just show up at my house, unannounced. "Do you know this girl's name? What did she look like?"

"I think she said her name was Tina? Tasha? Something like that. You know I'm not good with names."

A weight seems to drop from my mouth right into the soles of my feet. Tiana. Tiana is at my house. In my room. My fantastic mood disintegrates, and a feeling of dread cultivates like a fungus in the pit of my stomach. What on earth is she doing here? I try to maintain a neutral expression in front of my mom and nod. "Okay, I'll go and talk to her."

As I make my way to the stairwell, my insides are tying themselves into knots. I doubt Tiana is here for a peace treaty; her motives have a tendency to be much more malicious. How does she even know where I live? By the time I'm at my bedroom door, my insides really have sunk like lead. Swallowing my nerves and pulling on a brave face, I step inside.

"What are you doing here?" I hiss, the moment I spot her standing by my window.

227

"It's a shame that Alec's window is shut," Tiana replies casually. She doesn't look up to acknowledge my presence. "Drapes closed and everything. I'm sure he'd enjoy listening to the conversation we're going to have. My heart goes out to him, really."

I stare at the girl with icy contempt. "Tell me why you're here."

Tiana finally turns to look at me. Unlike me, she appears completely collected and calm. A small smirk tugs the corner of her glossed lips upwards, and her dark hair is razor sharp. "Well, well. The kitten gets her claws out." Tiana leans away from the window and takes slow steps towards me. "You aren't as good as you let on, are you, Riley? You act like a saint, like you're above the rest of us, but you *really* aren't." Tiana's laughter is melodious and intimidating. She's a sed predator. My chest tightens at the words she is saying.

She knows.

She knows.

"What do you mean?" The only words I can force out.

"I think you know exactly what I mean." She stops in front of me, and my chest begins to rise more quickly as my thoughts spin into overdrive. *Toby told her.* "I was always under the impression that Kaitlin was pathetic and unable to grab what she wanted when she had it. Little did I know that she might have managed to if it wasn't for *you*. Because he chose her before he chose you, didn't he? But you couldn't have any of that."

"Toby told you." My voice comes out as a whisper of defeat. I stare at the floor, praying that the guilt will stop devouring me slowly and simply swallow me out of existence.

"You always were a genius."

228

"It's not as bad as it sounds," I plead. I can't bring myself to look up at the smile I know is on her face. To know that she takes joy from this, from my pain and from Kaitlin's. "It was just kissing . . . It was at a party. They were together and I was hurt. I thought I loved him, and I know I was selfish but –"

"You're very good at stealing men, aren't you, Riley?" Tiana interrupts.

I stand in silence for a few seconds as I work up the nerve to speak back to her. "What do you want from me?" I lift my chin slowly, looking her in the eye. Shame bubbles inside of me, and the smug pride in her eyes does nothing but accelerate it, but still I stare. "Did you come just to torture me with my past, or do you actually have a reason to be here?"

"Oh I have a reason all right." A slow, wicked smile grows on her lips, like a sickening mould of happiness. "Like I said, I want you to stay away from Alec Wilde."

"Of course you do."

Tiana glares at me. "I want you to erase him, to ignore his presence with every atom of your existence. I want you to forgive Toby for what he's done to you tomorrow at lunch, and I want you to agree to go on a date with him. Lord knows you two shitheads deserve each other, and it will make him shut up with his babbling. Any opportunity that could push you and Alec apart, I want you to take."

"And if I don't?" I already know the answer.

"If you don't, I will tell every single person at our school that you and Toby are the reason that your cousin died. I will tell everyone about your little affair at the party. Everybody you know, or have ever known, or ever will know. I will tell them all. Does Violet know? Does your *mom* know?"

Tiana folds her arms. She has it. She has me in a perfect, silky spider's web of a trap.

"It was an accident." I try to defend myself, but it's useless. I'm scum in her eyes, as much as I am in my own. "Please, I just –"

"Tell me, why did she run out into the road?"

"Because she saw me kiss Toby." I force out the words.

"She died after she saw you, her best friend, her *cousin*, kissing the boy she was in love with. If you hadn't done that . . ."

"She would still be alive."

I can't force myself to defend my own name. The guilt has stolen my words.

"Make the right decision, Riley."

"I-I'll ignore him." The words physically hurt me as they leave my mouth. My chest clutches at the thought of avoiding Alec, of hurting him willingly. Does my pride mean so much to me that I'd sacrifice his feelings? I'm even worse than I thought. "If you keep this secret, Alec is all yours," I tell Tiana as I'm being torn in half. My heart is shredded. I know I shouldn't care about what people think, because they don't know the full story. The idea, though, that everyone would know . . . it's just too much to bear.

"Pleasure doing business with you," Tiana says, smiling innocently. "Your mom's cookies are good, by the way. My compliments to the chef." Laying a perfectly manicured hand on my shoulder, she pushes past me and exits the room, leaving me alone in a hurricane of emotional turmoil and guilt.

Somehow Tiana has stumbled across the single largest regret of my life. My worst nightmare is that anybody else finds out. What's strange to me is that the thought of ignoring Alec is almost as painful to me as the idea of everyone knowing.

I guess I'm in deeper than I thought, and it's coming back to bite me.

I wait and listen for the sound of the front door slamming before I give in to the tears.

I can say honestly that there are only three times I have felt utterly and truly lost in my life. The kind of lost that makes me question my ethics, my beliefs, myself . . . alongside the volatile world around me.

The first time?

Strangely enough, it was my first kiss. That kiss I shared with Toby, at a party with my hair hanging loose and my morals hanging looser. Kaitlin and I both had pretty huge crushes on Toby, but they were in a relationship. It killed me a little inside, but deep down I was content for them. They were my best friends, and all I wanted was for Kaitlin to be happy, so I didn't say anything. A little bit of vodka and a whole lot of cider later, I was dancing with Toby at someone's party. And it happened: I kissed him.

It wasn't anything special, which makes it even more of a regret in my mind. I think he was just as surprised as I was. I pulled away pretty sharpish. That's when I noticed Kaitlin standing opposite with her mouth hanging open. She hadn't originally planned to go to the party, but I guess she must have decided to surprise us. She turned and ran out of the room. I followed her, trying to explain. Toby too. She fled the house, ran into the road without looking. The car was going too fast. It didn't stop.

Before I knew it I was screaming. Raw, agonising screams.

When she was gone? That was the second time I felt truly lost.

The third is ashamedly and undoubtedly right now.

I haven't spoken to any of my friends today, just as Tiana asked. I'm not sure I could stomach facing them even if she didn't ask me to avoid them.

Am I doing the right thing by saving my own ass? Of course not. I'm hurting people because I'm not strong enough to face the idea of everyone knowing about my mistake. I want to be able to do the right thing, but I don't think I'm able to. Lost. I am utterly lost. Lost without my friends' guidance, lost in guilt and sadness and longing.

I enter the cafeteria, clutching my tray and I know that things are going to get a lot worse the moment I forgive Toby. I see him instantly, leaning against a pillar in the corner of the room with his headphones in. My heart beats painfully in my chest.

Violet is sitting with the boys at our usual table, and she's spotted me. Alec looks up too. Ducking behind my hair, I pretend that I haven't noticed them and I feel a sting as I do. *This is such a bad idea.*

"Riley, can we talk?"

I glance up to realise that Toby has moved and is now planted in front of me with a pleading look in his hazel eyes.

"Okay," I mumble.

"How are you doing today?"

"I'm okay, thanks."

"That's good," he says, "Okay so . . . I know you haven't really given me much chance to apologise so I'm going to take what I can get. I'm sorry for what I did to you. You have no idea how much it haunts me, and I want you to know I've changed. I know you don't want to be anything more than friends, but I'll do everything I can to be part of your life again, Riley."

Honesty shines clear in his words, so much so that I'm startled.

Surprisingly, I actually feel myself soften. Not enough to consider forgiving him for real, but enough that his sincerity has spoken through to me. Can I trust him? Hell no, but I'll accept his apology. "Thank you," I say, nodding at the floor. "I appreciate that."

"You're welcome," he says. He shoves his hands into his pockets almost nervously, and I realise that this is the first time in almost a year that Toby and I have been on vaguely good terms. Albeit, it's mostly a façade on my part but still. I don't know whether to feel sick or satisfied. The cafeteria is buzzed as usual, but I can feel eyes on my neck. My friends are all watching this little affair, and that's just what Tiana wanted. I feel myself shrink in my shoes.

"Where is it that we stand now?" Toby asks.

"I don't know," I sigh. "I will never be able to trust you, and that's a fact, but I accept that you've said sorry. I forgive you, for the sake of putting grudges behind me and moving on with my life." The words burn as they leave my mouth. They sound robotic.

Loss of my ethics.

"Thank you, Riley. You have no idea how much that means to me." Toby smiles a little. "You know, Tiana suggested yesterday that I ask you out on a date, as an official introduction to the 'new me'. I told her she was crazy." Toby twists his body awkwardly and can't look me in the eyes. "Was she crazy? Do you think if I did ask you out, you'd say yes?"

"I think I'd consider it."

Loss of my beliefs.

Toby stares at me in shock, "Really?"

"*Really?*"

Alec's voice sounds from behind me and something within me turns frosty cold. I spin round slowly to see that his face is hard, solidified into a gut-wrenching expression of horror, anger and disbelief. "Really, Riley? You're going to go on a date with him?" Just watching the emotions on his face has my mind writhing in pain. All of the boys, and Violet, are watching me in shock.

"I –"

"I think Riley can do whatever she wants to do," Tiana intervenes, entering the circle with a feline smile and a flick of her claws. "Toby and Riley have history, and Toby has changed for the better. Everybody deserves a second chance."

"Not him." Alec shakes his head adamantly. His eyes are pleading. "Are you insane, Riley? You can't seriously be thinking about this."

"I want to get rid of the baggage I have," I lie. My voice is soulless and deadpan. "I want to move on. It's a chance for Toby to redeem himself, and a chance for me to erase some of the dead, heavy weight I have in my life. It'll be good for me, I promise."

"But what about me?" Alec demands. My heart seems to freeze, melt and vaporise in an instant. It's reassuring to hear that I'm not the only one to know that there is some little spark between us, but it's also painful to think about what

I could be losing with this stupid act of self-preservation. I open my mouth to reply.

"You and Riley were never together, Alec," Tiana points out, interrupting me before I can speak. She's feeding ideas into Alec's head, and I want to scream at her. "You two are just friends, right?"

Alec looks at me for a long, heated second.

"Right," he says coldly, before turning and storming from the room. Part of me walks out with him, staring back at the rest of me in disgust.

And last but not least, the loss of myself.

As of now, I am completely alone.

20

Liar, Liar

I, among everyone really, have been prone to a bit of gossip in my lifetime.

A juicy rumour you overhear in the bathroom stall. Something A called B while their back was turned, or the fact that A slept with that guy B she swore she'd never sleep with. Something you don't see very often is a person stopping to think about the victim of a rumour, about how this twisted story, be it true or false, affects the people involved. I am as much of a criminal of this as the next person. The attention, the loss of privacy and most certainly the bullying never occurred to me, and I wish I could say that I was selfless enough for that to be my first thought.

I am lucky to be able to say that in my life, I have never been bullied. Disliked, sure, but bullied, no. But, as of now, I feel pretty damn close.

"I heard she dumped Alec, right out of nowhere."

"Apparently she was cheating."

"She likes that Toby guy, doesn't she? Alec was just a challenge to her."

"She tamed the bad boy, and now she's broken his heart. What a bitch."

I'm taunted by whispers as I stumble down the corridor. They egg me on, to carry on walking straight out of the doors and never come back. To sleepwalk my way off a cliff, or dig a hole in the ground and hide in it. There're so many voices in my head, so many comments, that I can't even decipher which are other people's and which are my own.

The only thing that keeps me walking is the fear that should they find out my other secret and had I not accepted Tiana's deal, the rumours would be even worse. This, I convince myself, is the lesser of two evils.

I've never been a very convincing liar.

"Violet!" I hear myself call as I spot a familiar face at the end of a corridor. The sight of her is literally a breath of fresh air, and I find myself doubling my pace as I reach out for the one person I know that I can trust. I ignore the glances of bystanders, the whispers and the dirty looks and sigh in relief the moment I reach her and she turns round. She organises her books in her locker and doesn't face me as I smile at her.

"Vi, thank goodness. I thought I was going insane."

"Hi, Riley."

"You haven't been answering my calls and texts. I need to speak to you."

"About what?"

My excitement plummets. I can feel it by the way she's speaking – she's upset. She, like everyone else, is more than wondering why I decided to accept Toby's offer. I wish I could tell her my situation, about the blackmail. If I did then she'd be able to see my side a little more. Although I can't truly say that I don't despise the choice I'm making and that

Violet wouldn't despise it too, at least I'd be able to give her a little bit of an explanation. Everything . . . everything was so good at the weekend. Now it's all fallen apart.

"You know, about the whole thing with Toby and . . . and Alec."

"Ah, that thing. I couldn't care less about Toby," Violet says, as she purses her lips and stares determinedly at the contents of her locker. "But Alec I actually really like. And you're acting like a complete and utter idiot – abandoning everything you've ever stood for, all you've ever said, ignoring me and the rest of your friends for the whole day and then hurting Alec seemingly out of nowhere?"

"That thing," I say tightly, waiting for her to turn.

"Riley." Violet sighs and finally looks at me, slamming her locker shut. "He told me you guys kissed. What the hell are you thinking?"

I say softly, "I did it for a reason."

"I know that." She nods. "Because otherwise you would be hurting Alec for nothing. But right now I can't think of a good enough reason for you to throw away what you had with that boy just to give a jackass another chance. So this 'reason' better be good." Crossing her arms, she leans against the locker and waits for disappointment.

"I can't tell you it."

"Are you kidding?" Violet scowls. "Why not?"

"I just can't."

"Well then, what the hell did you want to talk about?"

"I wanted to talk to you because," I struggle, "because I need you to trust me . . . I need you on my side. I don't care if the whole school hates me as long as my best friend doesn't."

"Riley." Violet closes her eyes for a second and opens

them with a new kind of fire in them, and I suddenly understand that what I did yesterday hurt her as well as everyone else. "I want to side with you, and back you up, but I can't until I know your reasoning. Alec is my friend too, and you hurt him yesterday. Tell me why, and I can help."

The fact of the matter is that the only way I can hope to escape this situation is to tell her. If that leads to questions about my past, about what I'm hiding, then so be it. I've gone through a whole lot worse than this before; I can manage it again. "All right, I –"

My words disintegrate as Tiana walks past and positions herself on the opposite side of the corridor, pretending to use her phone. There's no doubt that she's heard the entire exchange. Although she doesn't say anything, her cool smile tells me everything I need to know. It's a warning. *Tell Violet, and I tell everyone else.* And suddenly, all that I was about to say dries in my throat. I turn back to Violet before she notices that I was looking at Tiana and cough lamely.

"I just can't tell you, so I'm asking you to trust me," I finish.

Tiana approves. I can sense Violet getting irritated.

"Well, can I know why you can't tell me?"

"No," I wince.

"You're testing me here," Violet mutters, "I trust you with my life and you can't even tell me *why* you can't tell me something? I'm your best friend!"

"I know you are, but this is different. This isn't a stupid confession, or a piece of gossip. This is big, and you're going to have to trust me based off what you know already. I can't give you any more."

Violet throws her arms up. "All I already know is that for

239

some random reason yesterday, you went back on all you've ever said to anyone for the sake of some fool that hurt you! I trust that you must have a good reason, because otherwise you wouldn't be who I know you are. However, I can't stand by you while I'm still in the dark. You have to give me something. A reason to root for you." She leans forward, searching my face for the answers she so badly needs.

"You're not going to help me?" I ask, purposefully avoiding the question. "If I can't ask for my best friend to trust me, who else can I ask?"

"Riley, I trust you, but I can't fight blindly! I won't ever act against you – you know I wouldn't do that – and I'll try my best to persuade Alec that you had a good reason but . . . but you know as well as I do that unless you explain it to me, or to him, that my word means little to nothing. You want people to sympathise with you, but you haven't given them anything to go on!"

I want to be offended that she won't help me like I want her to, but I can't do it. Violet, I've always said, is one of the most opinionated people I know. If I gave her a cause, she would fight tooth and nail for me. Not doing so right now isn't a cause of our friendship and trust not being strong enough, but because of her nature. She can't fight for me unless she has an opinion, and I support that. I wouldn't want her to change her beliefs because it's why I admire her so much, so it was silly of me to expect differently from her.

"I understand, Vi, and I wish I could tell you more, but I can't," I say softly. "I'm sorry. Tell Alec that I'm sorry."

Violet pulls me into a tight hug.

"You can talk to me about anything, you know that. Please don't shy away."

"I know, and I'm trying not to. It's a bit hard, though, when everyone hates your guts."

"I'm sure that you have a good reason for doing what you're doing, and if it's what you want and it reflects who you are as a person, you shouldn't care about what everyone else thinks. It's just a bit of gossip, and their opinions don't matter."

But it's not and it doesn't.

"Thanks, Vi," I mumble into her shoulder. I can see Tiana walking away in the distance, satisfied in the knowledge that I won't tell anyone.

"Anytime."

It takes my mom approximately 0.2 seconds to hear me crying.

After having thrown my bag onto the bed, I slump into the pillow and let loose. All the fear, the anxiety, the loss purges out of me like a tidal wave and my body wracks itself into a ball with sobs. I hate this. Words can't describe how much I hate this. *Why?* I think to myself. *Why can you not hold your head up high and allow others to think badly of you? Why have you let Tiana win, sacrificing yourself and all of your relationships just for the sake of pride?* I clutch my knees and muffle my sobs into the pillow. I'm the biggest coward I know.

I'm a coward.

It was an accident! my mind screams. *Don't let her have this kind of power over you! Who cares what people think?*

"Riley?" Mom rushes in, kicking the door shut and making her way over to my bed. "What's the matter, sweetheart? Why are you crying?" Sitting at the edge of my bed, she pulls my upper body up until it rests in her lap. I can just about make out her concerned face through the blurred haze of salt water. "Has someone said something to you?"

I shake my head and wipe my eyes with frustration.

"Well what? Come on, what's got you in this state?"

"I've sc-sc-screwed up," I gasp. "I-I've hurt people. My friends hate me."

"Of course they don't," she says, hugging me tightly. "What a silly thing to say. Your friends love you to pieces." Her reassuring words calm me a little, and I manage to sit up, pushing myself against the headboard. Mom hands me a tissue, and I hurriedly try to wipe away the evidence of my outburst, only for more to come. I can't stop crying. I physically cannot stop.

"Mom, I screwed up," I choke, wiping my eyes. "I've made all the wrong decisions, but part of me doesn't want to fix it. How do you deal with that?"

"That depends on the situation." Mom wraps an arm round my shoulders and squeezes. "Come on, let it all out. I'm your mom; you can tell me anything." Mom and I have always been incredibly close – she's like an older sister to me. Dad is gone, aside from the cheques he sends monthly, and I haven't got Kaitlin to talk to now. Me and Mom, we rely on each other. If I can tell anyone about this situation, it's her.

You're a coward. You don't deserve your friends anyway.

I glance at her with watery eyes and instantly feel a wave of comfort. I can tell her. She won't hate me.

"I made a mistake a year ago," I say slowly. "And I think I'm paying the consequences for it."

"What mistake?"

"It was when Kaitlin was alive." I analyse the sudden

sadness in her expression at the mention of her niece, sniffing. "I kissed Toby . . . when he was still in a relationship with Kaitlin." I watch fearfully as Mom takes this in. She's shocked, that's clear. She takes a deep breath.

She's disgusted by you. What kind of person does that?

"Okay, well that's not a good thing, but it's not terrible. Did it happen on more than one occasion? Did you tell Kaitlin?"

"No," I admit. "It happened once. I was a bit drunk at a party, but it only needed to happen once. She saw it . . . she ran, out of the house and into the road –"

"Oh, Riley," she sighs.

"She *died*."

Mom remains silent, looking away

"I know. You don't have to tell me. I know how awful it is, and I hate myself for it."

Coward. Coward. Coward.

"Listen to me, Riley." Mom turns back to stare at me and her voice is stern. She refuses to break eye contact. "It was *not* your fault that she died. You made a mistake, and fate played a horrible twist. You are not responsible for her death; you are not responsible for the way she ran into the road. You made a mistake. A mistake. We all make them, we feel bad about them and then we move on. That's the cycle. The fact that you made that mistake *once* and you feel so guilty about it counts for a lot. You've learned, baby. You feel bad about your actions, and I'm sorry that Kaitlin's death has amplified your guilt. It's time for stage three – you need to let it go, accept it and move on. Kaitlin wouldn't ever want you to hate yourself over something so small. You two were fifteen. It was a *crush*."

243

"Mom, she ran away from us," I whimper. "She ran away. She was so desperate to get away that she ran into the road. She died, running from me."

"What brought this on, Riley? Why are you so upset about this right now?"

I hesitate.

"Someone found out," I whisper, sniffling. "They found out and they're using it against me. I can't speak to any of my friends, or they'll spread it across the school. I can't tell anyone anything, and part of me doesn't want to. I don't want anyone to know about it."

Mom squeezes me again. "Riley, do you trust your friends?"

"Of course I do."

"Do you trust that they'll stand by you?"

"Well yeah but –"

"Well yeah but nothing," Mom finishes. "There's your answer. You tell your friends everything, and if this nasty creature spreads it then you stand and you hold your head up high."

"I don't think I'm strong enough for that, Mom."

"You might not think it, but I know you are. Have a little faith in yourself, Riley. God, the amount of mistakes I've made in my life. At the end of the day, you're human. Now, who is this person? I'll go down to the school right away and speak to the principal – I'll see what I can do."

I watch her hands tense up, and I can tell how angry she is at this situation.

"You can't," I say wearily. "It will make things worse. Her family are tied in with the school board. She won't be expelled; it'll just make her angrier." I wipe the remnants of my tears away and breathe slowly outward. I feel emptied of emotion, exhausted.

"Why does she have this vendetta against you?" Mom demands.

"She likes Alec." I smile sadly at my Star Wars sheets. "She wants me to back off."

"Girls these days are batshit crazy. If it were my day, there'd be none of this blackmailing business. Playing dirty is never a way to win a man, Riley."

"Mom." I giggle.

"Well, I'm sorry but it's true." She chuckles. "It's no way to win anything else either, my girl. Now, what would you like for dinner? We can order in if you'd like."

"I'm not really hungry."

"Nonsense. I'll order us some pizza, okay? For Jack too. Watch some films, take a bath. Cheer yourself up and get a good night's sleep later. I promise you'll wake up feeling better." She kisses me on the forehead and gets up to leave.

"Thank you, Mom. I love you."

"I love you too, more than anything."

I stand by my window, shielded by my drapes, and look over at Alec's room.

Surprisingly, his window is open. His drapes aren't drawn. He's sitting at his desk, listening to music and studying, and never before have I wanted to dash over and hug him so much. To tell him that I'm sorry and beg for another movie and takeaway day together.

I'm not sure what it is that alerts Alec to my presence. I'm pretty sure I don't move a muscle – I don't think my wearied body can physically handle that. Under the weight of my

245

eyes, somehow, he turns and glances out. Our gazes lock, and I feel boiling hot and frozen all at the same time. My heart pounds in my chest.

Mixed expressions cross Alec's beautiful face. Pain. Anger. Acceptance.

And suddenly . . . nonchalance.

He slides up from his chair and makes his way to the window.

I can't breathe.

Just as I feel that he's going to speak to me, he reaches up, grabs the handle and slams the window shut. The drapes close shortly after.

And just like that, my hope and determination dissolve into ash.

21

No Time

"Riley."

I turn at the sound of my name, managing to pluck up the sides of my mouth ever so slightly at the sight of my ex-boyfriend. He stands before me in a crisp white shirt and dark skinny jeans, his blonde hair tousled and his hazel eyes happy. Toby grins at me, "I'm surprised you came, actually. I thought you'd stand me up. You look stunning."

I smile back half-heartedly. We're standing in the entrance of the Elephant Bar. Bamboo lines the walls, with cosy, mismatched furniture, statues and water features everywhere in sight. The atmosphere around us is buzzing with activity. This is possibly one of the liveliest places to host a first date, but I feel anything but lively. The thought of trying to pluck up excitement for this date is exhausting. I'm numb inside. My gestures seem doll-like, my face a mask. I feel *fake*.

"Thank you," I say. "Shall we sit down?"

"Definitely." Toby holds out his arm and I reluctantly

place my hand in the crook of his elbow – allowing him to lead me to our table. My hair is down and curled, and I even forced myself into a dress. Simple, understated, but a dress nonetheless. I'm not sure why I made an effort, but it was certainly not to please Toby. Maybe I thought it was courteous. Maybe I thought there was a chance of Alec charging in, in a jealous rage, and stealing me away from the dragon. Or maybe, just maybe, I'm so goddamn lonely that the thought of any attention, be it from Toby or not, is better than the week of solitude I've just survived.

Sadly, the last is the most likely. I haven't had the best week. Head down, trying to dodge the dirty looks and never summoning the courage to speak to my friends. I wonder if I ever will. I know I told my mom I would, but it's so daunting.

"I see you've already ordered drinks," I say, eyeing up the green-tea spritzer he bought for me. This used to be my favourite drink in the world. I'm surprised he remembered. Toby tucks my chair under me, role-playing a gentleman, and chuckles.

"Yeah, I hope you don't mind. I know what you would've wanted."

"I usually have lemonade," I mutter softly.

"Oh, sorry, do you want me to send it back and ask for a lemonade?" Toby asks, not at all fazed by my impoliteness. It's disconcerting, this friendliness. After everything he's done, it makes me uncomfortable for him to be kind to me or vice versa. I shake my head and stare at the table. I don't want him to be kind to me. I want him to shout, so that I have an excuse to shout back, storm out and leave this date.

"So," Toby asks as he tucks himself in, "how have you

been?" His face is flushed. He's happy to be here; this is what he wanted all along.

I should play nice. It's not like I'm a saint myself. Besides, it's kind of nice to be able to talk to someone, even if it is him.

"What do you think?" I ask, wryly. I take a sip of my drink and taste nostalgia. Nostalgia over the person I used to be, when I was with him. When Kaitlin was still alive, and I had an all-consuming crush on Toby Charlton. The selfishness, the moodiness, the loss. The pain of my life back then, amplified by hormones. The drink is bitter, and I put it down.

"I'm gonna say not too good," Toby says softly. "Do you want to talk about it?"

"Not really." I play with the rim of my glass, unable to look him in the eye. *Stop being nice to me. You told Tiana about the kiss. You cheated on me. You're the reason Tiana hates me. You're why I'm in this mess right now.* I struggle to keep my mouth shut.

"Fair enough, but I'm here if you do want to." Toby clears his throat. "Things haven't exactly been easy for you this week, and I understand that."

"Because you know me so well." I sip the drink again, trying to mask my irritation by not meeting his eyes.

"I'm not saying that. I'm just saying I understand it hasn't been easy."

"No part of my life has been easy," I snap at him before I can help it. My hand slumps from the glass onto the table with a loud and painful smack, and I welcome the pain.

You're lying. Those moments of your life with Alec were easy.

"I know," Toby mutters, staring at his lap. "I deserve that."

"You deserve a lot more than that," I growl. "You told Tiana about how Kaitlin died." This isn't going to plan. If Tiana hears about this . . . well, I'm a bit screwed. I seriously need to regain some control over my emotions. If I let the anger in, I let the hurt in, and I can't deal with that right now. Plus, Tiana wants me to try again with Toby. That means I at least have to try.

"How do you know that?" he asks sharply.

He's shocked.

I falter. He doesn't know what's going on between me and Tiana. He doesn't know why I'm here right now, instead of hanging out with my best friends or with Alec. I have to admit, this has caught me off guard. I thought Toby had a little more to do with this whole process, but apparently he has no idea about what's going on behind the scenes. I wonder what he'll think of Tiana when he finds out. At least I can tell him what's happening, even if I haven't mustered the courage to tell my friends quite yet.

"Because Tiana's blackmailing me with it," I tell him, stirring my drink with the straw. "And I made the link. We were the only two people that knew about the kiss, so math dictates that you must have told her." Toby doesn't even seem to hear the last part of my sentence. His eyebrows have furrowed.

"She's what?"

"Blackmailing me," I sigh. "That's why I haven't spoken to any of my friends in over a week. That's why –"

"That's why you're here, on this date," Toby finishes, deadpan. "Of course. It makes perfect sense now. I knew it was too surreal to be true."

"Yeah," I say softly. I feel a small amount of guilt for

Toby, which I shouldn't because of everything he put me through. However, to find out that I was forced to come on this date when he was evidently so excited for it must be painful, and I empathise with that. It's not like he knew that Tiana was going to blackmail me.

"Right." He grimaces. "So I'm her charity case, and you must be angrier with me now than ever. *For goodness' sake.*" He meets my eye after a second of brooding, and he looks . . . defeated. "I can promise you that I didn't mean to tell her about the kiss. We were at her house and she was probing for details about my relationship with you. It just kind of slipped out, and I'm sorry."

"It's okay." It's not okay at all, but we all make mistakes.

"So she's blackmailing you into staying away from Alec, correct? And I'm the ticket into pushing him and your other friends away. God, I feel used."

"Yeah." I laugh slightly but not because it's funny. "Sorry." I stir the umbrella round my drink mindlessly. At least now I have one person who knows what it feels like.

"Riley, I need you to tell me something." Toby grabs my hand, surprising me. His eyes glue themselves to mine. I can't look away. "We have so much history. But I can see you don't want to be here right now, and it's okay for you to say there's nothing between us any more. We've changed, and I was a jackass to you, so I understand that all this is my own fault. Just tell me. Am I stupid to think we could be a couple again?"

Think before you reply.

"You aren't stupid," I tell him slowly. "Once upon a time, we had an amazing connection. Strong enough that I kissed you even when you were with my cousin, because I

251

liked you so much. However," I draw out the word and look into his eyes. "That time has come and gone. You cheated on me when we got together, and the moment I found out was the moment that you and I ended for good. I can see that you regret it, and maybe it wouldn't be a bad choice to start afresh – I doubt you'd hurt me like that again. But it wouldn't be the right one. We aren't right together any more. I'm not sure if we ever were." As I speak I understand how the whole nature of our relationship was wrong, somehow.

Toby is silent for a moment, before replying.

"You love him, don't you?"

His blunt question catches me off guard.

"Love Alec?"

I think about it for a second. We've known each other for less than three months. He irritates me to no end, and I fluctuate between annoyance and adoration when it comes to him. He grates on me like no other person has grated on me before, and sometimes I want to slap him silly. Yet, my days without him are miserable. I think about him continuously. I feel safe, and happy, whenever he's around. He manages to make my stomach flip and give me girly squeals of excitement when I think about him (very uncharacteristic of me). If I could, I'd be with him 24/7, getting high off the buzz in my chest.

When he helped with my panic attack. When we talked about our pasts at the train line. When he punched Toby and defended me. Well, not that he punched him, more the defending bit.

Do I love him?

"Not yet," I tell Toby truthfully. "But I'm falling hard."

I've said it aloud, and my stomach flips. Have I even told myself how far deep I was in until this moment?

"Tell him." Toby smiles slightly. "Just go and tell him everything. If you feel like that, then he deserves to know because the chances are he feels exactly the same way about you. Everyone can see it, Riley."

"What about Tiana?" The mention of her name is enough to make me dismiss the idea. "She'll spread the thing about Kaitlin."

"I can sort Tiana out," Toby promises. "And if she spreads it, I'll say the whole thing is none of her business. It'll look like Tiana's just being spiteful. Nobody will believe her."

My heart begins to beat furiously, with hope, with excitement, I don't know what. Toby has offered me a way out. "Why would you do this for me?"

"Believe it or not" – Toby releases my hands to tousle his hair awkwardly – "I do care about you, and I want you to be happy. I have a funny way of showing it, I know, but I do. If he's going to make you happy, and there's no chance for us to ever work out, then that's something I need to accept. Riley, I'm not a bad guy. I've made mistakes, a lot of them, but I wouldn't hold you back like that. Kaitlin would have wanted you to be happy, so it's the least I can do given the circumstances."

"What if he hates me?"

"He couldn't. It's not in him to hate you. Now go." Toby gestures to the door. "The sooner, the better."

"What, right now?" I ask him in surprise.

"No time like the present," Toby says dryly.

I slide off my seat, wrap both arms round Toby tightly

and squeeze my gratitude. My heart is racing with excitement and determination – this is just the boost I needed. The courage to tell my friends, to hold my head up high whether Tiana tells the world or not. If I think I'm falling in love with Alec, then I need to do whatever it takes to be with him. If that means admitting to my mistake, then so be it.

"Thank you," I murmur. "Thank you, Toby, for letting me go."

"Excuse me – sir, madam – may I take your orders?"

I pull away from Toby to see a waiter standing nearby, tilted awkwardly to the side to see Toby's face. "I'm actually leaving, I'm afraid," I say. My voice sounds breathless. I almost – not quite, but almost – sound happy. "Thank you for the, um, wonderful service and the spritzer, though. I think we're finished here." I glance back at Toby for approval.

"We're finished," he confirms.

"Oh okay, well in that case, have a lovely evening." The waiter bids us adieu, rolling his eyes when he thinks we can't see him.

"Thank you," I say to Toby again, grabbing my bag from the table.

"You don't owe me any thanks, Riley. Just go."

I nod and make my way towards the entrance, nerves settling in the pit of my stomach. It's time to put my trust in other people.

Just as I reach the entrance, I spot a familiar flash of blonde hair at a table to my right. I waver for a second, deliberating over whether I should just leave, or whether I could try to talk to Dylan. I don't know if he'll even want to talk to me, if he's angry or what. I can't help but gravitate closer towards him, until I can see over the edge of the cosy booth down onto my best friend's dark form.

Dylan and Violet?

Candles are set out on the table between them. She's laughing at something he said. An inexplicable warmth spreads through me. *They're on a date.*

"Hey," I say as I approach. They glance up in surprise, and I feel slightly ashamed for imposing on what appears to be their first date together.

"Riley," Dylan says dumbly. "What are you doing here?"

"I was actually . . ." I trail off and glance behind to where Toby was, but he's left by now. I turn back to the pair with a slight smile. "I was just fixing something with an old friend. How about you?"

"I think it's pretty obvious what we're doing, Riley," Violet deadpans.

"Just wanted the confirmation." I grin. "I'm happy for you guys."

"You seem chirpy tonight," Dylan notices. "Every time I've seen you this week you've been so down. I wanted to come and speak to you, but I couldn't do it to Alec. I hope you understand."

There's them and then there's me. They stuck together, and I've excluded myself. I need to fix that.

I nod. "I am happier. I'm actually on my way to fix things with him right now. Explain why I did what I did . . . I hope he listens to my side."

Violet's ears seem to prick up at this. "Can we know too?"

"Yeah, you can, but after your date. I'll call you later, I promise. I hope you two have an amazing time, and I'm so sorry for ignoring you recently. I can explain everything,

255

but I won't ruin your date with that now. Make sure you treat her right, Merrick." I glance at Dylan, before looking to Violet. "You behave yourself."

"You make me sound like a toddler," she scoffs.

"That's because you are one." I walk away.

I feel determined, ready. I trust my friends to stand by me no matter what, because I would do that much for them. If Tiana spreads rumours about me, I'll survive. If she doesn't, great. A nervous energy burns in my chest. This is terrifying, but I need to do it. Alec alone is worth more than any possible comment that can be thrown my way. It's just strange that it's Toby who's given me the courage to see that.

"Go get your man, Riley!" Dylan calls as I reach the doors.

Oh, I'm planning to.

22

Chocolate Bars

Okay, so maybe I should have thought this plan through a little more.

"Alec!" I bang on the window, my eyes squinting in the rain. I'm kneeling on his windowsill in my dress, my curled hair hanging like rat's tails in the heaven's downpour. Some may call this torrential rain an omen. I call it an obstacle. Teetering slightly off balance on his window in the pouring rain – what could be more romantic than that? It shows determination. It shows endurance. It shows my willingness to fight for love.

It shows that you're an absolute tit, that's what it shows.

God, I hate it when my subconscious is right.

"Alec, please open the window." I tap the glass again. His drapes are drawn and his window locked. For all I know, he may not be in there. It's Saturday night, after all. He could be asleep. He could be out. He could be with a girl, I suppose, although that's something I prefer not to consider. Rainwater is seeping right through my clothing now, and my

257

hair is plastered to my face. I'm struggling to see through my wet mascara. *Maybe I should just abandon this plan, go home and have a nice hot shower. I can send him a fax or something instead, apologising.* I tap a few more times, lazily.

Just as I'm retreating back into my lair of rejection, the drapes are pulled apart.

Alec stares at me in shock, and it seems like he's cursing, although I can't hear through the window and the rain. I'm glad that he's only just discovered me here. That's a lot less embarrassing than tapping at the window for five minutes in a thunderstorm, while he sits listening in his bedroom. At least this way, there's hope that he wants to speak to me.

Alec gestures for me to move across so that he can open the window. He looks irritated. Then again, I probably would be too if the person I was annoyed with was sitting outside my bedroom, bashing my window like a deranged woodpecker in the pouring rain. Cautiously, I shuffle left, until I've moved enough that he can pull in the large window. I take an eager step towards shelter.

Rookie mistake.

My bare foot slips from the drenched ledge to the abyss below, shifting my balance dramatically as my whole leg follows it. I yelp, grabbing a hold of the window frame to steady myself. I attempt to pull my leg back up, but the windowsill is so small and soaked that I can't get a steady enough point to lean on. *R.I.P. Riley Greene, who fell off the side of a house while trying to break into a boy's room.* Frantically, my leg claws the wall for support to push up from but finds nothing. *Shit.*

Strong, dry arms loop round my waist, and Alec's

comforting scent envelops me suddenly as he pulls me up just enough to give my leg a support, so that I can scramble back up the ledge. "Jesus, you're clumsy," he mumbles in my ear, tugging me roughly through the gap in the window and into the dry. I fall forward, collapsing on his carpet like a sack of potatoes onto the floor while he shuts the window behind me.

This is when the awkwardness hits.

I sit, dripping a circle of water onto his carpet, unable to turn my eyes to meet his. This is the first time we've spoken in over a week. *What if he hates me?*

"Well," Alec starts, offering me a hand up "I can see that your coordination hasn't improved since we last talked."

"I don't think it ever will." I laugh awkwardly, taking his hand. As I'm pulled up, I blush at the proximity between us. I am standing flustered and soaking wet against him – our faces are mere centimetres away from each other. I still haven't managed to look him in the eye. My dress drips on the floor. My make-up must be halfway down my face, and my hair is stuck to the back of my neck. "I'm sorry," I say softly. It's the only thing I can think to begin with. I finally force myself to look up and meet his gaze. Those dark, brooding cobalt eyes stare back at me with a mixture of disbelief, hurt and annoyance.

And I realise in that moment just how freaking much I miss him.

"That doesn't explain why you did it." Alec looks away.

"Then let me explain for you now." I swallow. "You may want to sit down."

Alec stares blankly at me for a second, before leaning against his desk and folding his arms.

259

Better just get to the actual explanation then, Riley.

"I've told you before that Toby and I were childhood sweethearts," I swallow. My mouth is dry, like sandpaper, and I'm forcing myself to get the words out. "There's a little more to that story. Something I haven't told anyone, ever. I gave you the impression that Toby liked me and only me, and that it was as simple as that. I let you think that it was me all along, in his eyes. That wasn't really the case." Rubbing my hands together, I brace myself for this next part.

"Kait and Toby were dating first. We both had liked him, and I was jealous that he liked her. I was fifteen years old, and I thought I was in love. The night of her death . . . they had been dating for over a month. Toby and I were at a party. Kaitlin had skipped it, and we both got drunk. I kissed him."

Alec sucks in a breath.

"It was quick. It ended really quickly. But when . . . when I opened my eyes, Kaitlin was standing there. She'd come to surprise us, she'd seen the kiss and she ran. I chased after her. I was screaming, pleading for her to understand, but she kept running. She was so desperate to get away that she ran out of the house, into the road and . . . and she was hit by a car."

I finally look up at Alec but his expression is blank, emotionless.

"I never got the chance to tell her how sorry I was," I choke. "And I regret that kiss so much because if it hadn't happened, she could still be alive. After her death . . . I sank into anxiety and depression. I was going to regular therapy, having panic attacks. I couldn't leave my room for weeks I felt so sickened by myself. Toby visited me, and he was the only one who could almost normalise me again. Against my better judgement, we started dating. A few months in, he cheated on me with Tiana and then he moved to Chicago."

I look up at Alec. My face is burning with shame.

"How does this link to the past few weeks?" He stands still, arms crossed, leaning back.

That's all he has to say?

"Tiana found out," I mumble, and Alec nods as if it confirms his suspicions. "Toby told her. She was black-mailing me with it, to get to you."

"Me?"

"Yeah. She told me to distance myself from you so that she could get closer to you. She made me go on a date with Toby because she knew it would push me and you apart. If I didn't, she was going to spread my secret across the school. That's why I haven't been able to talk to you, and why I accepted Toby's offer of a date. I didn't want to hurt you, I felt I had to, and I'm so sorry for that."

"What changed?" Alec asks bluntly.

His lack of reaction to this news is worrying me. He doesn't seem angry, but he doesn't seem happy either. He's completely stoic.

"On the date earlier Toby found out about the black-mailing. He said he'd help me stand up against Tiana, and helped me realise that you are worth so much more to me than the opinion of lots of strangers." I look down. "I know that's corny, but it's the truth. I'm not like you and Violet – I do care too much about what people think about me. It ruins everything. I see that now."

Alec doesn't reply; he's quiet, as if he's taking the news in.

"Talk to me. Tell me what you think," I beg.

"I think it's okay to make mistakes," Alec admits, finally looking at me. "And that sometimes the only way you can learn is by making them. I'm not a saint exactly; I've done a lot of things I regret, but that makes me human. It's what makes you human too. As for the more recent events . . . I wish you could realise that you are worth a million times more than what people think of you. Opinions, rumours, reputations, none of it matters. It's all so *shallow*. You can trust us, you know that. Just don't let Tiana push you around with the fear that other people define who you are, because they fucking don't."

"I won't. I know they don't. I've learned my lessons I promise." I rub my arm to smooth down the goosebumps. I still feel awkward – I don't know what to say, what it means for him.

"Good," Alec says, and for the first time he cracks a smile before crossing the room in a few strides. His arms wrap round me securely, and I don't even notice when mine wrap round him too. I feel so small, so safe when he's hugging me. I kind of never want to let go. I feel him rest his chin on top of my head, and I close my eyes.

"I missed you," I mutter. "Too much."

After a second he replies, and I feel his muscles relax under my arms.

"I missed you too."

I almost screwed this up.

"You're amazing." He tilts my chin up to look at him. His eyes are focused on mine, and his hand still cradles my face. "Your mistake, it doesn't define you. I'm glad you told me.

Whatever *this* is, it's worth more than what anyone thinks of it."

"I know."

One day after my reunion with Alec, and already I can say I'm feeling a lot better.

I decide that it is time to tell my friends about my past, to tell them the reasons behind my actions this previous week or so. Of course, they think that it's absolute crap. Violet gives me a hug and tells me never to leave her again. I get a lecture from Chase about all of the mistakes he's made and how he just has to deal with that every day. Joe and Dylan don't seem to know how to handle it, so they just buy a chocolate bar from the canteen and present it to me in a small show of kindness.

As for me? I finally have the relief of saying that my friends know everything about me, and they don't hate me for it. It sounds stupid, but when you hold on to something for that long, it's hard not to blame everything that's happened since on that one mistake. I obviously can't let go of the guilt that easily, and it will take me a long, long time to get over Kaitlin's death, but it's a start. I'm at least going to try to let this go.

Unfortunately, my issues aren't over quite yet. There is the question of what Tiana will do with the information. Whether she will let the whole school know about my past or not.

Luckily, I have the help of a lenient ex-boyfriend, a school prankster, a badass best friend and a champion bad-boy bra thief, and between us we think of a plan to bring Tiana down.

Step one of the plan – kid her into thinking nothing is out of the ordinary.

Using my Oscar-worthy acting skills, I've avoided my friends all morning. I've kept my head down, stuck a permanent pout on my face and sulked around very convincingly. Luckily, it seems to have worked. Nobody, apart from our little group, knows that we are all back on good terms again. I'm still receiving comments and glances from all of Alec's fangirls, and Tiana has sent her progesterclones over to check on me every so often. They've reported back to her that my date with Toby went "okay".

It has kind of sucked, to pretend for another day that I have nobody by my side. I miss my friends. I looked at them earlier, walking around together and laughing, and it stung a little even if I did know that it was part of the plan.

Step two of the plan – Alec lures Tiana into an ambush.

Cut to present, and you have Toby, Chase, Dylan, Joe, Violet and me waiting in a classroom for Tiana and Alec to arrive. For this step, it's Alec's job to lure Tiana to our classroom (probably with his classic Alec charm) where I can confront her. I'll tell her that we're all friends again, and that she can spread the rumours if she wants to. Then, with any luck, Toby will step in and say that he won't allow the rumours to be spread anyway. I'm hoping that at this point, Tiana will at long last give an inkling into why she hates me so much. She seems to have a vendetta against me that's about more than just the closeness between Alec and me. I want answers from that girl.

Violet is sitting beside me on a desk, swinging her Doc Martens below her. She's more excited than she should be about this. Then again, she's always loved the idea of defeating the social hierarchy – and if anyone personifies that very thing it's Tiana.

"Are you nervous?" Dylan asks me, approaching with a shy smile.

"A little bit," I admit. "Not so much about the confrontation – about why she hates me so much. She's gone to great lengths to make me feel like an outcast. She must have a reason." I release a breath. The story between me and Tiana is anything but simple. Toby cheated on me with her. He left the both of us to go to Chicago with no warning, leaving the mess of his mistakes behind. I have every right to hate her, but what right does she have to hate me? As far as I'm concerned all she's done is cause me pain.

"You're right, she must have a reason," Chase agrees. "But that doesn't necessarily mean it's a justified one."

"Guys." Joe smirks. "If we make her sit down, I could so put a whoopee cushion on her chair. Or, if you're into some more hardcore stuff, there's always superglue. I've got some in my locker. Maybe gluing her to the chair will bring her down to earth."

"Dude." Chase laughs, fist-bumping his friend.

"No whoopee cushions, no superglue," Violet says, twisting her nose stud.

She has her game face on.

"What's taking Alec so long?" Joe whines. "He's so bad at this seduction game."

I begin to laugh at this, just as Tiana pushes into the room with Alec behind her. We all hush the moment she walks in. It takes her a second to realise exactly what she's been pushed into, but by the time she turns round and tries to escape, Alec is standing blocking her exit with a smug expression on his face. I sense Violet stand up. It's time.

"You jerk!" Tiana hisses in outrage, glaring at Alec. "I can't believe you tricked me. Let me out right now!"

"Now, now, that's not very nice." Chase chuckles.

He sounds so creepy, like a Disney villain or something.

Tiana goes still at the sound of his voice before turning slowly to face us all. She looks more dishevelled than her usual ice-queen appearance. Her eyes rest on me, and her face contorts with rage. "Riley, what do you think you're doing with them? So help me, I'll tell everyone – "

"Tell everyone what?" I interrupt, pulse racing. "That I was the reason my cousin died? Go ahead. I can face it." Her eyes flicker between us all. She's figured out by now that they all know my secret. I share a look with Alec, who's leaning against the door with his arms crossed. She is completely blocked in.

"You seem to think they won't care." Tiana steps forward and raises her arms in exaggerated gestures. "If what you did gets out, you're screwed. Everyone will exile you. So I suggest you rethink whatever plan you and your 'buddies' have concocted and keep your head down."

"No one will exile her – because we'll stand by her," Toby says quietly. "I won't let that happen. I'll tell everyone you're just an attention-seeker. Maybe you deserve that, after all the bullying you've done to other people."

I glance at Toby with respect, glad to see that he isn't just thinking about me. That girl Chelsea, who was kissing Alec when Tiana humiliated her? She was kicked off her basketball team because Tiana had a word with her family on the school board. There are other people too, people who have crossed Tiana and lost. She's selfish and a bully and she thinks she has free rein over us all. That needs to end.

"Even if you did tell everyone." I step forward. "Even if the worst of everything happened, I wouldn't care, because being disrespected by the whole school is better than disrespecting myself enough to allow you to push me around. I know I did an awful thing, with awful consequences, but still I'm better than that."

Something lightens in my chest as I speak the words aloud, and I'm not just convincing myself anymore. It's true. I've been through a hell of a lot worse than some snide comments from strangers. Violet grips my hands and squeezes. I can tell she's proud of me for saying that, and so am I.

"Are you, Riley? You think you're better than everyone, don't you?" Tiana is clutching at straws now; I can see it by the look in her eyes.

"Says you," Violet points out.

"Fine, fair enough," Tiana snaps. "Yes, sometimes I put others down to push myself up, but that's *life*. It's all very well for you to stand here now and judge me for what I've done to Riley, but none of you know what I've been through to put me in this position. Do you know why I want to isolate her?" Tiana stares at us individually. "Do you?"

"No," I say. "So tell us."

"You." Her eyes are cold and fixed onto mine, freezing a path of ice down the back of my throat and through my veins. She fills me with dread, even when I know she's got nothing on me any more. "I wanted to make you feel isolated, because that's how I've felt my entire life. There was a time, last year, when I met a boy in a coffee shop. He made me feel less alone. We talked, and for the first time in my life, someone seemed to understand me, to have respect for me. We had sex, and I fell in love." She glances at Toby,

267

accusatorily. "Only, when I told him this, he panicked. He told me that he was already seeing a girl and that he was in love with her. Then he ran off to Chicago."

Toby. Toby, no.

I gawk at Toby, only to see him staring down at the floor mutely. He should be ashamed. His actions didn't just hurt me, or Kaitlin. They hurt her too.

"I was alone then," Tiana hisses. "I accepted that, but I always hated you, Riley, for taking away my shot at happiness. Then guess what happened? Alec arrived. I spoke to him in class, and I liked him. He was the first guy to notice the fact that I'm actually really smart. He asked me why whenever the teacher asked me a question, I'd get it wrong, yet I'd always have the right answer written on the page below me. He noticed!"

She looks behind her at Alec, and I watch her expression soften. Then she turns back to me.

"And then" – Tiana scowls – "I heard that you and Alec were a thing."

I can do nothing more but look at her, dumbfounded. My mouth doesn't have the capacity to shape words. My brain can't function. I had no idea Tiana felt like that. It can't have been easy for her. However, I can't shake the feeling that nothing is an excuse to treat people the way she has. She wants to make the world miserable just because she is, and the stuff she just told me isn't a reason to hate me. It's an excuse to. I can see why I'm the ultimate person to blame, but that doesn't mean that I've done anything wrong to her.

"Have you looked at things from Riley's point of view?" Violet asks, walking towards Tiana with a cold expression on her face. She's going to make an amazing lawyer someday.

"Because, if you did, you'd realise that the object of your hatred has done nothing to personally offend you. She lost her cousin this time last year. She's been through pain too, and yet you don't see her treating you like crap, despite the fact that you were the reason Toby cheated on her."

Tiana glares. "That's not my fault; I didn't know."

"I know you didn't, but that's not the point," Violet argues. "The point is that pain is no justification to treat people badly. It's all well and good to tell us all how difficult your love life has been, but if you removed your head from your ass long enough to look around, you'd see that everyone deals with some horrible stuff, and you can't blame Riley for everything bad that's happened in your life."

I see the rage ignite in Tiana.

"You're all blind," Tiana hisses. "She's blinded all of you."

"Just shut up," Violet hisses right back.

Dylan reaches for Violet's hand. Joe is suddenly by my side, bumping my shoulder lightly. Alec's arms uncross and he's looking at me. As all this goes on, Tiana stands, blinking in shock. A realisation seems to dawn on her as she watches all of these interactions go on around her. She looks around, and all she can see are our relationships. Friendships. Bonds.

"I hate you all," she says softly. "I hate you."

Then she turns, shoves Alec out of the way and storms out of the classroom.

23

Cootie Brownies

"Alec, I don't think it's supposed to look like that."

I frown down at the pale lumpy gloop in the bowl and the sight makes me gag. I guess this is karma for making brownies freestyle, without using a recipe. I'm pretty sure that chocolate brownies are supposed to be made with cocoa powder, and they're not supposed to have clumps of butter swimming around in them. We didn't have any cocoa powder, so Alec improvised by using Horlicks – a bizarre powdered drink that tastes kind of like a hundred-year-old diluted chocolate bar. The result doesn't look good.

"Me neither." He frowns. "But I'm sure it will taste good. Should we add more sugar just in case?"

"Alec. You added enough sugar to make all your teeth fall out with one bite," I deadpan, coughing a little bit at the end of the sentence. In reaction, Alec swiftly takes the bowl from me, frowning and covering the mixture to protect it. He and I are currently attempting to make brownies to feed Millie and Jack, who we are supposed to be babysitting. Even though I suggested good old sandwiches, Alec wanted to "live a little on the edge" and make brownies. If the brownies do come out as bricks, the fault is entirely his.

"Don't cough near the brownie mix, Riley!" he whines in a playful voice, shielding the bowl from me as though it's a baby or something. "No one likes cootie brownies."

"Cootie brownies?" I cough out a laugh. "I apologise if I'm allergic to your bullshit. Let's stick the mix in the oven and maybe it will turn out better than it looks now." I wrinkle my nose dubiously at the mixture as he pours it into the tin. I don't think Alec believes me. Heck, I don't even believe me. That mixture looks like something a very old cat would puke up.

Ew, I don't want to think about that right now.

It's been a couple of weeks since the confrontation with Tiana and things are almost back to normal. Almost. I'm sitting with my friends again in school, and I can't explain how much of a relief that is. I feel a lot happier now, happier probably than I've ever been thanks to my mind feeling looser, less constrained. I even messaged Tiana to tell her if she ever wanted to talk about stuff that I'd be there for her. She didn't reply of course, but the offer is there. Nobody should feel completely alone, no matter what terrible things they've done.

I would be lying if I said that it's like nothing has changed. Something has formed between Alec and I, a kind of awkwardness. Now all the obstacles have disappeared, it's like we don't know what to do with ourselves. I'll catch him looking at me, but the minute I do he'll look away.

I've been trying to keep the conversation light and nothing too heavy, but it's beginning to worry me. Did he ever really like me in the first place, or were we just friends after all? If he did, does he still like me now?

271

"Done." Alec slams the oven shut with a flourish. "Fifteen minutes should do, right? I guess we should probably start cleaning up."

I turn to survey the kitchen. It's not that bad. There's a little bit of flour on the floor, and Alec accidentally dropped an egg, but apart from that the damage is fairly minimal. I glance over at the open bag of flour, suddenly having an idea. Yeah, it's pretty obvious what I'm planning to do.

"Sure," I murmur, leaning over to grab a handful of flour behind my back. Alec bends down to put the baking powder back (that we used five teaspoons of – I hope that's enough), and as he straightens up again I catapult the handful of white powder straight into his face. It's only as I throw the flour at him that I realise I have done so with too much enthusiasm . . .

"What the actual –" Alec yells. "Why did you punch me?" He inhales sharply at the pain, breathing in the flour that I've thrown all over his mouth before he dissolves into an insane coughing fit, clouds of white billowing everywhere. I watch the situation, my jaw comfortably resting on the floor. Oh crap. Oh crap, oh crap, oh crap. You've done it now, Riley.

I take a risky step back. Alec's gaze snaps up to mine as he coughs away the last puff of flour, and his eyes narrow dangerously. I just punched him in the nose and almost suffocated him. If looks could kill, I would be six feet under right now. On the bright side, he looks like a snowman. You'd have thought it would be hard to take him seriously at this point, but the look Alec is giving me is deadly.

I am so screwed, I'm practically a screwdriver.

"Oh, that's it." Alec's voice is hard as stone now, his eyes never leaving mine. I watch in horror as he plucks an egg from the carton. We all know what's coming next. My head is screaming at me to run but my feet don't obey, and in less than a second Alec's hand comes down on top of my head with a loud splat. The egg gunk runs down my face and I close my eyes in disgust as I feel it dripping through my hair, cold and slimy. Alec begins to laugh.

"Ew," I squeal. "Grasshole."

"Well at least I didn't punch you when I did it." He smirks, slinging his arm over my shoulder. "Come on, we better get this cleaned up before my mom gets back." He releases me to grab the remaining utensils that are strewn across the counter, giving me a horribly clichéd pang of sadness at the loss of contact. Ah, I'm so cringey. I take the mop from him, following as he lugs the bucket over to the sink to fill it. Water runs from the faucet and splashes angrily into the bucket, filling with bubbles when the washing-up liquid is added.

"I'm gonna need to go home and shower again," I complain, running my fingers through the goo and shell in my hair. "I already showered this morning."

In response, Alec scoops up some of the bubbles from the bucket and sloshes them against my cheek. "No need."

I'm about to scoop up my own revenge and splash his face with it when we're interrupted by the sudden ring of his mobile. It's easy to recognise his ringtone – it's My Chemical Romance.

Alec frowns, fumbling in his pocket and pulling out a sleek expensive model. He presses the button and checks the caller ID, face puckered with confusion. However, as he registers the words on the screen, he instantly presses the "end call" button and puts his phone on the counter. His eyes won't meet mine as he takes the mop from me again, and his skin has paled. What is wrong with him?

"Who was that?"

"My dad," Alec mutters after a few seconds.

"Your dad?"

My voice is masked with surprise. To be perfectly honest, I've never delved properly into that topic with Alec. I know the basics – his dad left them when he found out Marie was bisexual – but I never realised he kept in contact. It makes me feel incredibly self-absorbed for dumping all my problems on Alec when I hardly know a thing about his issues. I watch him as he concentrates remarkably hard on cleaning one particular tile.

"Alec, are you okay?" I ask, not really knowing what to say to him.

"Mhmm," he replies curtly.

An awkward silence falls. If he doesn't want to tell me, he doesn't have to, I remind myself. Still, I can't help but compare it to everything that I've told *him*, and I feel my insides shrink a little in disappointment. Evidently, I've not quite broken Alec's walls down yet.

"Riley," he sighs.

"Yeah?"

"I'm sorry, I just . . . I find this difficult, okay?"

I turn to look at him. "You don't have to explain yourself, Alec. I know what it's like to want to protect your vulnerability. It's okay."

"My dad is a dick," Alec states plainly. "There is nothing else to it. Yes, he tries to keep in contact with me. Emails, phone calls. Yes, he pays child support . . . but he completely ignores my mom. He hasn't spoken to her since the day he

274

left. He doesn't want anything to do with her, and as a result, I don't want anything to do with him." He sighs again, realising that he's splashed water all over the floor in the midst of his rant.

"I don't blame you," I finally say. I know that he doesn't want to talk much more about it. It must be so difficult for him, to be so detached from his father. I know what it's like to feel a little disconnected, but at least I'm still on relatively good terms with my dad. I can't help but wonder if my mom was right – that maybe Alec's trouble with his dad has made him insecure, has made him less able to trust.

I take the mop from Alec and begin to clean the water he's spilled. We're almost finished now, and then we've just got the counters to clean before we can change clothes and make ourselves presentable again. The egg trail left on my neck is drying by the second – cracking and crumbling every time I move. Bubbles pop on my cheek.

A comfortable silence rests on us. I glance over to Alec and he appears deep in thought, so I just hum his ringtone under my breath and continue to scrub the tiles. All I can smell is egg from my clothes and hair, and it's hard to keep a straight face when Alec's eyebrows are flecked with flour. How does he manage to look good even when he's covered in flour? I'm sure I look a total mess.

"Riley," Alec says after a minute, very quietly. "How do you do that?"

"Do what?" I look up, surprised to see that he's watching me. "Mop the floor?"

"No." His eyes burn into mine – deeper than an ocean, and frankly much prettier as well. His voice is serious and awed, unlike my teasing tones. "You just . . . you know exactly what to say to me. How to manage me. I tell you about my dad and how I don't want to speak to him, and you just . . . you just understand. You don't push me to try to get a better relationship with him, you don't pry or ask too many questions. You listen, and you know what I need in the moment. How?"

He leans towards me.

My throat tightens. "I don't know." I shrug awkwardly. "I just know where to draw the line I guess. Sometimes you have to know when a person needs you to comfort them or just to shut up."

His hands slowly pull away my mop, and he drops it to the floor.

"Do you think," he breathes, putting his hands behind my waist and pulling me to him. "Do you think it would be okay if we shut up now?" His lips are just inches from mine, and I revel in the feeling. The electricity of the air, the burning in my chest.

I nod slightly, and Alec doesn't hesitate a second. His lips press onto mine again, and the delicious warm feeling spreads through my veins once more. I've missed it. Kissing him, it's amazing. My arms loop up round his neck, and his hands pull my waist to press tightly against him. The sun feels like it's beaming from inside my chest, and I wonder if every kiss with Alec will feel like this, if this amazing feeling ever really goes away.

Beep. Beep. Beep. Beep.

I glance at the stove in surprise. Looks like our brownies are ready.

Reluctantly, I pull away from Alec to turn the timer off, my hands shaking. I release a breath, grabbing a towel and pulling a tray of very strange, pale brownies from the stove. I place them onto the cooling rack. I don't care about the brownies right now, or anything for that matter. *Alec kissed me again.* My skin feels hotter than the inside of the oven, my pulse racing. Even though I can't bring myself to focus on anything but the boy behind me, no part of me can bring myself to turn round and face him either.

Why hasn't he said anything?

I stand there dumbly, staring at nothing.

Finally, I feel a hand wrap round my arm and tug me round. Fingers lift my chin up and I find myself staring into a pair of deep cobalt eyes.

Alec releases a short breath, and his scent fans over my face. Slowly, after evaluating my reaction, he closes his eyes and rests his forehead on mine. "Is this real?" he croaks.

I let out a short breathy laugh. "Apparently."

It's so hard to concentrate when a drool-worthy boy has his forehead pressed to yours and is looking into your eyes, let me tell you. Already I'm starting to overthink. What are we going to do now? What if he's not ready to commit? His eyes close and his eyebrows furrow. What about –

"I like you," he says, and his eyes open.

My heart hits the floor, and I have to fight to remain calm.

"I really, really like you in fact, and I'm a jerk for not admitting this until now, I know . . . but I can't say that I love you yet, because the truth is that I'm as inexperienced as they come in that area. I have no idea what love is, how to show it . . . and one of the reasons I've left it so long to tell you this is the fact that I know you can do better – you can find someone who'll love you back the right way. But at the end of the day, I'm crazy about you. And if there's

277

a chance that you feel anywhere near as strongly as I feel, then I honestly think this could work. I want to make this work."

His eyes are earnest and my heart is exploding.

Somehow I manage to find words.

"I want this. I want you."

As he registers what I've said, his expression morphs into the most stunning smile I think I've ever seen a human wear, and it's too much. Way too much for my feeble heart to cope with. His arms wrap round my back, and he pulls me towards him like a magnet. All space between us is gone in a second, and I bring my lips to his to reignite the flame. It's stronger this time – maybe because I know for certain that this is it now, we're a thing. Maybe because I'm above cloud nine. Maybe because this is the first time I've initiated a kiss with him, and the ecstasy that overwhelms me when he returns it just as eagerly is the best feeling in the world. I smile against his lips, and his hands shoot up to cup my face and everything is perfect. So sweetly, deliciously perfect.

"How many times did you practise that speech?" I smile. My pulse is throbbing at the strain my heart is under. Honestly, if I ever do date Alec Wilde for real, then I may suffer from some kind of heart disease – they'll have to keep me in hospital day and night, I swear.

"Just a couple of hundred."

"Favourite movie?" I ask Alec, rolling the green Skittle around on my tongue as I wait for his reply. I'm lying sprawled across his chest in my rainbow leggings and my favourite big blue sweater. My heart is still fluttering at the fact that this beautiful, sweet and irritatingly cocky boy is holding me, and I can't quite help but marvel at my luck. Today has been the epitome of perfection. Alec's arms tighten round my waist.

"Probably something like *The Fast and the Furious* or *The Dark Knight*," he admits, grabbing a Skittle from the bag nestled in my lap. Words can't describe how cosy I feel right now – I'm in my softest clothes, with my crush's arms round me and a bag of Skittles in my lap.

"What's yours?" Alec asks me.

"*The Dark Knight* or *Gone in 60 Seconds*." I grin contentedly. "Favourite food?"

"Steak," Alec replies. His fingers unconsciously trace the skin of my arms, causing me to shiver. "What's your favourite song?"

"'Misfit' by High Dive Heart," I decide after a hesitation. To be honest, my favourite song changes every day – but so far, that has been my all-time favourite. "Favourite colour?"

"Probably navy. Will you be my girlfriend?"

I freeze. "What?"

I turn round in his arms to look at him, but his eyes show no sight of deceit or teasing. He's offering me a small smile, and his eyes are glinting darkly in the dim lighting. The freckles on his cheeks, which I once didn't realise were there, are now a prominent feature on his chiselled, gorgeous face.

"Really? You want me to be your girlfriend?" My eyebrows fly skyward, and excitement bubbles in my stomach as his smile enlarges.

"Yep. Do you have a problem with that?"

"Not at all," I reply innocently. "But aren't you going to win me over with a line first? C'mon, Alec – you have to bring out the big guns here."

Alec pouts. "You want me to think of a line?"

I grin cheekily. "Of course."

He sighs exasperatedly, but I can tell he's only teasing. He knows as well as I do that I'll say yes no matter what line he pulls on me, but sue me – I'm curious as to which one is his best line. Alec turns me round in his lap so that I'm facing him, and I eye his excited face curiously.

"Honey, you're so sweet that you'll put Hershey's out of business," Alec drawls. "And speaking of Hershey's – how about a kiss?"

"That was your best one? Seriously?" I can't help it – I'm not impressed. After all the other hilarious lines he's given me in the past, this can't be his best.

"No," Alec snorts. "But I already know you want to be my girlfrien."

"You mean girlfriend," I correct him.

"What?"

"You didn't pronounce the 'D'. . ."

"Oh." Alec smirks. "Don't you worry about that. You'll get the D later."

Oh my God. I fell straight into that one. I curse and smack his chest, watching as Alec bursts into deep peals of laughter. That was bad, and I can't believe I fell for it.

"You're a jerk," I tell him. I bite my lip and look away, giggling.

Alec feigns surprise. "The ice queen fell for my little pickup line? Does this mean you'll be my girlfriend?"

"Maybe."

"Okay, let me rephrase that." Alec clicks his tongue daringly. "Would you like to be my girlfriend? If yes, then breathe. If no, then lick your elbow." He pulls me closer, a defiant smirk on his lips. Instantly I take a deep breath and he grins.

"Now that's settled, I should probably get going." He climbs up off my bed and over to my window, and I watch him go with an air of nostalgia around me. A few months ago, he did exactly that with my bra in his hand. Reluctantly, I peel myself off the bed and follow him over to my window to say goodbye. After pressing a light and sweet kiss to my lips, he jumps over to his own windowsill with his reflexes as catlike as ever. When he reaches his room, I smile shyly and go to press the window down.

"Oh wait!" Alec cries out as he remembers something, and I spin back around to see him fumbling just below the windowsill. He grins when he finally grabs whatever object it is, and then looks up at me as he chucks it carefully onto my windowsill. "Here, have this back."

I step closer to examine the object which is now hanging from my window.

Holy macaroni cheese.

On toast.

With extra ketchup.

It's my Mickey Mouse bra.

I stare in pure shock at the bra I haven't seen in four months.

"Where did I hide it? If I told you, I'd have to kill you." He grins as I stare at him, speechless. This annoying, cocky, infuriating bra thief is now my boyfriend. I think people should pray for me – I might not survive otherwise.

Or at least, my underwear won't.

24

Kissing the Bride

"Do you, Fiona Hughes, take Marie Wilde to be your lawfully wedded wife?"

Fiona smiles. Her eyes are bright and sparkling even from where I'm standing, her hands clasped romantically in Marie's.

"I do," she replies easily, and I can see the shake of Marie's shoulders as more joyous tears escape her eyes.

Marie looks absolutely stunning; her white dress is modest yet so pretty – long-sleeved with lace detailing. Her wild curls are tamed into a gorgeous studded bun, with tendrils escaping, and she looks more beautiful than I've ever seen her. Fiona wears a more understated black dress. Alec told me that she's never been drawn to the glitz and glamour of weddings, but she's tearing up just at the sight of Marie. I think everyone else is too.

Gah, this emotion is too much for me to handle.

"And do you, Marie Wilde" – the minister turns to Marie with a smile that crinkles the corner of his eyes – "take Fiona Hughes to be your lawfully wedded wife?"

"I do," Marie whispers.

I can't see her face at the moment; I'm standing angled behind her, along with Natasha and Millie.

We make up Marie's bridal party, alongside Rosa – the maid of honour. All of us are clutching small bunches of orchids, and our dresses are a gorgeous silken grey, each in a unique style. I share a small smile with Natasha as Marie says the words, tears pricking the edges of my eyes no matter how hard I fight to restrain them. Since Fiona came back for good, Marie has been the happiest I've seen her in the short months I've known her. Fiona is by far the friendliest and funniest woman I think I've ever known, and it's safe to say that Alec was under-exaggerating when he described her as "nice". It's clear that the whole family worships Fiona, and from what I can see of her face right now as she gazes into Marie's with complete and utter love – the feeling is mutual.

How can I stop myself from crying when everything is so perfect?

"Then I now pronounce you wife and wife," the minister announces, his face breaking out into a smile so large that I'm afraid it will break out of his delicate, thin-skinned face. "You may now both kiss the bride."

And Fiona does. She uses their intertwined fingers to pull Marie closer until their lips meet. I can see only the back of Marie's head from where I'm standing in the bridal party, but by the cheering and applause coming from the crowd I can tell that everything is pretty spectacular. I catch eyes with Alec, who is standing beside Fiona and grinning as he claps with everyone else, his eyes trained solely on me.

I blush. You'd have thought I'd have gotten used to him looking at me by now, wouldn't you? I mean, we have been dating for eight months. Still, none of the effect that Alec used to have on me has faded, and I have to say I'm glad about that. I grin widely at him, ignoring my bunch of flowers as my own hands collide in congratulations for the newlyweds. Marie and Fiona turn to face the crowd, and for the first time in half an hour I see more than the back of Marie's head. Her face is tear-stained, but her eyes are shining, and she looks absolutely gorgeous. With linked hands, the pair begin to walk back down the aisle, and the audience stand up. The wedding is over. The vows have been said.

"Oh my Lord, that was so beautiful," cries Natasha beside me.

Her mascara is halfway down her face, and her thin black hair has been twisted and pulled back in an intricate design. I never pictured her as a hopeless romantic, but apparently she is. I guess I should've expected it – Joe's turned into a right romantic recently under her watch, and the pair have been dating for just under a month now. She was the one to man up and tell him first, believe it or not, and he obviously accepted. I really admire her courage, and sometimes I wish that I could've been the one to ask Alec out first – it might have saved a lot of my confusion and his anger if I did.

Ah well, I guess everything's worked out well in the end.

"I know." I smile to Natasha, wiping the salt trails away from below my eyes. "They both look so beautiful."

Natasha nods before pulling me into a hug and resting her chin on my shoulder.

"It's been nice seeing you, fellow bridesmaid." She grins through the tears. "I'll miss you. Alec doesn't bring you to visit often enough! The wedding preparation has been so much fun, though."

I smile nostalgically at this. The last month has been hectic with rehearsals, bridesmaid training, dress fittings, etc. Rosa, the maid of honour, has been coping astonishingly well, and she's been the rock that both the brides needed to get through all this. More often than not, Marie has taken the planning headlong – with my mom as a trusty helper. I glance to the side and see her, sitting happily in the second row and talking to Jack. She and Marie have been closer than ever recently, and I wonder if Marie regrets not asking Mom to be part of her bridal team. But that's such a small detail. The whole wedding has gone according to plan, and it would take a fool not to see how happy Marie and Fiona are with everything.

I glance around the room as people begin to climb out of their seats. It's time for the wedding after-party, which is being hosted next door in the main room of the country club where the engagement party was held. I'm not going to lie, I'm looking forward to going back – that place was so glamorous. With the way I'm dressed up now, I feel particularly excited. I glance down at my bridesmaid dress. It's the same grey as Millie and Natasha, but where mine has a gorgeous studded neckline, Natasha's is strapless and Millie's has spaghetti straps. Millie turned five recently and she's the cutest little five-year-old in the world. Her hair is longer now, curly and darker like Marie's – and it's twisted into a fancy updo which closely resembles mine.

"You look very grown up," I tell her, squeezing her hand. She looks up at me with a grateful toothy smile. "Are you happy that your mommy and Fiona are married now?"

She nods excitedly for a second, but then her expression turns crestfallen.

"They won't let me go on holiday with them. I want to go to Paris!" She pouts, her eyebrows furrowing cutely.

On her fifth birthday, I couldn't resist but buy her a new tea set. It's the biggest set the store had, and it's pink – her favourite colour. I bought it to commemorate the time when I first met her, when we played with the tea set, which is now chipped and old. I thought she deserved a new one, and I was right – she adores it.

"Aww." I frown. "Yeah, I want to go to Paris too, but you know what? You get to spend the next two weeks with Auntie Rosa, Natasha, me and Alec. That's a pretty good holiday, isn't it?" I kneel down and offer her a smile, poking her gently in the ribs to make her giggle.

She nods shyly.

I dread the day when this little angel grows up, I honestly do.

I stand back up and release Millie's hand, only to have arms wrap themselves round my waist from behind and lips pressed to my collarbone. Alec. I spin round in his arms with a smile on my face, staring up at the gorgeous boy in front of me. His lips are cracked into a cheeky smirk, his eyes brighter than usual and staring down at my face. His role at his mother's wedding? Well, he gave her away; he walked down the aisle with the bride. Unlike me as I walked, he was resolved and calm and did all the right things. I looked like a bit of a mess when I did it – it was a tremendous struggle not to trip over my dress in the heels, despite the amount I've practised in the past month. But in the end I didn't fall over, which I consider an achievement.

"Alec Hughes." The boy in front of me wrinkles his nose as he says his new name. "It doesn't have quite the same ring to it as Alec Wilde does it?"

His fingers stroke the small of my back tauntingly, and he pulls me closer to peck me on the forehead.

"Well," I point out, smiling, "your mom did say you could keep your surname if you want to. Just because she's becoming a Hughes-Wilde doesn't mean you have to, too."

"Ah," he sighs. "But you're missing the point. I refuse to have a wife one day called 'Riley Wilde'. The sounds are too monotonous. 'Riley Hughes-Wilde' sounds better, even if it isn't my original surname. I'll get used to it."

He shrugs, but by this point my jaw is on the floor. *Did he seriously just joke about getting married to me?* My heart thunders in my ribs, and I can feel a blush spread across my cheeks – thick and crimson. He can't be serious. Is he trying to make me die of heart failure?

"W-what?" I choke out, eyes wide as I stare at him. Recently he's begun to grow a little stubble on his chin, and I'd be lying if I said that it wasn't the sexiest thing for miles around. I guess it's his new look for senior year, and he's turning eighteen soon.

Alec cocks an eyebrow at my reaction, smiling smugly. "Riley, don't pretend you don't want to be my wife one day. It'll probably happen whether you like it or not." His confidence is amusing, and I let a chuckle escape my lips as he holds his chin proudly high.

"You stole my bra, and now you want to steal my last name away? Don't you think you're being a little greedy, Alec Wilde?" I frown. "You never did tell me where you stashed away my best Mickey Mouse bra."

"If I tell you, you've got to promise not to tell anyone." He gazes steadily into my eyes, and his finger rises up to press down on my bottom lip. "This is my darkest secret."

I watch wide-eyed as he glances either way to check who's watching us. He's actually going to tell me. I feel a buzz of excitement deep in my gut, and I lean closer for him to whisper to me. His breath tickles my earlobe, and he brushes away the wisps of hair tucked behind my ear, which causes me to shiver. I can't be sure whether he's teasing me or not. I never really am when it comes to him.

"Don't tell a soul," he whispers, "but I hid your bra . . . in my boxers."

I jolt backwards.

"What!" My eyes ping open even wider, and I nervously glance down at his lower half.

Please tell me he's joking.

Alec takes one look at my horrified face and bursts into laughter – making it very evident that he was stringing me along. It reminds me of when I was doing a similar thing the day after I drew on his face. Speaking of which, I still haven't uploaded that photo . . . Maybe I could do it on his birthday. That would be a cool little surprise, wouldn't it? At the moment, my profile photo is a selfie of the two of us. I didn't upload it. Heck, I hate that photo, because it reminds me of how particularly ordinary I look next to Alec. However, Alec stole my phone a couple of months back. He uploaded that photo, making me look like the world's clingiest girlfriend, and then proceeded to upload a picture of Mickey Mouse as his profile picture.

Needless to say, it didn't get as many likes as his last shirt-less picture, but he found it pretty hilarious. Grasshole.

"You actually believed me." Alec sobers up from his chuckles, letting out an almost pained gasp for oxygen. "You actually believed me. What kind of person do you take me

288

for, Greene? I'm not that disgusting." He wrinkles his nose, and in synchronisation, his fingers grab my bra straps and ping them. I'm pretty sure it's not just me; don't all girls find that incredibly irritating. I scowl up at him.

"Where did you hide it Alec? If you don't tell me, I might just have to upload the boxer story . . ."

Alec's laughter disappears instantly. He edges towards me, a malicious smirk tugging up at those beautiful sculpted lips of his.

"Are you threatening me, Riley Jessica Greene?"

"Possibly."

"What are you going to do? Try and blind me with body spray again?"

Ah, now that's a good story. I nod happily, and his gaze narrows.

"I hid the bra –"

"Hey, guys!" Joe interrupts, and I look to the left to see his arm is casually slung round Natasha's shoulders and she's grinning like a cat who got the cream.

Most of the people have exited the room now, leaving us and a few others behind. We should probably start heading next door for the party, but dammit! I was so close to knowing the location of the place I searched for so hard. Where did he hide my bra? He's never even joked about telling me before, so this is exciting.

"We should probably get moving." Natasha smiles. "C'mon. Let's head off. Chase and Dylan are already over there."

Since Dylan and Violet started dating, he has returned to his old self. He's charming, sensitive and logical. Recently, I've encouraged him to ditch some of the clubs he doesn't want to attend anymore and catch up on his sleep for once. He used to put way too much pressure on himself for the sake of his reputation, and as Alec stated that one time – reputations really don't matter. I can be the spokesperson for that lesson.

We're on the brink of senior year now and thinking about college. Everybody plans to go to different colleges, and it breaks my heart to think that I may be separating from all of my friends in just a year's time. However, it means that I'm a million times more excited to spend time with them during senior year. The way I look at it, this is a chance for a fresh start after Kaitlin, Toby, Tiana and all of last year's events, and I plan to make the absolute most of it before college starts. I know I'll have finals, and I know I have college applications to worry about, but I have Alec by my side for both. This year better be kick-ass.

Okay, I'm going to stop now before I puke at the cheesiness.

"Riley." My thoughts are interrupted as Alec tugs at my arm, willing me towards the door where Joe and Natasha are waiting for us. "C'mon, daydreamer, we need to go to the party."

"Right." I nod. "The party. Let's go."

"Riley!" Fiona greets me, a grin spreading across her face. Her hand is locked into both of Marie's, her eyebrow piercing glinting. "You didn't trip down the aisle!"

"Tell me about it," I agree with a laugh. "It's a freaking miracle!"

Since Fiona arrived back in Lindale and started living with Alec's family again, everything has kind of changed for the better. She got a job as a firefighter, as Alec told me, and by the sounds of it she's the happiest woman in the world. I'm not sure whether she experienced any emotional trauma from her time as a soldier, and Alec doesn't know either, but she seems happy enough from day to day so we both just leave it be. When Fiona and I first met, we started really well, and I'm happy to say that I'm a close friend of hers and Marie's now. That means that Fiona is well aware of how unbalanced and clumsy I am. It's been a kind of inside joke between us that I was going to trip down the aisle.

"Hey, Fiona," Alec greets from beside me, squeezing my hand. "Did I ever tell you about the time that Riley tripped over a –"

"Let's go," I hiss to Alec, interrupting him, before turning to Fiona with a courteous smile.

"Congratulations. You and Marie are made for each other."

I don't even give her a chance to do anything other than smile before I pull Alec away to our designated seats. The country club is decorated slightly differently to when I last saw it. The tables and chairs in front of the bar have been grouped together to form a collective horseshoe shape facing the stairs. The dance floor has been cleared, and everything is decorated with white ribbons and fairy lights. In the dim lighting, it looks even more beautiful than when I last came here.

The tables are dressed with fresh white tablecloths, and orchids – matching the bouquets that the bridal team carried. My place is sandwiched between Natasha and Alec, who has taken his position next to Fiona. A little further along, I can see my mom and Jack climbing into their own seats, and even further still are Dylan, Chase and Joe. They look especially awkward in their tuxes, sipping from champagne glasses. On every plate is a fortune cookie. I think that's an amazing idea for a wedding favour – it's so different to the usual ones.

I turn to Alec, gesturing down at the fortune cookie. "Are you breaking yours now?"

Alec frowns and picks his up to shake it. As if, somehow, that will give him the answer. What an idiot. "Yeah, why not?"

I pick mine up and break it, revealing a thin strip of white paper.

How can you have a beautiful ending without making beautiful mistakes?

Alec frowns at the words, before turning to look at me. "This is a beautiful beginning, not an ending."

Unable to think of anything to say, I lean forward and kiss him lightly on the lips.

Alec smiles and breaks open his own fortune.

Your fortune is as sweet as a cookie.

"Huh," I say. "That's a cute one."

"Do you want to know where I hid your bra?"

I come to attention immediately, head snapping round to look at Alec. I nod eagerly.

"I hid it in the bottom of your wardrobe."

"What?" I ask. "My wardrobe!"

"It's the one place you didn't think to look – in your own bedroom." Alec smirks.

"But what about when you first stole it? You ran out of my bedroom and into yours," I frown, remembering. "It must have been in your bedroom then. When did you put it back into mine?"

"After I'd stolen it," Alec tells me, "I hid it under my mattress, but I knew you'd try to find it at some point or other, so I waited for you to leave your bedroom the day after. You, your mom and your brother were coming over to meet us. Then I slipped in and chucked it at the back of your wardrobe, where you wouldn't think to look. All I had to do then was to get back into my own house and act surprised to see you." He shrugs. "It's actually quite worrying how you didn't find it in the space of four months."

Hey, in my defence, my wardrobe is a mess. The flooring of it is covered with shoes and boxes of games from my childhood – it's no wonder I haven't seen my Mickey Mouse bra in there.

"I can't believe this!" I look up at him, and he smirks infuriatingly back down at me, taking a sip from a glass of champagne. My fists clench in frustration.

That damned bra was in my wardrobe the entire time and I didn't know about it? How stupid is he making me look?

Alec wriggles his eyebrows playfully.

The food is going to be served soon. Marie and Fiona are taking their designated seats at the heads of the table.

"I don't believe it!" I slap him on the shoulder "You – you son of a barnacle!"

"You love me really." Alec leans slightly closer. "More than Minnie loves Mickey."

He's got me there.

A bad boy stole my bra, and I couldn't be more thankful.

Alec freaking Wilde, you manipulative grasshole.

293

Lauren Price was born in Coventry in 1999 and remembers spending her childhood with her nose in a book or creating short stories. In her teens she first posted her writing on the online platform Wattpad and soon gained a devoted fanbase for her funny, playful and, in Lauren's own words, "frankly quite weird creative voice" – she enjoys bringing a smile to her readers' faces! Lauren likes to draw, watch films, travel and hang out with friends and family. As a self-confessed book lover, she intends to study English at university.